AN AUTHENTIC DERIVATIVE

I0547523

A CALEB COY "NOVEL"

A profusion of thankfulness to Bud Thomas, Luke Guard, Trae Bailey, Joshua Ball, Ryan Hogan, Seth Terrell, and my family.

FIRST EDITION, AUGUST 2015

ISBN-13: 978-0692479421
ISBN-10: 0692479422

Printed in the United States of America

calebcoy.wordpress.com
@CalebCoyGuard

Cover Design: Bud Thomas, Junior Design Co.
@juniordesignco

NO PROMO

For my son
and every generation after

AN AUTHENTIC DERIVATIVE

There is nothing so pretentious as an epigraph. For those readers who don't dig why I didn't have one, now you know. I recall Turkish novelist Orhan Pamuk, who said it best: "Never use epigraphs, they kill the mastery of the work." I would no more need an epigraph before a decent book than I would need a tuning fork before hearing a decent record. They are gimmicks for the kitsch and the predictable. One might as well fill a page with all the quotations they could find about whales. This practice of adornment through pilfering is no different than the many teensters who emblazon their social media with quotations from their favorite blockbusters as if their own musings were worthy additions to the monuments that came before.

When we epigraph we are merely pinning the jewels of another's genius at the top of our page, as one would tie a bow, to signify that we are as profound as our predecessors, repackaging the social capital of our imitative work for more than it's worth by stamping it with the de-contextualized words of another as if it were a mere motto, or worse, a brand. It's profusely cliché. George Eliot ostentatiously used over eighty-six of them in one book, and I can tell you that nobody reads *Middlemarch* unless they're told to.

Epigraphs are for people who don't have the patience, or the mental faculties, to thumb from one page to another and hear the work speak for itself. So if you don't have the patience to flip the pages, you've come to the wrong place, my reader. The author is still unknown—the title and cover were just edgy enough to grace your virgin bookshelf.

I'm writing this book to release the burden of a narrative that was bestowed upon me. A passage from Publius Ovidius Naso that still haunts me—you may know him as Ovid, the Roman author of *Metamorphoses*, although few are familiar with his work in *Epistulae ex Ponto*—was one my grandfather highlighted in the front of a book he gave to me on my graduation:

"Our songs will escape the greedy funeral pyre."

I considered it a challenge from my grandfather, to escape banality, mediocrity, Hell—what have you. It's haunted me in a way I think it would haunt anybody who's heard it, and let it simmer for such a long time that it really began to define, in a way, the essence of what's really coming out of our generation. We plagiarize and obfuscate our affectations, the lot of us, and I am in no position to adjudicate my generation.

I'm being pedantic.

But I will judge the unfolded narrative of Garrett Sedgwick, a chronicle that will change the way you drink your coffee. He has been described as "a restored, antique seismograph whose finger was on the pulse of a generation," but I find that to be both patronizing and hyperbolic. I don't hate Sedgwick—or as those of who like to think we knew him personally, "Wick"—I really just hate the cannibalistic smog that tended to follow him.

When I first heard of Wick, he had just released his fifth independent label album, *Gravity Waltzes: A Study in Velvet*, one that garnered mixed reviews, which in my opinion are the best reviews. Before he released the album exclusively online, followed by a vinyl release, he paid his producer out-of-pocket to release all nine tracks in a limited edition box of 3 1/2 inch microfloppies (twenty-seven of them, it took), which the music community interpreted either as a bold sign of retro-techno avant-garde genius or as an audacious commentary on the elitist drive of fans who would go out of their way to either purchase a 1990s PC or an Imation drive, merely because it was rare and lo fi. There were not enough for it to become a collector's item, not even for those who professed to have gotten the irony of the release.

The unofficial first release of the album actually happened before all this, when the album leaked online and a local radio station played the entire set on the air at midnight on low fidelity the day before the official release. Wick called in to the station, who predictably aired the call, and in no kind words berated them for committing sacrilege against the industry by airing the leak. This act legitimized his integrity among high school dilettantes, while for others it was an obnoxious publicity stunt that created serious blowback, which itself created such a controversy that even more devout fans, professing that they hated loving him and loved hating him, expressed their ambivalence in such terms that his status as a multi-faceted icon was further cemented. Either way, he was clever and talented, but still too recognized for his earlier work, which sold more compact discs at Best Buy and FYE than his more mature endeavors. As he himself ranted on the air, "if it's some *American Idol* star's big label record, you'd call it theft, but if it's an indie artist putting food on his plate, you call it promotion? Is that it? Is that it?" Yes, that was it.

Mojo hailed *Gravity Waltzes* as "absolutely noble" and gave it a 9.5. "With a fuller, more inviting sound," said Ben Silver of *Nashville Scene*, "*Gravity Waltzes* rubs it in our face that Sedgwick will never grow stale. I've already listened to it six times." *GQ* suspected it would be their last positive review: "He's not spreading himself thin so much as plunging his talent too deep. Surely he's maxed himself out with this one." *Guitar World* was also none too flattering, proclaiming that "you can't grow tired of his new methods, but give it one listen and you'll think *he's* grown tired." Benny Griggs cast a metaphor both hurtful and complimentary in *Rolling Stone*: "The melodies linger, yet they play like hardcore amusement rides: Thrilling and memorable, but not made for more than a couple rides a day." The iTunes review tried a little too hard: "There isn't a genre Garrett Sedgwick doesn't know, and in *Gravity Waltzes* he covers the last frontier. He goes back to the basement, offering a street food buffet of raw sounds like a carnival barker in a time-traveling jallopy. He's no Rumpelstilskin, but he weaves only gold." Writing for *Blender,* Lisa Rowe said of the new record that "a thematic, meditative optimism permeates his latest album, so much so that it is a breath of fresh air, a rare gleam amidst a sordid parade of gloomy releases. Haters will hate; This record is genuine."

The most advantageous to his continuing career came from *Pitchfork*, whose passive aggressive refusal to praise the album to its fullest came in the form of a pithy spat:

"Old maestro; New licks."

They gave the album an 8.5 out of 10. After many reader complaints, they changed it to a 9.

I say all this to say that this was the talk of the scene and the state of things for Wick when I ran into him. A few years ago I moved to Nashville. I slept on an air mattress in an apartment loft, with nothing but a Macbook Pro and a pile of books about design. That and the Ovid text my grandfather had given me upon getting my Master's, a month before he died. I had just graduated, taken a job offer, had a grandfather die, and began looking for an apartment all within the span of a month, all the while having the feeling that everything was uncertain fermenting in my head. This helps us frame the narrative, for though I am not the protagonist—Wick is the protagonist—I do carry the equal burdens of perspective and hindsight.

My name is Neil Oberlin, and the narrative is my burden. I've elected to record the narrative in the vintage Lapiz Lazuli Parker Duofold fountain pen that was a graduation gift from my father, but I will eventually have to transfer it to digital text.

I'm being discursive.

Before I actually found an apartment I stayed for a weekend with an old friend who had moved to a neighborhood in South Nashville. I came to look for an apartment and meet with my first client. I would have stayed with my cousin, who had moved to Nashville three years prior, but she was out of town. I slept in a slim loft office in a sleeping bag with a single alcove window over me. I browsed dozens of articles on graphic design trends, and tried to get a feel for the city. One has to have friends who are well read, well cultured, well educated, tolerable.

My friend was Greg Dickey, whom I had roomed with for a year as an undergrad before transferring schools. He had not changed much, the same self-professed odd ball I had known him to be, an amateur photographer and ukulele player, an Asiaphile and a gamer who shared my taste in music—Radiohead, Of Montreal, New Pornographers. He had become a high school science teacher, and was a suited to disperse factoids to students with zeal as he was to overanalyze relationships. He even kept a sketch book for his theories on relationships, which often included intricate graphs. His students called him "Mr. Savage" after the Mythbusters host due to his resemblance in both form and essence—that is, when they were not calling him "Mr. Dick." He was the son of a preacher, the deer-in-the-headlights variety. He once rambled about the complexity of the universe as proof of the existence of God, which I challenged as a clear case of *ad ignorantiam*. Once, when I once explained Nietzsche's concept of eternal return, and he claimed it was merely borrowing from Ecclesiastes and its "nothing under the sun" routine, I called him a swine and he called Nietzsche a sociopath.

Still, I would have grown permanently misanthropic towards him were it not for his optimism and his taste in music, the latter of which made us kindred spirits.

Greg and I went out for sushi and, after moaning about how girls play the "low self-esteem" card on everything, he convinced me to go with him and his roommates to go "stalkin' the Hag"— that is, hit up a Merle Haggard show. I would have declined, as it was not my scene and I could not afford the tickets, but the ticket was free, and I was a guest of Greg's. It occurred to me, also, that attending such a concert would indeed be a novel experience I could not pass up, as I make a rule for myself to refrain from passing up novel experiences, especially when I can get a kick out of the characters they draw. On top of all this, I was looking forward to attending a show where it was less likely that someone would mistake me for Ben Folds.

The opening band bombed, but Merle Haggard, whom I had actually never heard before, was decently vintage with a rugged authenticity I could not bemoan, and the edginess of his outlaw persona I found to be a precocious veneer until I heard from Greg's roommate, Hank, that Haggard did indeed spend time in prison, which cemented his legitimacy and allowed me to enjoy the concert. Still, it was not my scene; I stood out in my Che tee.

Because I ended up enjoying the concert, and because I was still seeking to initiate myself into the scene, I obliged Greg in attending his church with him the following Sunday. I was in the nexus of the Bible Belt, after all, and my trip would not be complete without the obligatory concert and church combination. This was not to say that I had no interest in pursuits of faith. I am not fan of organized religion, but I would qualify myself as a seeker — or perhaps more of a ponderer.

The congregation was large, as expected, and the building was an uninspiring, drab slab of brick. The hymns were sung in a capella fashion and all the men above the age of forty wore a cheap sport-coat. They had a crisply spoken and a paternally watchful preacher, one who knew his text well, but his sermon did not stimulate me intellectually. The narrative of this church consisted of the typically fed lines that immersion into a new mode of existence through a supreme being full of grace and hope was a salvation from eternal damnation, and I recalled being a child and hearing that same narrative, that same anthology of mostly harmless untruths that kept old people in their pews. The folks were nice, though, and they were in love with their text—or rather their tradition of experiencing their text. One old woman gave my hand a good squeeze and told me to come again. As we left an elderly man told us boys to take care of ourselves, drive careful, and "don't go on any wild tangents." These people amuse me. Still, it was not my scene; I stood out in my Nietzsche tee.

They let me pick lunch, Greg and his roomies. I mentioned a bistro I wanted to try downtown, but they didn't want to hassle with the traffic. They teased me, asking if I had heard that Jack White liked to eat there. I made the mistake of sarcastically mentioning that we could go to Shoney's when I saw one up the road. My sarcasm being too subtle, Shoney's it was. I didn't speak up, so as not to offend them, but they finally became attuned to my sarcasm when, after we sat down, I contemptuously complimented the breakfast buffet's homestyle grits served at room temperature for being "just like my grandmother made them." Brunch then became awkward, and for my penance I ate in silence.

I internalized the experience of eating at a buffet not as an act of eating but as a commentary on how we eat, which, like Warhol and his cheeseburger, was a joke understood by no one else. I ate the buffet not to please Greg and his friends, but to ironically savor the entertainment of actually scraping the thirty-minute-old eggs and potatoes out of the pan and onto a cold plate as a commentary on the absurdity of mass produced, mediocre food culture. My condescending amusement may have only offended anyone who noticed. The brunch took me back to my days of eating at the school cafeteria, and I was beginning to feel misanthropic. I wanted to go home and read Kafka.

I'm being melancholy.

After talking about the concert the night before, Greg and his roommates, Hank Scott and Mason Leary, began discussing music, and I forgot that I was eating derisively. Greg was far more enlightened on the music scene, while he was appreciative of more commonplace artists. Hank was a throwback fan, a firm believer in the old school heroes of Country Music—Merle, George (Jones more so than Strait), Charlie, Willie, Waylin. It was a family tradition to him, and his father had named him after Hank Williams—the first Hank Williams, that is. I knew nothing of these artists, but he was humble and passionate about his opinions. He also wore a hip pair of prescription horn rim specs that boosted his authenticity. Mason had a catlike air about him. He spoke seldom on the matter of music, but spoke sharply and sincerely. His era and genre of choice were the Grunge and Alternative scenes of the 1990s. But he had recently purchased an album called *Gravity Waltzes* that he recommended, and it was then I was first introduced to Garrett Sedgwick.

I tell you all this, readers, to tell you that I would eventually be introduced to Wick in the flesh, as well as to tell you that though these new friends were not in my scene, they would come to resurface again. The three of them agreed that he was talented, and though I was having a miserable day after attending a concert, a church and a buffet that were all not to my liking, it struck a chord with me that Greg, Hank, and Mason would all give such an artist a rave review. They burned me a copy of the album and I played it to myself in the loft bedroom as I hunted for apartments. I had to give Wick two listens in order to make a decent judgement.

This is no prologue, readers. This is how the narrative must unravel, where it begins: If it was not when I moved into an apartment in downtown Nashville, it was when I first heard of a local artist named Wick while dining at a Shoney's just south of the city.

I'm being sentimental.

1
"YOUNG FOLKS"
feat. a reluctant Marxist apology

According to Hank Scott, one of the most revealing moments in Country Music history was the infiltration of Ashton Kutcher into the Country Music Awards in 2012, in which he sang the only Country song on the stage that night, George Strait's "I Cross My Heart," and sang it poorly. People said he was poking fun at the genre, which he was, but he was mocking the very crowd that had forgotten its roots. By appearing in the traditional garb of a Country singer and singing off tune, this prankster with no connections to the genre defied an entire industry to dare examine its own trail. His ten gallon hat was derivative only of the original style, and the award which used to bear its resemblance. The only Country he had ridiculed was the one that had already lifted its feet up off the grass it had once walked on.

It wasn't KISS presenting an award that angered the crowd, but a man who dressed and sang like the only one who should have belonged there. I can't help but be intrigued by the implications upon any other given scene. It almost made these struggles of such a stale and predictable genre seem almost, one might say, universal. I tried to imagine the reaction if Bon Iver were to play at the Source Awards and the crowd booed at Kevin Hart for dressing like Grandmaster Flash, or if the Latin Grammy audience was treated to Flogging Molly, but hissed at George Lopez for presenting an award dressed like a Mariachi. Kutcher blurred the lines of what Country thought it was supposed to be, so that nobody knew what exactly he was mocking, not even himself. It had reached the point where such shenanigans were no longer shocking, they were just awkward.

I was not fortunate enough to find an affordable place in the blossoming neighborhood of East Nashville, where I had originally set my sights. Once I was able to establish myself, my goal was to eventually find a cozy bungalow with a modest veranda, within walking distance of a grocer. It was a more realistic vision than the house on the coast I would design, the coastal house from which I would embark on all my projects, ruffling the fur of a dog or cat by my side as I sipped choice drinks and filled sketch books. For the time being, a one room apartment would do. I passed up the opportunity to have a roommate in order to have a quiet studio. I can work in any wifi hot spot, but a designer needs his space. Mine had hardwood floors, well-aged brick and a view of the Pinnacle undergoing construction.

Before I could get about to making friends I met with my clients and set about to carving a work schedule. A local bank had hired me on to do illustrations for them, a series of sketches around trades meant to draw new, younger clientele. They clearly wanted to expand their business toward a developing market, and my portfolio had matched the style they were seeking. I set to work on a number of rough sketches to pitch within the next few days.

I am not a sellout because I chose to take my work to a lucrative business rather than labor on artistically confrontational pieces for art galleries and civic fairs. I am not so idealistic as to assume that working for money is anything other than making money. I am doing the same thing the bohemian painting on the street is doing, and if I were asked to perform any task that violated my integrity I would gladly step away from the contract. I dress like a communist, and I work for a capitalist. I am neither. Not everything is a business, but everything must have a business model. Any institution exists to provide a product, and every product has a market. I do not have the luxury of not having to work for revenue. Those who claim no revenue are dependent on someone, somewhere. A starving artists is not any more holy than a well fed one, but only less fortunate. It may be the fault of a society enslaved by commodity that art is not well appreciated, but it is not the fault of the employed artist for finding a way to feed himself, so long as he keeps to his principles. Entrepreneurship is dead without creativity. I have no qualms with art behaving as a business. It always has and always will be. The creative community must meet the challenges of the new economy, and to do so, one must consort with economists. If it is any consolation, readers, the bank was a local lending institution, and not a multi-national corporation.

I'm being condescending.

*   *   *

Also living in the city were my cousin Tabitha Redding-Davis and her husband, Virgil Redding-Davis, the latter of whom I had never met because there was never actually a wedding. I had grown up in Florence, Alabama and Tabitha had lived the next county over. She was a quiet one in high school, sticking mostly to her books. She dated no boys, but had been a passive aggressive butterfly, the kind who had dazzling wings but still remained in her cocoon. With the combination of being pretty, mysterious and disinterested, she tantalized any boy that went after her without even trying. The pursuit was all she wanted. She had developed a fixation on Brad Paisley when she went through a Country phase. All her crushes had been either famous or fictional since she was little, but she eventually outgrew such nonsense. She had gone to school to study foreign language and business, and had thought about going into international law, but her move to Nashville had changed those plans. She now worked as a librarian's assistant at Aquinas College, where Virgil was enrolled.

Virgil was the first man I had known Tabitha to date, let alone marry. He was from Louisville and five years older than Tabitha, and as if his beard was not enough to make up for his balding head, he had a premature man bun focused like a stunted, swelling halo. He was impressively well read, and was climbing academia toward what he casually announced would become a Ph.D in Theology. He had gotten a Master's in Old Testament studies at Harding in Memphis, where he had met Tabitha, and was close to receiving his second Master's in Theology from Aquinas. Tab would mention later that Virg had hoped to be accepted into a doctoral program by now, but adjusted well into settling for a second Master's.

They invited me over for dinner once I moved, and served a sustainable meal of organic bean pasta. Tab had taken on buying only organic produce, which they purchased weekly at the Farmer's Market off Eighth. It was clear that Tab and Virg Redding-Davis longed to move to a more cosmopolitan metropolis to immerse themselves in the academic, cultural and theological scenes therein, and had settled for Nashville for circumstantial reasons. They had an acutely insatiable ambition to be caught up on all things print and pregnant with implication, so much so that one could not read a trending article that they had not already spoiled.

"You'll have to give me some good reading recommendations," Virg told me. "I'm still recovering from reading the most horrible book last week on Biblical Hermeneutics. It's the closest I've ever come to saying a book ought to be flat out banned."

"Why?" I said. "Because of the fallacious doctrinal suppositions?"

"No," he said with a wave of his hand. "Because the writing is just so pedestrian."

"Oh."

"Have you read the biography of Bonhoeffer? Not the one by Metaxas. It's tedious and heavily biased. I'm referring to the Schlingensiepen one."

I read no biographies of theologians. "I'm familiar with it," I said.

"Mmm." Tabitha savored pasta and her recollection all at once. "I read this article in *The New Yorker* about the unique history of homicide in America. Startling."

I waited patiently for her to continue on about it.

"Neil," said Virgil, "you have to read this *HuffPost* article. I can send it to you. It's all on how professors have the least stressful jobs in the country. I guess I'm in the right line of work."

He laughed out loud at his own line, his furry eyebrows ruffling behind his Buddy Holly frames. I could not tell what Tab was thinking but Virg, being more transparent, would no doubt plow through text after text after text, luxuriating them by the stack like bottles in a cellar. There were those competitive couples who played one another in tennis and then either copulated or altercated afterward, sometimes both. Rather, Tab and Virg must have raced one another through dense volumes with a glass of Sauvignon Blanc and an evening of NPR.

"Read any good novels lately?" asked Virg.

"I've tried to get into *This Side of Paradise*," I told him, truthfully realizing *post facto* the incidental play on words I had just uttered.

He nodded his head, as if to move on to discussing the novel, which he didn't. "Have you read *The Evening Redness in the West*?"

"Not yet. Been meaning to."

"Oh, I tell you," he said, brimming with delight, "it's a brutal read. You almost have to be in a certain mood to move through it. McCarthy is just a master." He paused long enough to gulp down his food. "I'm really telling you, Neil, that you need to jump into Maritain. He will change your world. The legacy he left us..."

Tab leaned over to me to explain. "He's doing his capstone on Jacques Maritain. The monk?"

Nodding, I said, "He sounds delightful."

Most of the evening consisted of conversations like this. Among the established upper class, the customs of signifying one's worth based on one's possessions was rooted in an insecurity of the self, of the need to be validated by what one had gained, or inherited. Such is not the prerogative among the cultured, educated debtors such as ourselves, who live as middle class citizens on money borrowed, inherited, or gained from our newfound and indeterminately temporary occupations, enslaved to repay whatever we do accrue, even supposing we are fortunate enough to land a job in business, academia, or the fine arts.

It Is imperative that we maintain a collective narcissism in order to live day to day. We do not have vast tracks of land to show; what we have are vast stores of cultural capital. When we say, "I've read a nice book lately (as well as understood and analyzed it)," we are, if cultural capital is the equivalent of financial capital, equated with the one percent who say, "this house used to be owned by a tycoon," or "this car was manufactured with only one hundred like it in the world, it goes very fast, and it is very shiny both inside and out."

For us it is a defense mechanism, a way of establishing that, whether or not we care how little capital we possess, the cultural capital we possess is by far more enriching. In this way we have supposedly supplanted the moral high ground of the financial elite, oblivious to the reality that we have dropped quite a fortune of debt on the obtaining of this knowledge. We hold the keys to class determination, we tell ourselves, yet the keys are growing ever more extortionate and ineffectual, an aristocracy of triviality which seeks to compensate for the expenses of our pursuits by speaking outside our areas of expertise. We have signed in blood the payment of great sums of capital in order to declare ourselves literate. We cannot resist declaring what we find lying around. Our texts are our show horses: We do not have to have ridden upon them, so long as we have them resting in the stables, shelved away.

I'm being tangental.

*   *   *

Tab and Virg had a Boston Terrier they always took for evening walks after dinner. They were ecstatic about their new pit bull terrier, whom they had proudly converted to vegetarian food and given a washable diaper. They named it Caraway, after the herb.

As I walked with them I caught them up on my life, and they caught me up on theirs. The little dog trotted ahead of us on his leash. We walked out of the way of Hillsboro and the noise and lights of the noisy joints. I was happy for her, that she had found Virg and settled into a city with a sufficient launch into her career, happy for the little dog too. The scene was treating them well enough. Virg answered a phone call from a friend who wanted to talk about the poetry of Blake, so Tab and I strolled behind slowly. She stared away from him, away from me, off into the dusk, as if she was sighing on the inside.

"You know Virg isn't Catholic," she blurted out, as if in defense of something I had said, breaking out of her usual murmur. When she saw that I didn't care, she apologized.

"It's just this whole—you know my parents. I mean, you knew them enough. They didn't get Virgil. They thought he was just meddling and drifting. When he told them he attended a Christianity and Zen conference, it was like I had come out lesbian or something."

"So why did you marry him?" I said. "I mean, I don't care. But if your parents didn't approve—"

"He's just so smart," she said. There was more she wanted to release, but resisted articulation, not out of a lack of words, but a lack of the perfect way to form them. It had been one of her more grievous traits for years.

"You don't have to defend yourself to me," I told her. "I remember your parents were shocked that you brought him home. I would have come to a wedding. I get it if you didn't have one because of them."

She hesitated. "It wasn't that," she said. "They would have come and supported me. I mean, they didn't disown me or anything."

"Was it Virgil's parents?"

"No, they even took it well that we swapped each other's last names. And it wasn't money either, if you're wondering. Virgil could explain it to you. We just—we've decided that marriage has just become—"

"An outdated tradition, right?"

"No, no," she said, shaking her head. "We're married and everything. And part of it was money, just the expenses, not that we couldn't afford them, but if you add up the money spent on a dress and the decorations and—it's complicated. I wanted to make sure it was for the right reasons, and I love Virgil. It was a decision we made together."

"Like I said, you don't have to explain yourself to me."

"I've just opened my eyes a lot, that's all," she said, perking her shoulders. "You understand." She knew I understood. We all understood. We were young people who's eyes had been opened. "You would understand more than a lot of people. Oh gosh—the people at church! All they want to know is when we're going to have kids."

She stopped herself like she stopped at the dinner table when they mentioned the new church they had joined, stopped when Virg had brought it up and I could tell she was about to invite me. It was the same look she gave me when she knew I was no longer a part of that scene and did not want to burden me with an invitation, almost did not blame me for forsaking such a scene whose relevancy had dwindled in our budding years. I was emotionally stable and intellectually well-rounded enough.

"Things are just different now," she said to me. "Virg is just so smart, and I don't think they understand."

"That's the thing," I said, comforting her through agreement. "People are so hegemonized."

"They just don't appreciate—" said Tab, and stopped herself. She sighed with the anxiety of sophistication and didn't say another word. Even now she could not talk to me, only because she could never talk to anyone. I was glad for her that she had found in Virg a man she could talk to, or even better, a man whom she could listen to—listen to for hours—more than her own father, more than her cousins, more than any other man in her life. She laughed and beamed from underneath her leather flat cap, as if by introducing me to her lover-husband she had hoped to gain at the very least my approval, asserting that she had joined, and had perhaps always been privy to, a distinguished generation of misunderstood cosmopolite pioneers. I didn't care either way who she married. She was happy, and she had a dog too.

I found it more than difficult to improve upon a symbol that communicated both the security and community of a small lending institution. I worked on my client's designs for two days straight before joining Virg and Tab again at the Farmer's Market where they helped me select some produce. They had brought along a friend, Kenna Rothchild, and I had a suspicion they would try to fix me up with her. She was a friend of Tabitha's from high school, a gossip and a scenester who never left home without a trilby and never put down her iPhone. Kenna was a wedding photographer and a music blogger, but she treated them both as hobbies. She dressed like a true vintage queen, all outfits complete with a leather belt.

Friendship with Kenna was Tabitha's guilty pleasure, and you could hear it in their laughs, as Tabitha exchanged her maturity for that of a high schooler, and they were absorbed in each other's musings.

"Oh yeah, this durian looks like a f—in' sea urchin," she'd remark, and Tabitha would laugh.

If you think I am engaging in self-censorship, readers, because of some deep-rooted obligation to the moralism of my raising, or some subconscious impulse to actually conform to the repressive and superstitious standards of decor thereof, you would be wrong. No, I clearly do it for ironic reasons, as the breaching of an artistic expectation that will cause you, readers, to question the very purpose of censoring art, as well as pausing over my intentions.

Kenna found me interesting enough, repeating with her masculine voice "you kill me, Neil" to every one of my one-liners, or explanations of my work. Kenna was momentarily enthused by every trending observance, so I wasn't flattered. I felt like a tourist attraction, that Kenna was a girl who treated this whole town as if she'd grown up here, and that the tourists were what amused her. Although Tabitha kept her modest tongue since she was a child, Kenna swore casually and frequently, not because it came natural to her, but as if she had most recently left the nest and discovered that she could not only swear, but that swearing was a rite of passage she had to prove she had long grown accustomed to, like a teenager pretending she wasn't smoking for the first time among friends. She was a reminder of why I prefer girls with large vocabularies anyway.

"That tee shirt is a f—ing riot," she told me, and snapped a picture with her phone. I was charmed in an odd way by her audacity.

Kenna's latest news was that she had gotten tickets to a Garrett Sedgwick concert. "I'm killer stoked about it."

"Garrett who?" said Tabitha, who had never heard of him.

"Are you kidding me?" said Kenna. "Wick? He's all over the f—ing place. How have you not heard of him? Oh my G—, Tab. You are going with me."

"I can't," said Tab. "Me and Virg have this thing—" She gestured to Virg to confirm, but he was babbling over the phone while he juggled a lime. She turned to me, and the obvious finally surfaced.

"You could go with Neil," she said. "Take Neil with you."

I laughed at the prospect, but I had not been to a Nashville concert since Merle, and I needed a different scene, a real chance to break in, find new friends, and get a taste closer to my own.

"Sh—. You're going with me," said Kenna. "Have you seen him? Tab, come here, you need to see him."

Kenna pulled up a clip of Wick playing in concert from the last show she had been do, to which Tabitha shrugged with indifference. "Yeah, you should go with Neil."

"Yeah, I gave *Gravity Waltzes* a listen," I said. "It was decent."

"You have to see him live," said Kenna. "Let's do it. I'll hook you up. You'll love Wick. He's totally deck."

I feared this would turn into a first date, because I had been at the wrong place at the wrong time, and Tabitha had become more engrossed in relaxed parties than new music. But I was curious about Wick, and couldn't say no to the concert. Besides, I heard a decent band was opening for him. I was a bit perturbed that Tab had played the cupid and sprung it on me, but I was getting a free show out of it. I had just spent fifty dollars on fruit and a baguette. I needed something for free.

2
"FOOLS BY YOUR SIDE"
feat. 3rd-person omniscient
present tense excursions

At the Sedgwick show, I was introduced to a crowd so charmed that they were compelled into an almost reluctant frenzy like apprehended draft dodgers gone patriots, opting out of dancing and clapping, instead nodding their heads hypnotically as if a Mahatma was lecturing them at a summit on human rights, so that at any moment they could effortlessly shift to shaking their heads and shrugging their shoulders should they spot one another being enthused. I remained in their midst so I could bypass the noxious air of screaming fan girls and frat boys who knew three of his songs and half of which didn't know which show they were at.

Sedgwick was currently touring with his current band project, Gargamel Epic, but played mostly songs from his fist LP, *The Miquelet*, which he recorded with another project, The Hymnists. It was raw enough that he was playing mostly another project's songs, but it had become common for his shows, since he formed another band for each album, and humbly released each one under that name. His credibility grew exponentially as his name got out despite it's flying under the radar of each release, as if he had planned it to be so.

AllMusic called *The Miquelet* "a fresh and versatile parade of impressive stomps balanced by beautiful ballads." A review in *The Tennessean*, confirming an aside made several issues before, confirmed that Garrett Sedgwick had indeed been an upcoming artist worth paying attention to. As it goes, such a mention gave him more of such attention. *The Nashville Scene* predicted that Wick would win Best Local Artist of the year, which he didn't, and though he was never nominated, the unofficial title remained spoken among various circles. Walt Bowen of *Pitchfork* called the album "a raucous debut made for a crowd hungry after something previously unable to satiate: In a land far away, a demi-god rode in on a T-Rex and delivered a child to human parents. That child emerges as mysteriously as he came with the honky-grunge record that astonished Music Row." Music Row didn't really pay much attention to it.

Upon the release of his first LP, Sedgwick's swift popularity threatened to catapult him into a saturation of omnipresence that caused a nearly suicidal blowback of adoration and frustration with such salient adoration. A business mogul hosts a pool party in which the entire album is played on shuffle, and a fight ensues in which a girl is nearly electrocuted to death by being nudged into the pool simultaneously with a speaker. Two Belmont dropouts are seen dropping fresh copies of the vinyl down a storm drain after a Humvee rolls by blasting the single, "Chimeral." A high school Homecoming princess soils her reputation by losing her virginity with the bedroom door open, and the one facet of the story everyone and his mother tells the same way is that the boy impressed her with his knowledge of Wick's musical influences as the album glows softly in the corner like a lamp. A sophomore at Vandy creates a new logo for the campus radio station, modeled directly after the cover of *The Miquelet*, and a cease-and-desist order from the label causes the station to revert to their original logo, although the damage has already begun as tees bearing the logo spread across the campus. Two years later one of the shirts sells on Craigslist for seventy dollars.

I saw the design, and admit I was a little jealous. To describe it as a solid orange imprint of a steampunk robot struck by lightning in the style of a Mayan relief would not do it justice.

It was a decent show, held at the Fontanel. Sedgwick's band was one of three playing, like it was some mini-festival. Kenna related to me that Wick never played big arena shows without pulling in another couple groups. He mostly stuck to small venues by principle, with few exceptions. Hosting other local bands as if they were headliners and not opening acts was seen as both a humble gesture and a motion of pretense, since everyone knew who they were there to see. He even made his set list as short as those preceding him. We heard Jeff and the Brotherhood, followed by Pujol, both of which were letdowns.

I should have expected that I couldn't go through a night without someone spotting my mistaken celebrity. "Hey! Ben Folds!" a random girl shouted at me as I walked by with a fresh bag of popcorn. "What are you doing here?" As if she knew me, of course. Or, knew Ben Folds. But if I was Ben Folds, where else would I likely be?

"I came for the popcorn," I said, and trotted away.

We weren't anywhere close to the stage, but I ran into an old friend who introduced me to a few people who I thought would make a decent batch of droogs. There was Samantha, who came with her husband Sam, and it was no shortage of confusion in how they were both referred to as "Sam." They were high school romancers who had just gotten married and gotten back from a honeymoon at Coachella. They hung around one another with the freshness of a childlike nonchalance, like they were best friends who had once dated before they were best friends who had once dated before they were best friends. Samantha worked customer service at the Omni, and Sam was a barista. Samantha had a pink smirk and Sam was lanky. They were funny to watch together, like they had just chased one another out of a song by The Moldy Peaches.

There was the great bearded Julius, who had just divorced and had been getting out the blues by attending shows with Joey, who himself was splitting with his wife over various cracks in the relationship. Julius was a bank teller, though he was seeking work in the theater. He had killer sideburns and brewed his own beer. Joey was the old friend who introduced me to the others. We had met in college and almost became roommates at one point. Despite his pending divorce, he seemed his usual, convivial self. He was now a marketer for *The Tennessean*, although his dream was to travel abroad and, well, do something abroad while traveling, something involving mostly reading in other languages, though he had not picked up any he was fluent in. His Beatles haircut was stuffed under a black beanie he seldom removed.

There were Frances, Amanda and Cline, who all roomed together. Frances, whom they called "Frenchy," was a short girl in a fur cap who always let the covers hang over her ears, making her look like a small puppy. She worked at an artisan bakery where they didn't mind that her arms were ridden with tats. She smoked Parliaments and carried a purse almost half her size so she could smuggle in forties, which she shared with everyone. "They never check my bag," she said. "They're always checking out the hat." Amanda and Cline were baristas who were always together and bickering, but weren't dating. Everyone chastised Cline for being a John Mayer fan, which he found more tolerable than years of being bullied for his owl-eyed glasses. Amanda must have believed it was her duty to perpetuate the stereotype of the fiery redhead. She vaguely sassed me, as I was told she did with all her new acquaintances, just to discover early if she would like me when I made her angry. It made her a little too coquettish.

They were interesting cats, each of them. I discovered I shared enough interests with them, or that if I didn't I at least shared the same outlook on the concert, and we were all well practiced at endlessly articulating our complaints. None of them admitted to being fans of Wick, or at least the Wick who now had put out five records. He just happened to be the only decent show that night, and they had all come upon the tickets incidentally. Rather than tuning in to the stage we shared one another's favorite groups, dropping their names and matching them up like hands in a game of Gin Rummy we were playing in the back corner. Anecdotes about Wick were exchanged:

Before he started out Sedgwick had dropped out of music school with a single credit remaining because he had broken two fingers in a bar fight the night before his jury recital. He had to buy a new cushioned wing chair every time he wrote a song. He painted his own equipment orange because he has an obsession with the color, proven by its heavy presence in each album, mostly appearing in a checker pattern, as well as the name of his debut EP, *Orange*. When asked by a radio host, he once said he planned to put out an album named after each of the prismatic hues, and never affirmed that it was a publicity stunt. He'd done uncredited guest recordings and surprise performances with artists like Bright Eyes, Arcade Fire, Neutral Milk Hotel, Sufjan Stevens, Nick Cave & The Bad Seeds, My Morning Jacket, M. Ward. He'd once covered Cohen's "Bird on a Wire" and began crying, unable to finish the concert, and not a single fan demanded their money back, for they had all been privileged with such a raw moment. He didn't drink, smoke, eat any meat other than fish, or have sex, all out of boredom with the banality of such indulgences, unadulterated dedication to his craft, and as a spiritual-seeker experiment he was performing as part of a personal journey. But we agreed that the performances had gotten lame.

I'm being ostentatious.

After the show, we made plans to hang out, but not where or what to do. Kenna had already acquired everyone's number, anyway. She had actually shot the wedding photos for Sam and Sam. It seemed before long she would have listed contacts in half the town.

"If you don't get a job in music, get a job in the wedding industry," she said. "You make a f—in' killing. I shot Sam and Sam's a month ago for two grand. And that was a three grand job, but they were super cute and it was a small deal."

"They look made for each other," I said.

Kenna shrugged. "I give it a year. Maybe less." There was not even a tone of pessimism, but only an entrepreneur's remorse. "F —. I probably make bank on remarriages half the time. I kid you not. I shot the same girl's wedding twice within like three years. If she'd seen that coming she could've gotten a package deal."

"I think I'll remain in the throes of bachelorhood," I said. "I can just divorce myself. I'd take some killer photos."

Kenna took a drag. "You kill me, Neil."

The show had left me less than enthused. Kenna had only touched on an epidemic with glosses of commercial appeal, and we discovered we were both cynics. Our generation was raised in a hegemony of instant gratification and objectification of both the female form and the female mind. The objectification of the female form allowed the social institution of marriage to become a rite of passage for men seeking to obtain flesh as a permanent, though risky, signification of social capital, whereas for women the institution of marriage was marketed as an experience requiring a satisfactory number of purchases whose value would need to be equaled in the waning years of the inevitably perishing relationship by the continuing purchase of household products, expanding a rift in the relationship already brought on by the continuing purchases of the groom meant to satiate our culture's expectation of a growing domain. The desire to expand and modify the domain expands into the relationships the spouses have with others. We have sought to avoid this by minimizing both the capital spent on the ceremony and the upkeep of the household that follows. In lieu of that, we have maneuvered past one obstacle and into another.

We do not stand on the serious formality of ceremony, but sit playful on the motions of it so that any vestige of guilt for moving in together may be sent to a place where vows are pinkie promises. In doing so, we have less to lose. But we can still take some outstanding photography.

I wanted to watch other people revel in a good show, one that would last for at least a week. I hadn't bought the ticket, but I'd spent my evening. I didn't have a right to complain because I met some interesting people and had a great time, but I went home that night feeling surprisingly misanthropic. I decided to stay up and read some Wallace.

Julius and Joey called me up the next day and invited me out. Joey wanted us to go to PechaKucha Karaoke night, and Julius just wanted us to hit a bar. We could have just done both of these things, but what we decided was that we would do both of these things, only in reverse order. It happened just like that. We said, "hey, what if we went drinking and *then* went to PechaKucha Karaoke night?" I had only heard of PechaKucha, which was very simple—twenty Powerpoint slides, twenty seconds each, six minutes and forty seconds to cram your message. It was a simply genius pop presentation format devised by some architectural engineers in Japan to keep pitches short enough for an increasingly fast-paced professional world. Add in the element of Karaoke, and you have an improv speaking exercise to entertain millennial white collar workers. Plus, Joey said, "it always looks good on a résumé." He was right about that. You can make anything look good on a resume. I took a one-way suitcase to Europe for a semester of college because it would look good on a resume.

I only remember intending to order three beers at Santa's Pub, a cozy trailer of a place with wood walls, harsh lights, and poor karaoke artists, so poor they were a riot. It was a novelty experience, not just for the Santa kitsch, but also for the smokers. After my first beer I asked

Julius why they only served beer, and he said it was because liquor only made people do dumb things, and we laughed at the karaoke singers butchering "With A Little Help From My Friends." There wasn't one type here. It was a roadside attraction for all manner of folk. There were scenesters and geezers, and bankers and bikers (both of the motorized and pedestrian persuasion), Vandy preps and TSU geeks, uneasy out-of-towners and skanky party girls, creeps who'd lounge around the bathroom but didn't hit on any girls, a bassist whose claim to fame was having once toured for Country legend Hoyt Murdock, a vagrant who just wandered in, because everybody wandered in and we all wandered in. Nobody knew anybody by name, but we were united by oddity and ale. It was oddly cozy, like sneaking into your strange uncle's garage Christmas party, in June, and it was like some mystical experience.

It was at Santa's that Julius told me his story, laid it out like it was a stage play he had just seen, and no doubt he was thinking of turning it into a stage play. There were three acts:

"Act I: We marry and do the same odd sh— we always did, live in the same apartment we always lived in, see the same venues, eat the same foods, sleep in the same bed. You know, no conflict. It's a slow first act.

"Act II: We grow tired of one another, which grows increasingly frequent. Conflict escalates quickly, but subtly. When the conflict builds to a certain point we just leave and get with a friend, a pattern with an irresistibly exponential rise, scene after scene.

"Act III: We are with friends more than each other, and treat each other more like friends than lovers. Each realizes that neither cares, that perhaps the two of us are just friends, and one day I am living in a new apartment, and so is she. This scene splits the stage, and each of us carry on our own scene. The audience is actually split too and must watch only one of us live out our lives. And this was the freest moment of my life. My side of the audience is treated to it. Hers, what the H—. I hope they enjoy the show."

It was a comedy, an egregious satire. Julius laughed at the end of it and downed another beer. We all laughed. Julius bellowed. Joey still had a bright soul, I could tell from his giggle. He would point something out about you and you knew then that he knew you had a bright soul too. I was glad I'd run into him once again. I had stumbled upon the best. I wanted us to just get up and amble outward into the street after one another, or after the town, wherever it was going, but whenever I thought of it they snared me into some unnecessary philosophical abstraction, Jules gripping my shoulder and Joey kicking back in a schoolboy laughter I had to partake in. I was sipping nectar with Bacchus and Pan, I was with the Ghosts of Christmas Present and Past, and I was the Ghost of Some Obscure Holiday Yet To Be Future Conditional Pluperfect Subjunctive, and we would have been traveling through time and space if we could. It was the North Pole, it was 1893. It was El Tabernaculo in Grenada all over again, with spiced beer and minced pork all around, except pork would have been superfluous. In every moment I felt amused and bemused by the liminal griminess of the place and its pilgrims. Still, it was a little kitsch.

It seemed we were there longer than we were before we left and took a cab. We were late to PechaKucha Karaoke night, and we were too drunk to know we stood out for our drunkenness. I hadn't been drunk many times in my life, having remained repressed for some time from my religious upbringing. I don't remember any of the slides they gave me, or the narrative I wove to attempt to tie them all together. All I know is that I was a hit. Joey was a natural. He smoothly blended the images like he was stringing up laundry to dry. But whatever I did, it won the crowd. I was up and speaking and I saw the pub singers up and singing and I was up and down, I was audience and participant. I don't even remember who I talked to, but by the end of the night I was given seven business cards and received two calls the next day. I was hung-over, and I looked out my window at the skyline holding all the others who peered out their window so casually, and I was with them all, trying to make it somewhere. I returned the phone calls and by the end of the day before I knew it I had two more clients, a men's clothing store and a regional barber shop franchise. I was going to be sketching a lot of dapper gentlemen.

3
"INTERVENTION"
feat. white self-disillusionment
to go around

Along East Bank heading past Parkway Terrace there was for a time a billboard above the old Cumberland railway that merely read "NO PROMO." Away from the towering cityscape and hovering over the rusted rail to the river's far side, you'd miss it if it weren't so out of place. This billboard is regarded by many as some sort of typo or a result of confusion between the billboard owner, an artist, and a business owner. It may have been a space that the owner was waiting for someone to buy out and had meant to send a message that there was not yet a brand or slogan, a vacancy awaiting new business. Many also believed the canvas to be already occupied, and that it was some viral marketing for an emerging company or product. Others suggested it was part of some anti-ad movement or an act of culturejamming vandalism that had yet to be corrected, or perhaps that it was a form of protest from a neighborhood association against the visual pollution of company billboards hovering so close to their homes, a PSA that failed to achieve the potency of an understood, heeded message. It became a byword tacked onto conversation, and only some understood the reference.

I first noticed the sign on the way to a gathering with Tab and Virg on the East Side, a picnic held at a friend's place. The friend was Lucy Calder, a Kiwi expat and a frugal minimalist whose only outstanding expense was a cozy bungalow with a modest veranda within walking distance of Turnip Trick, the organic grocer she had quickly found out she could not afford to shop at every week, but only in the preparation of special meals, which she would host for her friends. She wore an elegant and simple nineteen forties dress that was a sister to the one Tabitha wore. She was freckled and had a rosy smile that was not too coquettish. I took a liking to her traits before I realized she had a husband, Philip, who was a previous schoolmate of Virgil's. Philip was a keen banjo player and preferred to dress like a member of the working class whose clothes were never tarnished and hands were always washed.

Lucy and Philip hosted the picnic in their yard on a perfect day, and everyone brought a dish to help out. I was not a cook, so I bought a melon at Turnip Trick. I could see why both Tab and Lucy found it so expensive, and they lamented how dreadful it was to have to settle for the Farmer's Market on the west side, whose pastoral narrative was less transparent.

"The key is to always buy exactly how much you need to eat," said Lucy, and I could have bought a record of her telling me how to eat with her Kiwi accent. "I always tell everyone, think before, during, and after you eat. It's not just for the budget, it's for your body. Be minimalist, and be smart."

Her insistence on this minimalism had led Lucy to terminally and permanently forego all social media, shutting down her Facebook, Twitter, Pinterest, Flickr and Instragram. She kept her food blog running, and obviously kept her email and phone service. Tab persuaded her to reconsider, because email and phone were not enough to keep in touch with the pictures and links they had shared, and after several minutes of pleading she finally let it go. As Lucy reminded her, if anything, people need to have interventions for being too attached to their social media. They were at a social gathering, and there were people.

The other people included Benjamin Shearing and his wife, Kelly. The skinny, goggled Ben was currently a library researcher at Lipscomb, and I could tell, because he could name at least one excellent book on any subject named by anyone. He had moved here from Asheville with Kelly, who was a part time English teacher. Ben and Kelly had figured out a way to dispose of their garbage only three times a year. Ben was an environmentalist and a mycophile who could afford to shop regularly at Turnip Trick, and at every meal he would invite everyone to hunt mushrooms with him. Kelly maintained a regular blog on biblical language and theology, but was currently writing a diatribe for submission to the *The Observer* questioning the necessity of both Shelby and Hermitage golf courses where there had previously been a stretch of arable farmland along the Cumberland bank.

Obadiah and Emily Jenkins had just married. Emily was a social worker who headed up a children's ministry. Obadiah was an associate minister at Tab's church who quoted Chomsky profusely in casual conversation. He quite believed the World Wrestling Federation to be an operatic feat showcasing the true dramatic forces of Western power struggles and relationships, rather than a pompous specimen of low culture machismo. He was also the lead guitarist in his band, Cactus Jack and the Boiler Room Studs, serving a repertoire of covers from Dylan, nineteen eighties hair bands, and ironic ballads he had written based on the book of Genesis.

Everyone and their wife was at this picnic. I had expected Tab to play cupid again and provide a single female, but I was instead made to be the proverbial ninth wheel.

As we ate everyone talked with one or two across or next to them until a roundhouse series of compliments over the dishes brought melded into a unified discussion of food. Within seconds we were questioning the basic assumptions of the military-industrial-agricultural complex. Ben had been accused by a blogger of being elitist.

"The very notion that I — that we are propagandizers is at most quite base and at the very least hypocritically misaligned and offensively fascist," he said.

"So what did you say?" asked Lucy.

Ben shrugged. "I referred him to *The Omnivore's Dilemma* by Michael Pollan, wherein he distinguishes between myophiles and mycophobes. There are people who know what food is, and there are people who qualify as nutritionally and naturally uneducated. He said he didn't have time to read that trash and that it was probably full of leftist dribble."

"It sounds like an ad hominem," I said. "I mean, what member of the alleged foodie elite is a member of the one percent?"

"It's an evasion tactic," said Virg, smiling. "They want to avoid a serious debate, but it's already happening, so they revert to name-calling."

"The current industry being overly reliant on monocultures is a recognized threat to sustainability," said Ben, as if he were reading it directly from a tract.

Obadiah stroked his goatee. "The partisan politics game always pulls us into the same game. The military-industrial complex doesn't want sustainability." He began to giggle and fervently bang on the table with his palms. "If I ran for office, no more sick-eyed people hoarding their loot. There is no freedom without interdependence. It is the farmer who feeds us and the farmer alone who should be tax free. Rights come with responsibilities, and that's law. Open all vaults and cancel all wars. And never, under any circumstances, vote for a male politician without a beard."

Virg kicked his head back and laughed at Obie's speech.

"Do you mean don't vote for someone without a beard, or don't vote if you don't have a beard?" said Tab.

"I make no investment in partisan politics anyway," said Ben.

"Me neither," said Obie, "but solutions do not exist without political dimensions."

"I think maybe so," said Lucy, "but I think it really begins with interpersonal relationships and awareness."

"Which is why we all need scholars and researchers," said Ben, his eyes smiling.

"Have you read that article in *Patheos*?" said Virg.

"It's very true," said Ben, who apparently had actually read it. "When evangelicals get a PhD nobody wants their research. Between doctrinal issues and a desire for layman's literature, you're not likely to publish anything anyone is going to want to read. The job market for academics is diminished even greater for PhD's in religion and theology. Institutional evangelicalism is often antithetical to inquiry. Any chance at real scholarship is undercut by rigid, traditional doctrinal stances held by university donors and boards of trustees."

"That's why you should be an adjunct," said Philip. "You have nothing to lose."

Obie chuckled at his forming thoughts. "The student loan institution, the main source of oppression here, will also have to come down, regardless of how good a job you get."

"Here's to being blessed with a full ride," said Virg, lifting his glass toward Tab, who blushed. She had never liked to boast about her full ride.

"But that's true in any field," I said. "Academic pressure isn't exclusive to fundamentalist universities."

"I thought we were talking about food," said Lucy. "What do you think about not relying on political strategies but going on with things on a grassroots level?"

"Too many factory farm workers are underpaid," said Obie. "The people cannot stand if minimum wage cannot stand. I wonder, I do so wonder where all that subsidy money goes. Methinks it does no good. It is the migrants especially who suffer. Where are the workers and vinedressers?" He rose up his hands in a divine gesture. "I tell you that if the least of these does not have food on his table, you who feast on bread cannot be a disciple."

"You don't have to go and make a sermon out of it," I mumbled.

"He's just being funny," said Tab.

"But I mean, you're all sitting here preaching to the converted," I said. "Nobody's in disagreement that the food industry is a simulation of a food experience. Nobody denies the urgency. But if you can barely afford to eat these meals imagine what the rest of the ninety-nine percent is consuming."

"He's got a point," said Virg. "The hispanic community in American cities does not have the English literacy to begin to read the instruction labels on most packaging, not to mention the number of native born Americans who don't have the functional literacy to buy what is good for them."

Tab nodded her head. She had been more talkative while complimenting the dishes brought, but in the tension of the current conversation she could not express herself, and I wanted to hear what she had to say. Instead, it was mostly the men talking. If I didn't know better I would have thought I'd stumbled into a previous decade's patriarchal table. Rather, I knew it was the case that all the men had married introverts.

"But," I said, "it is a bit elitist to think that when someone receives the same knowledge you are privileged to that they will be filled with the same incendiary fervor."

"I think what he's saying," Philip interjected, "is that it won't be enough for us who are educated and financially stable to merely continue our own eating patterns, that this will only produce a cycle of middle class consumers of expensive organic food culture."

"I'd recommend Eric Schlosher's *Fast Food Nation*," said Ben. "It's a bit pedestrian but it treats the subject matter rather fairly."

"Can you imagine convincing Wal-Mart to replace the Doritos isle with a sustainably farmed carrots aisle?" said Obie.

"So let's be creative," said Lucy. "Let's think of ways to get the word out and connect communities these ideas."

"What if you started some kind of food education fellowship group?" said Emily.

"A good text to include as a reading group with that would be *Scripture, Culture and Agriculture* by Ellen Davis," said Ben.

"Is that the one you showed to me earlier?" said Virg. "I'm not entirely sure everyone in our congregation has the literacy capacity to endure the reading."

"Those with the capacity should be the ones to discuss the matter," said Ben, "and those without should put their trust in the educated to perform their tasks, just as I put my trust in any other professional in any other field. It is a mistake to expect anyone to understand the scriptures without the aid of scholars. People cry against elitism, until they cry out for the elite."

He probably didn't mean for it to come out the way it did. I wanted to ask him if he was positing a caste system of educated and uneducated, or if he thought professionals in any field should always trusted by default, or if he was admitting himself as an elitist. I didn't know how to ask all of these without sounding contrary, so all I said was, "you sure about that?"

Ben turned his head to face me, blinked twice, and said, "To which antecedent to you refer?"

It kind of peeved me, so I didn't say anything else, and neither did anyone else for a minute, not even the wives. It occurred to me that maybe we were all introverts. Everyone took the silent moment to recharge.

"I just think it's very important," said Lucy after that long moment. "God wants us to take care of our bodies."

"It's certainly an aspect of holiness code that goes neglected," said Ben.

"I read a fantastic article the other day comparing the various farming and dieting practices of monasteries throughout the centuries," said Virg.

Before Ben could recommend another book, and before I thought of how offensive I would sound, I butted in. "I mean if you're going to tie Jesus and religion into it you'd think you'd have some of the poor people out here with you." I said that words *poor* and *Jesus* like they were forbidden.

There came another silence, not nearly as long but three times as dreadful as the one I had created moments ago. Tab raised her eyebrows at me, eyes wide and cheeks blushing, but she knew I had just brought more stimulation to the conversation. She was just waiting for the silence to cease.

"Th bourgeoisie are living a farce," said Obie, slamming his fist on the table with a grin.

"I know, it's hard not to be a pessimist about the whole situation," said Virg. "It's hard to escape the trappings of our social strata and make a difference. Neil, I think you have a point. We have to address the question of bringing in people of underprivileged backgrounds to the table. Have you read Roedeger's *Towards the Abolition of Whiteness?*"

"No." No one else had either, though it was assumed everyone had heard of it.

"A more recent work you might want to take al look at is *Understanding White Privilege* by Frances E. Kendall," said Ben. "It builds on that study but goes further with modern implications."

"Right," said Virg. "I think the real problem is that we want to fix the social, economic and racial divides that exist but we also want to be comfortable."

"And a lot of white people think their culture is being besieged," said Philip, "so they're voicing their concern for the survival of their privileges. I know my grandpa sure does."

This brought smiles back to the table. Everyone had that grandpa, or that uncle.

"That's the real reason they all oppose abortion in all circumstances," said Obie, "and yet give no thought to the very real circumstances of lower class mothers when it comes time to cut government programs. After all, I'll be darned, 'the white woman is here just to make us more white babies.'"

"But the vast majority of abortions are performed on minorities," said Ben.

"I hope we're not just lapsing into self-loathing," Emily piped in. "Like that will get us anywhere."

Virg leaned over aggressively. "I think the idea is that if we don't do something about it, the white race, or at least the construction of the white race, will continue to be the dominant norm even in the face of rising blended families and immigration, that the continued, you know, discrimination practices will not see defeat in our generation."

"Yeah, but that will take time," said Tab.

"But whiteness is a construct to begin with," I said. "The definition has already shifted in two hundred years."

"But it's very much a core part of everything in America," said Lucy. "I mean, even in New Zealand there's prejudice against the Maori, but there's not a KKK or Black Panther presence or anything that just, I don't know, cements in the national consciousness like it does here. The definition of *white* is even different across cultures. It stays around, but you know, it's complex too."

"I think the essential definition is having a lineage of privilege," said Virg. "We can mitigate the injustice we perpetuate, but we're still privileged and it's largely because of our ancestors. Obviously none of us hates ourselves here, but we really have to come to reject, in a way, our cultural status, or upbringing."

Obie slammed a fist on the table. "Swat the wasp!"

"But for what?" said Lucy. "I mean, imagine if if we all just decided to ape blackness or something. I don't think it would pass as very real."

Virg laughed. "Yeah, what was it Yankovic said? 'I know that I'm white and nerdy'?"

Beaming, Ben said, "If you do prefer a casual layman's read on that there's *A Shadow History of Hip-Hop in White America* by Jason Tranz."

"The solution is to abolish the privileges," said Obie. "But let's get real. When will they write that one into law? We can hate people, oh yes, we can hate people all day. But dare not think of hating a system, no sir. No promo."

"I think I remember that quote from Ignatiev," said Virg. "Something like, 'Treason to whiteness is loyalty to all races.' I think that was it."

There was a nodding of heads around the table.

"Profound," said Emily, flattening the napkin in her lap.

"So I guess it's up to us," I said in soft derision, and everyone clinked their ice in their cups and picked their teeth with their tongues. It made me feel a tad pusillanimous.

So there we were, a table of white people dressed as white people and eating white people food and talking of white people things in a white people neighborhood in a white people city, giving a toast to the end of whiteness. After lunch we played Bocci Ball while Obie and Philip jammed on the guitar and banjo.

*   *   *

I didn't remember ordering any Sedgwick tickets. Nobody ever admitted to actually ordering Sedgwick tickets; You just told people you had gotten hold of some and asked them if they wanted to go with you ever so subtly, as if it was a privilege for Wick to have you attend, if it wasn't out of your way. Seeing as how I didn't remember ordering any tickets, and two tickets showed up in my mail, I could safely say that I had "gotten a hold of some Sedgwick tickets." What was a figure of speech for others was true for me. There had been no purchase, no contest. I had placed myself under no obligation to go, to take someone, or to arrive and at least pretend to enjoy the show; yet the sheer passive-aggressive serendipity of it placed me under a perverse sense of obligation. The admission tickets were also specially designed—simple, yet elegant—with repeated chrome chevrons alternating up and down, as if beckoning me to some mock art deco formal ball. Rather, I was invited to bring a friend out to Marathon Music Works for what I hoped was a more intimate show than the Fontanel. I would give Wick a second chance, as my first encounter had not proven fulfilling.

I ran into a serious problem in selecting a fellow attendee. I first thought of everyone I had met at the Fontanel. Surely they wouldn't mind another show. Julius and Joey were a trip, but if I took one I could not take the other, even though I had known Joey longer. I had the same issue with Sam and Sam. In either case I could have given my tickets to both, but I felt it necessary to attend myself. Frenchy would have been deterred by an indoor show where she couldn't smoke, and both she and Cline had to work. Amanda was too annoying on the day I thought to ask her, within the same hour alternating between the persona of the naive virgin and the experienced flirt. She also would have never taken Cline's shift for him, even if he begged the both of us.

Then there was Kenna. She had been thrilled at the previous show. Still, I had already taken her. Tab and Virg hadn't gotten the chance to go, but this was yet another weekend they were both busy, Tab driving down to see some friends and Virg attending a conference. There was also Greg, who had indeed introduced me to Wick. For that I might have owed it to him. And yet he never did express that he wanted to see a show.

These were the options I weighed for days. I could have just scalped a ticket, had I the nerve. I could have played roulette. I could have tossed them. I could have gone alone. I chose to take Kenna. She was somewhat loud, but I knew she would be free and it would avoid any dilemmas of contingency. She intimidated me. The invitation intimidated me. It made me jittery with curiosity. It was the hand-drawn pattern of chevrons like mustaches, appealing to my own modus operandi. I wanted to take a blank canvas and copy the pattern into perpetuity, arrow after arrow after arrow, conveying possibility upwards and downwards at the same time.

I'm being premonitory.

4
"RUNAWAY"
feat. one or two red herrings

Some attendees buzzed around Wick like he was a lantern who would scorch them if they hung around too long. But in a more intimate venue, they allow themselves to take baby steps closer to the stage. Marathon Music Works is glowing like some guerilla spot in a brewery. The bar is open, the privileged chatter incessantly around drinks, enthused over the names of groups whose songs they have forgotten. Vague tunes hover from an unknown source in preparation, merely warming the air for the show. A roadie darts on stage and several eyes dart toward him, only to draw away again. This repeats several times.

I'm a sucker for vinyl, and so I bought a vinyl of the third album. Recording with a get-together of artists he temporarily named The Follies, Wick spun out *Mutual Induction* in less than a week, song-writing at all. The album itself seemed fully dedicated to the mind of Michael

Faraday, as the single, "Faraday Cage," strongly suggested. He elaborated in an interview that his obsession was an artist's admiration for a craftsman in a completely different field, his own way of demonstrating his occupation with hobbies other than music. His words betrayed a subconscious, or perhaps fully conscious, comparison of himself to an idol from a separate discipline, a previous era:

"Faraday had, like, no formal education, which I can totally relate to, you know. Invented the electric motor, dreamed up nanoscience before there were even microwave ovens. He's just the perfect example of experimenting, pushing boundaries—but on his own steam. I mean, everybody knows Einstein's name at the drop of a hat, but this guy was like a precursor to him and Tesla and all those other crackpots. The Royal Society really screwed him over, and it's like he just gets tossed off to the side and forgotten. It's like all the parts of his brain were just hauled off to some warehouse somewhere. The guy should at least have a lighthouse named after him or something, you know? Because not every inspiration has to be from the same art. I think we can learn a lot from scientists, inventors, f—in' cave explorers, whatever."

In "the Faraday album," as some called it, Wick sang to his audiences as if he had only pledged partial love to them, under the assumption that he had committed himself to another squeeze. As one music critic put it, "*Mutual Induction* is ostensibly an apology to his own betrothed, as if he suddenly became aware of his fans in a manner like Jacob the Biblical patriarch, aware too late that he had married the wrong sister. Sedgwick shows his most layers yet, but this is only a chastening bluff. Is he holding back on us, or is he threatening us with backing off and fleeing the scene before he abandons the craft? Either way, when you play this record — with your eyes closed, mind you — the album, bearing its true shape, is a vast black hole with a groovy event horizon that envelopes all, and you found you have not only died, but become one with a sulking, collapsing star."

The release was marked by enough ironies of ironies to constitute what in any other universe may have been interpreted as convoluted, self-destructive publicity stunts: A woman whose record shop declared bankruptcy takes it upon herself to raid a Virgin outlet store and vandalize the Pop section, among her antics being the replacement of several CDs with a number of indie label records. *Mutual Induction* is the one album overlooked after the switch, and several copies are purchased, leading to the store manager's decision to restock the album in the front display, causing an unsavory chain reaction. A regional radio station selects Wick for a feature, and cuts his interview short, because he answers every question with either a two-word epithet or a verbal essay, but when they began to play his music, several angry callers prompt the station to cut the song and return to his interview, sparking the creation of a remix of his music using his unintelligible ramblings, one that becomes an internet sensation for a full two days.

From the moment Kenna and I arrived, she bought her first drink and laid down every fact about Wick she had not previously told. Either because of her volume, or because she had actually been recognized as a music blogger, a small congregation formed around us, and the anecdotes were traded like currency.

"You know sometimes this early he'll go out in the audience and mingle with everybody," said Kenna. "I know this guy who like just spotted him in the crowd with a fake beard, just messing with people."

None of us wanted to be the first to scan the incoming audience for a wayward star performer incognito, so we hid our glances in gulps of beer, tilting our heads at odd angles.

"Apparently he broke the world record for most musical instruments used in a single piece of music," I said. "But then, like, this composer in India broke it again like a month later."

"He's got an entire room that's just full of Victorian upholstery he's collected over the years," said Kenna. "He gets a new chair for every album, every tour. So deck. Like what does he do? Just sit in those chairs all day?"

"He cited his favorite actor as Marlon Brando," said one guy, which may have been true, as several of Brando's improvised lines from films had found their way into Wick's songs.

"Old Brando or young Brando?" I said.

"Young Brando. You kidding me?"

"He's got this weird celebrity fetish thing for Leslie Caron."

"Leslie Caron now, or 1940's era Leslie Caron?"

"Yeah, I'm pretty sure it's the latter."

"Did he actually date Zooey Deschanel?"

"Everybody dates Zooey Deschanel. But no, they actually collaborated on some project that never went through."

"I think he just has a favorite everything," said Kenna. "But if you like asked him his favorite anything he would just get up and leave the room. Like, he's that cool."

"Remember that time he had a random campaign he was a part of against the air-strike in Dhoble? Was that it?"

"Yeah, like, he never gets involved in random charity sh— or anything, then he's suddenly on stage for that one night with A Tribe Called Quest and Eddie Vedder. Like, his music isn't really that political. Not in the partisan sense, anyway."

"Well, you know, a lot of his music comes from his turbulent relationship with his father. I think he said that in an interview. But it's not like venting, it's more conversational. You can also tell he's widely read. He's got so much topical range."

"Ok, what's with all the requests not to take pictures, and then he goes and sells prints of his own show? That's like corporate sh— right there."

"No, man. He doesn't stop you. He just wants that focus, especially at the front crowd. He explained on VH1 once. He wants you to get the experience from his crew without worrying about snapping your own shots. Plus, his prints are cheap, and he doesn't take a cent from them. No promo."

"Did you guys read up on that story of how that one critic compared him to Wesley Schultz because of that one song?"

"Oh yeah, and like he went off about it on Twitter?"

"Yeah, but it was like this whole deconstructing essay thing, one tweet at a time. Like he totally tore the guy up. But then he agrees to interview the guy and they become b.f.f.'s."

The whole time nobody mentioned a single song or album of his, unless it was in reference to an in-song allusion or feature of the packaging art.

I escaped the trivia bar and went to the bathroom before the show started. There is no reason to mention a trip to the lavatory unless something of significance happens, or you see something written on the wall, but when I walked in I saw a giant salmon.

Before you assume I had ingested LSD, this sudden lapse into surrealism has its explanation. The evening's bathroom attendant was indeed a man in a giant salmon costume, sitting relaxed on a stool against the wall. A coral-colored fish had apparently swallowed a man who was talking out of the back of its throat. This fish wore a top hat and monocle. He heckled one of the other bathroom attendees as they were leaving, demanding a tip. He was almost like a poorly designed cat food mascot. He was so startling he made me giggle, even as I relieved myself. The salmon came with a full repertoire of juvenile jokes, directed either at those that wandered in or at Sedgwick.

"Hey man, what's your favorite Wick song?" said the salmon, its slightly muffled voice issuing somewhere behind its unmoving mouth. "Come on, tell me your favorite Wick song."

I had no response but a childish giggle. It was novel, it was audacious. I was hoping it wasn't just some video prank, that it would never be recorded, but only retold and recalled.

The fish continued. "Hey can you go grab me a beer? Dude, don't forget to wash your hands. I saw where your hands went."

Others walked in to hit the toilet, and experienced a similar reaction, or just ignored him.

"So do you guys actually like this trash or did you just come for the girls? Did you know Sedgwick pees sitting down? Oh yeah. He's a total *sitzpinkler*. Hey man, don't forget to leave a tip."

It is hard to hold everything straight and not miss while you know a fish with a top hat and monocle is haranguing you. I almost regretted not drinking more beer before walking in, but the fact that it was non-hallucinatory made it all the more pleasant, like a free sideshow. He seemed like he belonged in a dunking booth, only reversed. I afterward had the thought to myself that aping animals is the new minstrel show, but I didn't know what to do with it other than to write it down. It would come in handy whenever I could tell the story, "so I'm at the MMW and I walked into the bathroom and there's this giant salmon just sitting there by the sink..."

After the bathroom I lost Kenna but instead I found Greg Dickey and the girl he had brought as his friend/date, Shelly. He had attended the concert because he had expected a play-through of mostly songs from *Mutual Indution*, which was his favorite album by far. He compared it's thematic greatness and ingenuity to the work of BT's *Binary Universe*, a "brilliant electronic artist" whom I had yet to experience. It was farfetched; comparisons are odorous. Although I had no reference from which to contribute, he digressed into a discussion of electronic music as a whole, and when I say "discussion" I mean monologue. He went from praising BT to disowning Moby, and everyone had heard of Moby.

"It's like digital photography. Do you know much about digital photography?"

"Yeah," I said. "I have an art degree."

"I know, I'm just referencing. But you know, with digital photography, I hate most of it, because it just dilutes the art. You're no longer taking pictures because you're trying to capture something. You're just slapping on a lens and filtering anything into a pretty picture. It's like 'yeah, pretty to look at for a couple seconds, but where's the art?' It's just cheap tricks to tamper with an image. That's what Moby does with sampling. He takes a song and cakewalks a 4x4 beat around it. And they put it in commercials. Commercials!"

"Selling out like pop music," said Shelly.

Dickey winced. "Well, it depends on what you mean by pop music. You take The Postal Service or Death Cab. Now that's what pop is supposed to sound like. Aw, my mom bought their album for me when I was in the hospital, but I refused to listen to it until I was out because I didn't want to associate it with the pain of having my appendix burst on me."

"You could have made it a transformative experience," said Shelly.

"Yeah," I said. "Enrapture yourself in a cathartic episode."

"Well, they did have me on drugs at the time," he joked.

Dickey droned on until all three of us were able to settle on an even conversation, agreeing that while the debut of Velvet Underground was like any other 60's band trying too hard to avoid mainstream, and their sophomoric *White Light/White Head* sounded like pure heroine, their self-titled third record was "a gem years ahead of its time." Those were Greg's words. How they transgressed from practically inventing distortion to delicately wading into pop territory with such grace, we could not discern.

Dickey talked a lot to Shelly, not like a self-indulgent douche does, but like a well-meaning, passionate geek does. Even in the presence of a friend who may have been a date whom he was still trying to magnetize into a relationship, Dickey could not help but analyze the nature of relationships before the two of us.

"I've realized—I've realized that pretty girls are usually a bit more psycho than the average girl. And I have two theories about this, okay?"

"Let's hear it," said Shelly, with the look of a pretty girl just waiting to see how a boy would dig himself out of his own grave. She had the stature and hair of a small, blonde mouse, but by her sassy look I surmised her a strong-willed feminist, and estimated that it would not take long before Dickey's reductionist manifestations exhausted her.

"Hear me out," said Dickey. "This is either because they are treated differently, and haven't picked up on how pretty they are and therefore feel so insecure that they second guess their own social interactions—"

"Because they're not smart enough, right?" said Shelly, without so much as taking a physical stance. I winced. Dickey continued.

"Hear me out, hear me out. Or, all girls are crazy, but with the pretty ones guys have a defense mechanism for when they're rejected or things don't work out."

"I don't know if that bodes well either way," I said.

"There is a third option," said Dickey.

"I'm listening," said Shelly.

"The third option is that there's another reason that hasn't come to me yet."

"The third option," said Shelly, "is that the men are crazy, and there are endless defense mechanisms."

"I'm just verbalizing what I've heard other guys say," said Dickey, in a way that only he could get away with, as if he had come across an unfortunate theorem.

Shelly rolled her eyes toward me.

"Don't look at me," I said. "I have no investment in this."

"Of course there are exceptions to the rule," said Dickey.

Shelly cocked her head to the side. "Like?"

"You," he said, gesticulating like a magician in his prestige. "You're an exception to the rule. A girl can be pretty and not crazy."

"Nice way out," she said.

But Dickey had not learned when to stop. "Like, for example, my ex-girlfriend, Cameron—she was pretty, not the kind of pretty people in Hollywood thought were pretty, but pretty in her own awkward way. And she wasn't crazy at all, but when other guys started talking to her, even while I was dating her, her crazy side started to show."

It was excruciating. It was the first and only time the whole evening that I was actually desperate to find Kenna. Fortunately, she found us just after the show started, and something Dickey found repellant in her drove him and his date away.

Wick played what was inarguably a much better show than my first experience. Rather than play the more familiar orchestral style of "Ballad of the False Robber Baron," he opted for a performance that turned from simplistic to hardcore, and his show-ending rendition of "The Last Séance of Percy Bysshe Shelley" went on for a good twelve minutes. The show felt so intimate and true that nobody cheered over-enthusiastically for the first bars of "Faraday Cage" as would those casual fans who would have discovered him in a clothing store or coasting through Pandora. There wasn't a single glowing phone in sight.

As Adrian Dyer of *The Guardian* wrote, "with the full intensity of his harmless-sounding band, The Follies, Sedgwick reached into his distantly recent catalog with a sparking rebirth of nearly his whole previous album." Writing for *Spin*, Dewey DeWeese observed that Sedgwick "enlisted a slick lineup who, in perfect sync from beginning to end, streamed a constant, alternating current of both artistic lust and obsessive devotion to the fundamentals of song-playing, displaying full symmetry throughout the night." *The Tennessean* ran a review comparing Sedgwick and the Follies to "a spool from which platinum was spun in new, fresh arrangements." I wanted to congratulate *The Tennessean* on their lyrical metaphor. At least they were trying.

Kenna would later blog that the show was full of "captive ferocity tempered with a kindergarten ring of melody," a line I think she got help with at the bar, and concluded that "Wick gave us the same shadowy drama of every show, but seemed more eager than ever to waterboard the meaning out of his own songs as if someone else had written them. He played like he was the only one on stage and expected everyone else to do the same, and when the last note of every song was played, you were the only one in the audience. Were you there, you knew there was something special about that night." She was being hyperbolic.

However, the night did morph into something rare, and not necessarily because of the show itself. Well, there was the whole salmon thing. But during a "break" in which Wick fiddled with a guitar while his band switched equipment around, I caught a guy coming around to get a better view from where he was standing. I immediately recognized him as Ben Kweller, the rebellious ten-year-old boy squeezed into a pair of jeans with a haircut that only a musical genius in the lineage of Beethoven's hair metal band could attempt. I was never one for harassing celebrities for the mere sake of meeting them, but he wasn't necessarily a celebrity, and it didn't seem out of his way. I had nothing to say to him or ask from him, but the opportunity was there.

"Hey, Ben Kweller!" I blurted as cooly as I could. It was an introduction as immediately tragic as any honest fan's.

"Hey man," he said, tolerantly.

I punished myself for not knowing what to say next.

"Here to see Wick, huh?"

"Yeah…He's all right."

We both stood there like two people who have no business standing together, but have no reason not to move from their trance in whatever moving tableau has captured them, sharing a weak covalent bond consisting of a halfway greeting that is begging to be dissolved. I am ashamed to admit that I could not keep my pulse down in the physical presence of an artist not even rehearsing his craft, and I felt reduced to the immature mass of a swelling fanatic trying to keep their cool beside an otherwise indifferent and currently uninteresting bystander of something greater than the two of us.

"So what are you doing after the show, man?" This came from me, and I thought I had made it sound more like a curious gesture than a doorway to conversation.

He shook his head. "Just head back to my hotel. Smoke a cigarette. Mellow out."

"All right, man. Mellow out."

I used this as an opportunity to shake his hand and escape. His handshake was baked and limp, spending as few calories as possible, the opposite of what they would teach you in business school. I had to get out of there. I was being awkward.

So yeah, that's how I met Ben Kweller.

I tried to find Kenna back at the bar. Most everyone had evacuated. You didn't come for the beer, and you either tried to catch Wick backstage, hit up some open late place for food, or went home. I faced the brick and rusty pipes, just waiting for Kenna to show back up. I kept tracing with my mind the majestic, ridged, two-toned "M" logo leering in front of me, studying with envy the monosyllabic font of the single letter, nearly chanting it aloud like the all-encompassing *OM* of Siddhartha's warm-up chant.

I felt the gravity of a tall person two stools down, like the feeling that comes right before you realize a cop is tailing you for no reason.

"You think Sedgwick has an alter ego or am I missing something here?"

"What?" I turned. No, it wasn't Wick. That would have been amusing, but cliché. It was a tall guy, early forties, in a black button-up, thin black glasses, and black, gelled hair. He had that antagonistically optimistic grin that only a music business guru with an eye on the trending market would dare let loose in a venue like this. He looked like the next words out of his mouth were going to be, "why, yes, I am a tool." He stirred his finger on the rim of his half-drunk beer. Then came the leading riddle.

"What kind of guy reads Henry Miller *and* Salman Rushdie at the same time, owns a Gibson J-160 E but *prefers* a Les Paul, tells you that the best song in the world is 'Walking the Cow,' and plays the best cover of 'Iris' you've ever heard, even though he hates the song?"

I shrugged. "Is that the opening line of your feature?"

He traded my gaze at the "M" on the brick like it was a live game on a plasma screen at a sports bar. "Nice piece of work," he said, toasting it. "Don't you think?"

"Has everything it needs," I said. "Doesn't draw too much attention."

"Good work draws just the right amount of attention," he said. "You do any design work?"

Really? If this was the business equivalent of being hit on at a bar, he was no less creepy than your average desperate stalker.

"Yeah," I said, after a pause.

"Pecha Kucha Karaoke night," he said. "You were the guy with the killer presentation, I remember."

I couldn't remember him, much less my presentation.

"Well," I said, leaning over and pretending to whisper an obvious secret, "I *did* prepare it ahead of time."

He grinned playfully. "I just like how you didn't have a business card or a website because of all that artist integrity sh— you went on about. If I'm not mistaken you gave us your email on a cocktail napkin."

I was disgusted by this stooge. "Yeah. I try to stand out by not standing out. I'm not really into personal branding. It doesn't pay the rent."

He nodded. "'Cobbler's son has no shoes' kinda thing. I get it." He reached his hand out to shake mine. "Bruce Fey. I gave you my card. Still looking for clients?"

"What would I be designing for?" I said.

He stood up and brushed himself to flatten any wrinkles in his shirt. "You'd help come up with something for Wick."

"So where's the punch line?" I said. "Is this where the tickets came from?"

"You gave me an address," he said. "I gave you a card. The tickets were a bonus. I'd say take the shot. He wants to work with a new local upcoming artist. Know anybody else who fits the bill? I'll give them a call."

"I mean, I'll think about it," I said. "It's been kind of a surreal evening. Now it's getting Wonka-esque."

"So I'll give you time to think it over," said the ol' Slugworth, his eyes and mouth squinting in an attempt to read my mind. "Something to put on your résumé."

He spoke like a manager. Every word he said was an advertisement for his client. But if Garrett Sedgwick had a manager at all, I didn't picture it being this cardboard bozo.

"Yeah. I'll totally think it over."

"Sounds cool." He gripped my shoulder as he walked off, not even shaking hands, and I had the feeling I was just roped into a task I couldn't refuse, like I would wake up the next morning to an equine decapitation if I so much as thought about making any other plans. That or this guy himself had been pushed into approaching some unknown designer by a client whose wishes he couldn't comprehend or even read. I had yet to have a natural, comfortable encounter the entire evening.

Then Kenna appeared.

"Neil! Where the f— have you been? You missed it. I totally snapped a shot of Ben Kweller hanging out with Ben Folds. I am not sh—ing you. It was sweet!"

"I'm ready to go," I said. It would have been a mistake to tell her about the possibly phony invitation to do some design work for a Wick collaboration. I didn't want her to jump me. I ended up telling her that some guy who looked like he belonged at a Sting concert came up to me and either hit on me or offered me a job, which was true, but I was caught short of improvisation when she asked me who. The only other business card I could remember was from some pastor of a local megachurch. I should have feigned the strong buzz of oblivion.

"I've totally been there!" she bellowed. "Oh my God, taking you. I am giving you the hookup."

"You don't seem like the church type," I said.

She gripped my arm hard. "I know, right? It's Nashville. You can't live here without going to a church at least like five times a year. No, this one's pretty cool. You'll meet some people. Dude, you're so gonna be my church date."

One thing I learned was that you don't pass up an invitation to church in the South, even from the irreligious. It's better to avoid the complications of bad manners and bad kharma. And my mind is never closed to any ponderings, not even from the stale waters of Southern

American religion. It may be two hours of your life you can't get back, but so is a bad show, or a bad film. One can always feign sickness, or make plans ahead of time. But eventually, propriety somehow dictates a seat in the pew.

When I got back to my apartment and shuffled through my cards, the one from Bruce Fey was right there. When I googled him, several sites mentioned his name as Wick's manager. Also in the pile of business cards was one from the Community Church. It might have been the beer that simultaneously fabricated my story to Kenna from both truth and falsehood, but I had woven myself into the trap of meeting this potential client as well. This is what happens when you try to attach your career to everything. Between a phony manager and a megachurch pastor, I had the inkling that I was going to end up working for a tool.

I'm being pessimistic.

5
"JESUS, ETC."
feat. a fish quite out of water

The Community church Kenna took me to was large, both in audience and in structure. I will entertain no sermons on how a church is a people and not a building, because most Christians do not actually manifest such a paradigm. Much attention had gone into the ambient-friendly structure and the soporific tope of its walls, a color tone that eased attendees with a sort of papyrus color, but also functioned as a neutral palette for light shows to splatter themselves upon. A massive rigging of such lights gave the mind an anticipatory phantom scent of pre-lit incense. Most churches no longer connote a sense of the spiritual in their architecture, and so it's hard for me to believe that a religious experience is occurring when my eyes aren't met with a convincingly visual cosmic reality.

I was greeted with a few handshakes, as was the custom. I don't remember a single person I met. Before everyone had taken a seat, the lights dimmed and, rather than being hustled into our seats by a string of announcements as had been my experience growing up, we were prompted to look to the empty screen by the blasting of "Walk On" by U2, soaring vocals that attempted to evoke an emotional outpouring I was neither prepared to or motivated to summon. I casually glanced about the room, as some others did, while Kenna and others bobbed and closed their eyes as if Bono himself were in the room. A guy next to me held his hands up as if to receive a free T-shirt, and I saw the Music Rising bracelet on his arm, as well as the "Make Trade Fair" equals sign "tattooed" on the back of his hand in what looked like black marker.

It has apparently become chic to champion social causes attached to musicians as a method of establishing oneself in a karmic simulacra of deeds and rewards. T-shirts, bracelets, stickers, patches, retweets and profile pictures— there is a semiotic reference to the incarnational peace-warriors of good causes that bedecks the religious-spiritual among our generation and befuddles the skeptic as well as the fundamentalist. As image bearers, or fans of image bearers, they are under obligation to signify their values, though as non-didactically as possible, through a patchwork of artwork and album collections and the bonus, assorted, charity paraphernalia that come with. In their younger years they may have been found wearing tees that bore sacred verses matched with the attempted hipness of a provocative, perhaps offensive tag-line: "Life is short; eternity is long. Hope you know Jesus," or "wide-eyed, sanctified, Bible-totin', scripture quotin'." These children have graduated to the subversive, ineffable logic of sacred song lyrics coupled with logos and hyperlinks that, if interested, one could ask about or seek out at some other time, references that at some point may lead back to a devout expression, or murmur, of faith.

This sort of "bono chic" attaches itself to a crowd eager to incite curiosity, eager to support, eager to hear a good tune and not feel guilty about it. Nothing is allowed to approach propaganda, but must stray into the ascetic aesthetic of statements of faith and goodwill deeply embedded into counter-cultural messages, like a crossword puzzle stitched together from vaguely like-minded bumper stickers. One could just as easily purchase coffee at a Starbucks, grab an album from off the counter, notice the fine print at the counter reminding them of what non-profit organization-of-the-day they just supported via their purchase, and walk away having made the world a better place. Such a vast devotion and sacrifice categorizes a very involved crowd of concerned, optimistic youths who seek spiritual relevance in every concoction of art and culture.

Especially in regards to such a discursive space as the web, these decorations may add up to an appearance of devotion wherein being a fan is conflated with being an activist. Our digital and fabric signifiers enable us to become interested bystanders and dedicated workers all at once. The mystique of having set foot in various countries, spoken at various conventions, or merely moved boxes of any kind of aid around are irresistible. We have discovered the convenience of contributing to the solution of the various problems of the world by assisting others in the acknowledgment of and identification with our sociopolitical concerns. We are on a campaign to identify ourselves with campaigns, convinced that we are unlike the masses who every four years merely adorn themselves with either a red or blue pin and wait in line to stand in a booth. It is a most visible art form, and its adherents are so thrilled to be part of something so much greater than themselves that it is overwhelming to think of where to begin. To this generation, awareness is its own currency, one that has no set value, a priceless and harmless investment that does not have to be spent today.

One of the ministers rose to speak a quick message to the crowd — the youth minister, I think. It could have been the college minister, the student ministries minister, the community life minister, the preaching minister, or the middle school minister, but I knew it wasn't the missions minister or the audiovisual minister. I would later be meeting with the executive minister. The youth minister spoke before the hyped crowd.

"Relationships. What kind are you in? And I'm not just talking about boyfriend or girlfriend — that thing you click on Facebook. I'm talking about the relationships you have with everyone around you: Your parents. Your friends. Your youth leaders. Your community leaders. We walk in here and we can talk a lot about theology, or a lot about religion, but these people are here together for a reason. Ultimately, human relationships are what church is really about."

He gesticulated in such a manner as to indirectly direct everyone's attention toward the tattoo on his lower arm, a remembrancer of his trendy, connected role as leader to the crowd, or perhaps a hint at his personal narrative of a man who had been through dark times and overcome them, a man who had a story to tell, a story that begins or ends with a tattoo.

The youth minister introduced the praise band, who launched into their set with closed eyes and heads shaking back and forth with a rehearsed look of surprise from the grace they felt encompassing them. There was a song everyone and his brother seemed to know by heart, followed by a new song they were trying out that all but five people didn't know, but mostly the singing was kept to the praise band. Those sitting further in the back, like myself, were allowed a healthy distance with which to merely observe curiously with hands in our pockets, while those with a more readily summoned zeal for attachment to the songs had rallied toward the front. The whirring lights kept the focus to the stage. One could browse on their Smartphone without distracting anyone else.

Following the songs was a prayer, followed by presentation of rather forced inquiry assembled into a video package of patently intellectual retail music accompanying stock footage, mostly of people walking a busy street with no questions on their minds whatsoever, overlaid with scrawling questions and useless speculations spanning across the screen, addressing me as if I was previously unaware that I had ever asked such questions: "Do you ever wonder if you are alone? Do you sometimes wish others could know the pain you feel?" — questions that made me feel I was about to hear an advertisement for a medicine with a dozen side-effects, canned questions with canned responses made for tracts that middle-aged men in suits hand to you on the sidewalk on the first day of college.

Nonetheless, I was a little surprised by the executive minister's cautious treading around the very subject at hand, avoiding not only canned answers but any answers at all. I tried to focus on his presentation but I was distracted and then irritated by the hideous spinning logo that spun endlessly on the screen above him. It looked like it was trying to imitate a silvery burning bush, but was more like an awkwardly shaped ice cream sundae, rotating clumsily on the massive canvas as if we were to soon be hypnotized by it. I soon lost interest in the message of the very man I was soon to meet as I became tangental in my own thoughts.

As an early teen I felt valid and secure in my prayers, seeking in that void a figure adapted to my imaginations of that figure. It was not until I first began to be asked to lead prayers ("Son, you've got a way with words. Use that God-given vocabulary for the Lord.") that I concerned myself with the apprehensive notion that I would become inauthentic in front of crowds in an effort to please them. The burden of forming words from thoughts—not the difficulty of language, but the finality of pronouncement— hampered the virility of my expressions. They felt scripted, only for a human audience, not for divine ears. I was raised with a prejudice against spontaneity, and so when called upon I gave my litany, expressed my petitions, and then sat down. Eventually, the words were too bitter to say aloud, and rather than refuse their requests, I stopped going altogether. This is but one of many reasons for what no small number of people I knew growing up would call my "falling away" into agnosticism.

I'm being petulant.

But as the band started up again, I asked myself if this is what any performer, whether in prayer or in concert, felt when burning out from repetitive performance. Is it possible to perform the same act over and over again in public and still maintain the same fresh rawness of inner stimuli, that openness to honest exploration of a meaningful, defining moment? Should a musician be expected to play a hit on his set list if he cannot feel it in that moment? Should the lyrics and notes be thrown in the fire if they no longer carry any meaning to him, or never did in the first place?

Then came the closing song, the one that manipulates you into crying, if you have the tears. Some were led by a spirit to come down to the floor, or perhaps led by the incessant begging of the worship leader who persuaded them that what they had was a spirit. I will not judge what they felt. I didn't come to judge, but to ponder.

"Come on. Let's see those penitent spirits. Clap hands, hold hands. Let the spirit bring you in. Hug your brothers and sisters. Step out of that shy place and recognize one another in the love of God. Can you feel it? God is at work here."

And it was hard to tell when the worship was over and when the drifting toward the exits was allowed to commence.

After a good twenty minutes of brief and jumbled introductions and greetings with people Kenna either only knew by name or really only hung out with outside that auditorium, she suggested we head out for lunch. I reminded her that I had agreed to meet with the executive minister. I managed to catch him for a brief second in the midst of a sizable crowd and he told me to meet with him in the library.

"Let's head there," said Kenna. "These people kill me."

"You introduced me to like ten of them," I said.

"It's a big church," she said. "I hate the small ones. You can meet who you want here."

I was dragged as if toward a closet to make out. We mazed through the crowded, crescent lobby to a rather small library. Two people were already in there, a guy with neon shutter shades and a girl with a cassette tape strung on a necklace. They were at a wood table stacked with un-catalogued books. When we entered they were laughing to themselves and invited us in on the activity.

"What's the riot?" said Kenna.

"Check these out," said Cassette. "Look how old these books are. Can you believe it?"

"Are these just off the shelves?" I said.

"Like, these are for real," said Shades. "I couldn't read this one. I just couldn't." He held up a copy of a book called *How to Be Happy When You're Married: 10 Discussion Outlines*, with a cover depicting a couple embracing one another, one the author must have taken at his daughter's wedding in 1973.

"These are so classic," said Cassette. "Oh, jackpot. Right here." She held up three in a row: *God Loves the Single Person Too; Eat the Devil's Corn and You'll Choke on His Cob;* and *God's Guide for What To Do When the Mental Patient Comes Home*.

"Where do these come from?" said Kenna.

"They've been hitchhiking from church library to church library since like the fifties," said Shades. "We're supposed to be putting them all in boxes to like donate or throw away somewhere. But they said anybody can come by and take some of they wanted."

"Oh yeah," said Kenna. "They're converting the library into a media room."

"Who would take these home?" I said.

I glanced through some of the dusty titles laid out on the table: *Heart Diseases and their Spiritual Cure; Vine's Concordance; Miracles Defined; Old Testament Introduction; Roll On, Jordan River; Heretics of the Centuries; The Bible and Archeology; A Serious Call to a Devout and Holy Life; What To do When the Brethren are Drifting; Other Sheep in Other Pastures; Let's Explore Bible Lands!; The Cost of Discipleship; A Problem with Change; Shifting Sands; the Church Masquerade...*

"I'm sure one or two of these are worthy of salvaging," said Cassette.

"What would these go for on eBay?" said Kenna.

"Even Goodwill wouldn't have use for them," said Shades. "Look at this one."

"I don't know," said Cassette. "I mean, most of these were like donated by somebody, even before the split. Like, it's like letting go of our heritage."

"Letting go of your parent's doctrine?" I asked.

"No, not even that," said Cassette. "Just like tossing out what you know you came from. I mean, it's like a museum in here. Like, people for us actually read this stuff at some point."

"You weren't going to read it anyway," said Shades.

"Nope. No promo."

"Yeah, we oughta soak all this in formaldehyde," said Kenna.

In a moment the executive minister arrived, along with the youth minister with the tattoo. Kenna and the two other kids drifted off.

"Kip," said the executive minister. Up close it turned out his Guy Fieri hair cut was real.

"Cody," said the one with the tattoo.

I shook their hands and we circled up as if we had already agreed to work on a project.

"We're really excited to work with a young person with a fresh outlook," said Kip, himself at least a decade older than Cody. "And you said you were looking for new work. Man, you had a killer karaoke presentation."

"So I hear," I said. "So what are you thinking? A new church bulletin?"

This must have been the funniest thing Kip and Cody heard all day. "I love this guy, I love this guy," said Kip, clapping his hands together and bouncing his legs.

They must have liked my "Ithaca is Gangsta" tee as well, although I couldn't tell if they got it or if they wanted to venture to ask what the reference was for.

"We're thinking of a new design for our website," said Cody. "You do web work?"

"I do," I replied. "I mean, for everything I do I always do a sketch by hand first. It's important to my craft that I produce it with real graphite with my own hands. But I wouldn't make it in this world without web skills."

"I hear, I hear," said Cody. "Well, as you might have noticed, a lot of young people are just leaving the institutional church these days. They feel shackled down by these stagnant traditions, like they're not going anywhere and haven't gone anywhere, and won't go anywhere."

"Yeah, that's one of the reasons this church was founded," said Kip. "God wants us to be together, most of all, connect deeply, share real issues, things like that. You might've noticed we don't have traditional Bible classes. We have conversation hubs that form to just let the air out about various topics on everybody's minds."

"We feel it takes the pressure off of people," said Cody, "especially young people. Scriptures and traditions can be real intimidating, and sometimes it's just good to close them up for a bit and talk about the issues that matter to us right now."

I nodded and nodded.

"But eventually we open the Bibles up," said Kip, with a wink. "I mean, you can't have church without a Bible. But our efforts here are to make the Bible relevant, and relational."

"We actually came up with a term together," said Cody. He rubbed his hands together, and froze them still as if in prayer. "*Relevational*." They both tried to hide their grins at this one. "See, it also makes us think of Revelation. So, they'll be like 'what'? And kind of get caught off guard. But it still sounds Bible-y enough to get our focus back where it belongs."

"Okay," I said, still nodding.

"I mean, we don't have to use it," said Kip, wiping the word out of the air as if it had been smudged on a screen before us. "The point is, that's what we want our first impression to be, too. That's where our website comes in, because this next generation is all digital natives. One thing we're thinking of doing is actually creating a space that is like a hub where these discussions can take place."

"I hope you have an html guy for that," I said.

"Our IT coordinator's got that covered," said Kip. "We wanted to go to you for the imagery alone. We chose you specifically for this."

This piqued my interest, and I stopped nodding to reorient myself. "Why me?"

Cody put his hands together piously and gestured directly at me as if blessing me with saint-hood. "See, you're an outsider. You come from us with your own perspectives. You're not representing us, but observing us. You have that first-time visitor's perspective. I mean, maybe not with church, but here, anyway."

I felt the need to clear the air of something. "Yeah, you guys should know up front I'm pretty agnostic. I mean, I'll be a seeker if you want me to be, and all."

"Perfect," said Kip. "See, we want people to see us how you see us, so they see that we understand to be how they see us, so they can see how we see us."

Cody acted as an interpreter this time. "We want someone to approach our website, and maybe even ultimately our worship center—and I'm talking about someone with a lot of doubts and maybe even someone who's already abandoned the church—we want them come into this and say to themselves, 'hey, this looks familiar. They get me.' We'd like to show that we're aware of these perceptions, and maybe even playing into them just a little bit. Making it comfortable to talk about."

"That's a lot to be said in a web design," I said. "Have you consulted your PR minister about your 'About Us' section?"

Kip gripped himself in a tight hug and trotted in place with a vehement laugh. "See, I knew we had the right guy for this. We need something sharp."

They showed me their current idea for a design, something they said "wasn't what had to be done" but they thought was "a good starter idea, something that will give a feel for what we're looking for." The concept was simple, involving a visual commentary on the ancient art-form known as stained glass. They envisioned colored gel cells, fragmented and isolated, like jagged, wandering stones in a river, not forming the chromatic vision of a kneeling Christ or penitent disciple, but rather a mosaic spectrum of loosely fitting shapes struggling to form a cohesive caricature of a shifting resemblance of a faint hint at religion: Episcopal De Stijl.

"I mean, I could do some doodling and send you some samples," was all I could say.

"And like we said," Kip repeated, "you don't have to go with that. It's just a basic direction we thought of going in. But we'll trust you to pitch us some ideas of your own, if you're up for it."

"It's something to sink my teeth into," I said. "I thought you were pulling me in to talk about reworking your logo."

They shared a look of puzzlement. "Why? What's wrong with our logo?"

I got queasy fast. I needed to go home and read some Baudrillard.

I needed some time to think. I always need time to think. I hung out with Sam and Sam at the Bongo Java where Sam (the boy one) worked. The coffee was good and the wall art was not too intrusive. Sam and Sam were good for one another, and they were good for me, due to their shared, perhaps even duplicated, dare I say, exponentially multiplied optimism.

When Sam ended his shift he came and sat halfway on Samantha's lap and said, "what are you doing, Sam Schuler?"

She said to him, "I don't know. What are you doing, Sam Schuler?"

"Scoot over, Sam Schuler."

"You scoot over some, Sam Schuler."

It was as if they shared a soul that had just split into two, and this occurred every time anyone met up with them. Rather than feeling like a third wheel, I was casually romanced by their steady, blooming flirtation, like the kind between couples about to become official. Joey was with us, anyhow. He had been strumming his guitar and put it down. Ever perceptive, he could tell I had a lot on my mind, and so he asked.

"What's wrong with you, Neil? You have what people call 'the long face.'"

"I'm having a squeamishly abeyant afternoon," I said after a long pause, my arms limp at my side.

"Is your trauma psychological or physiological?" said Sam.

"Yeah," Samantha repeated. "Is your trauma psychological or psysiocolo — physi — "

"Ha!" Sam cut her off. "You messed it up. You couldn't say it."

They settled and returned to the question, but I didn't have a mind to divulge the details. I didn't want the pestering that came with the revelation that I might be working with or for Sedgwick on any sort of project, nor the disbelief and jeering that would likely precede such. I also didn't feel too right about the church design proposal, but it was the second conundrum on my mind. I needed to just ventilate, and I couldn't do it around Kenna, because she wouldn't really listen but tell me how much of a riot I was. I didn't want to feel like an exhibit at a menagerie.

"I went to a Sedgwick concert the other night," I said. "It was actually good, but I'm not sure how I feel about liking it so much."

"Was it better than the Fontanel?" asked Joey.

"It was better than the Fontanel," I said. "And it was just a different show altogether. I'm pretty sure Wick could play for another thirty years and still surprise people."

Samantha, texting, said aloud, "I imagine that, like, in thirty years he'll settle into complete tool music but everyone will still be listening to his records from right now."

Sam, also, was texting. "Only the people who have no idea who he is now, or hate him, will be blasting his sh— like it's the Beatles."

I yawned. "My dad always told me back in the day the Beatles could fart and everyone would love it."

"When I fart everyone loves it," said Sam.

"Ew," said Samantha. "I just tweeted you on that."

"Thank you, Samantha Schuler."

I continued my tangent aloud. "He has the tenacity of a cockroach."

"Can I tweet that?" said Samantha.

"I feel suddenly exploited," I said. "No, Wick is like that. He's almost reached the point of Lennon."

"Lennon?" said Joey.

"Okay," I said. "Maybe not Lennon. But Lennon was bigger than Jesus."

"Kanye is bigger than Jesus," said Joey.

"Everyone pretends they don't like Kanye," I said.

"Everyone pretends they hate Wick," said Sam.

"I do hate Wick," I said.

"Wick doesn't think he's bigger than Jesus," said Sam. "He should write a song about Jesus."

"Sufjan has songs about Jesus," said Sam.

"Wick should write songs about Sufjan; Sufjan should write songs about Wick," said Sam.

"Jesus should write songs about Wick," said Joey.

"Wow," said Sam, but then shied away from any chastisement.

I leaned forward, struck with effulgence. "Lennon couldn't picture religion outside of what he was doing. Kanye can't picture what he's doing without it being a religion. Lennon was just babbling on and knew it was a joke. Kanye is a joke but acts like he doesn't know it."

"Maybe it doesn't matter if you know it's a joke," said Sam. "If you know you can go mythic, you go mythic."

"Yeah," I said, leaning back again on the couch, and gazing at the swirls on the ceiling. "Yeah, yeah. Like Bono."

"Like Che," said Joey.

"I wanna be mythic," said Sam.

"I think I've clearly reached that state," I said. "I need something more...I've reached a plateau...I'm hungry..."

"They have really good scones here," said Samantha.

Then I remembered a critical piece of information I had to share with them.

"So I'm at the MMW and I walked into the bathroom and there's this giant salmon just sitting there by the sink..."

We giggled more than we should have. I squeezed every giggle I could from Joey and that couple. We laughed like we were high. We laughed at a painting on the wall, or rather our abstraction of it. We laughed at horrible movies. We laughed at Amanda's J Crew outfit she had worn. We laughed at memes. At some point I felt good about the day, and vicariously felt good about the decisions that lay before me. If I had the time, I would take on both projects. What could I say? They'd both look good on a resume.

6
"KING OF SPAIN"
feat. bad shisha

Slumped over a cramped corner table with his hands across his idle arms, Sedgwick, his battered hair draping — or perhaps dripping — over his round, transparent-rim glasses, looks almost like a grown up, alternative Harry Potter who, after a stint in rehab, is in line to audition as the BBC's next Doctor. A plaid shirt erupts from the collar of his black, buttoned blazer.

"I picked it up at a flea market," he says about the gold pin on his coat. "I have no idea what it represents."

Garret Sedgwick is on a touring hiatus in his Nashville residence, occasionally playing shows around town, but mostly relaxing in the wake of his fourth record, *Gravity Waltzes*, which, after an unsteady and brief career of hits and misses, somehow landed in the Top 40 for over a week.

For an artist who finally earned his respects around here, you'd think he'd be doing anything other than sulking. His face is a waxy blank slate, surrounded by the smoke from hookahs around the room. He has wandered off in thought and could return any minute having channeled any number of artists undercover: Ben Gibbard, Langhorne Slim, Isaac Brock, Beck. We are under the tent-like, dilapidated, hobo festival-themed Taboosh, the downtown hookah bar where he agreed to meet. Christmas lights and colored tassels enchant the rising smoke from infrequently washed pipes. Sedgwick sips his cinnamon tea. Himself an ex-smoker, he found an odd spot for an interview.

"I like to take other people where they like to smoke," he says, tapping his teacup nervously. "And sometimes I don't mind the secondhand whiff. I went out on the Kerry Gaynor method, so I'm not afraid I'll slip back or anything. And it's a good place to camouflage yourself."

Wick, who has admitted to hating doing live shows, is a monastic recluse, avoiding crowds whenever he can. Although he could have picked a better spot. The edgy allure of hookah and Indian food is enough to attract the indie crowd that has followed him thus far. He is almost begging to be spotted. However, the infestation of emo teens and Vandy frat boys doesn't seem to take notice of this prodigious enigma. In the corner across from his guest, he is more nervous than he should be. Every word and movement is intentional, fidgety, as if he is about to divulge his innermost thoughts and emotions in an interview so candid that it won't be released until years after his death.

"It was nerve-wracking coming into the scene, to say the least," says Wick, reflecting on the rise of his career. "It's a nebulous blur, to be honest. I truthfully spread myself a little too thin. I was enraptured with so many musical ideas all at once. I don't remember any fan reactions or what I did about them. Maybe I blocked it out like soldiers do in combat. I just harnessed what was pulling me forward. Sometimes it's easy to feel out of touch."

Wick doesn't sound like he's alone. Although his relative stardom has in no way reached the surface of pop radio, hit soundtracks, or your mom's mini-van, Wick is a special breed of over-reflective, hyper-self-ware, garrulous-about-their-own-craft, ungrateful artists who seem clueless about their fan base. They act surprised when they put out great tracks, and so do we. When we hate them, they're misunderstood; when we love them, they're conscientious.

As proof of this, *Gravity Waltzes*, equally Wick's most paranoid and passionate record yet, arrived just after a false alarm announcement that he was temporarily "retiring" from musicianship. It may have been a veiled memorandum that he was slowing down, pacing himself.

"My mom once put me on Ritalin," he says, shifting himself in his seat as if in self-parody. "If I'm not writing, recording, or touring I get this itch and I go out in the night and I'm worried I'll wind up halfway across the country with no memory of why my pants are missing."

If he's threatening himself with self-destructive behavior in order to remain prolific, it shows. He has yet to be arrested, check in to a clinic, or make the front page, and rumor has it he owns a safe with over 40 hours of unreleased material. Still, despite his average of an album per year, secret negotiations with a yet-to-be-named label are hampering an upcoming project.

"This is why I've avoided major studio labels," he said. "There is no such thing as an artist-friendly label. Unless you leap off a building. Then they'll release everything you've ever written on a box set, no matter how sh—y it is."

But the latest rumor is that, without the backing of the new label, Wick has already reserved three days of his own studio time, on his own dime, and has yet to invite another artist. Names float around, including the collaborators from his previous records—The Hymnists, Gargamel Epic, The Follies, Al Jazari. Known for his mercurial flexibility and intrepid penchant for mimicry, Sedgwick's next project could take off in any direction, with any number of collaborators. The mystery recording is still weeks away.

But Sedgwick isn't leaking any details, not even to his closest compadres. He's brought in a new graphic artist, an upcoming starter named Neil Oberlin, to produce the cover art for the upcoming album. Neil sits across from him, in a plain tee with the words "eschew obfuscation; espouse elucidation." No one has heard of this young artist. His name isn't even floating around. A casual fan of Wick, Oberlin only seems calm in the musician's presence because he's the only one smoking the ash-heavy apple flavor from the hookah between them.

"I wanted to go with someone who'd just come to the area looking to make it," says Sedgwick. "I remember what it was like when I was playing around town, just trying to get my name out and work with whoever I could."

Oberlin, unsure of what to say, gives a wincing smile, as if he's still unsure whether this Sedgwick is an impostor, roping him into an elaborate prank.

"Okay," he says after a long silence. "So, do you want me to give your demo a listen and see what I sketch out, or do you want me to give you some samples? I mean, I don't even think you've seen any of my stuff. This is uncannily uncomfortable for me."

Sedgwick nods and rolls his eyes, only empathetically, as if looking back into his own skull, somewhere into his past in order to identify with another human being. His eyes meet yours, try to get in touch with you, and then retreat into the heavens where you hoped he would take you. For a second you think you're looking at some redneck in a Halloween costume scratching his head because he forgot to recite a line. Although his antics have always been unpredictable, and sometimes, on the surface, counterintuitive, most established artists just don't insist on collaborating with some unproven up-and-comer whose work they haven't even seen yet.

Oberlin's inspirations range from the psychadelic art of John Maeda and Mark Weaver to the simplicity of Frank Chimero. "He has a kind of Wes Anderson feel to his work that I admire," he says, of the latter. "I think Wes Anderson has inspired me more than any visual artist. I like to begin my workday like a shot of one of his films. Just lay objects out on a table and sketch them as they are, laid out bare. I think deconstructing our tools and possessions really helps see the brand that we are."

Sedgwick nods in agreement, and an idea has come to him. He begins to pull small trinkets out of his pockets — a copper wire, a rechargeable AA battery, and a tiny magnet the size of an altoid. With the obsessive focus of a magician he wraps the copper wire into a coil. He snaps the magnet under the battery and stands it upright. He balances an end of the coil on the top of the battery and the coil begins to spin around it. Sedgwick's hands are spread away from it, and the small device continues as if it had a life all its own.

"It's a homopolar motor. The magnetic field propels the copper on a fixed axis."

The tiny MacGyveresque machine continues its smooth, silent loop.

"This was like Faraday's first motor demonstration. Everything reduced down to its components. Perpetual motion. As long as the current's in there. It could go on forever." He looks up at Oberlin, then back at his motor. "Who doesn't envy that?"

Oberlin taps the table, then interjects. "So you're thinking of a design like that? Harkening back to your Faraday album?"

Sedgwick rubs his hands over his face, as if this is a big decision. "I think. Maybe not literally a sketch. At first I was thinking a holographic image, but tossed it. Maybe something hand drawn. I don't know yet. It's a starting idea, you know. Just the concept. Something propelling itself on its own steam, you know. Like a brand new creation."

Oberlin bites his lip and begins to jot notes on a pad.

Sedgwick holds up an invisible idea in the span of his thumb and forefinger. "Faraday said that there was one kind of electricity," he says. "One kind. For everything."

"Yeah," says Oberlin.

"Yeah," Sedgwick repeats. "Everything being powered the same way. Think about that."

Such a symbol could mean potential for anything. Wick's roots are as mysteriously laid out as his projected directions. His influences are outrageously eclectic, casting him in some culturally postcolonial, post-American age, an impossible pigeon to pigeonhole. He seldom discloses his past, but occasionally drops hints here and there.

"Why would you bother asking Rembrandt what village he was born in or what his favorite coffeehouse is?"

he once said in a radio interview. "If people want to know these random facts about me, they can just look up my Wikipedia page or something, if they have that kind of time. I'm sure someone's looked into it."

According to his Wiki page and its few citations, Sedgwick was first discovered in Nashville as a street performer, mostly covering Daniel Johnston or anything passersby requested. He had dropped out of college when he met a professor from South Africa who "inspired me to quit my studies and make something of myself." A now defunct band called Monolith in Stereo took him on before splitting up, providing just the moment for him to be discovered by — well, here's where it gets fishy. Nobody knows quite sure who claimed his discovery first. The Eels? Cake? Modest Mouse? The Decemberists? Any name you can drop is flattering.

But after a long string of short-term, uncredited stints with various bands, Sedgwick used seed money from deceased actor Heath Ledger to make a name for himself with an ambitious, yet patched together EP, *Orange*. To describe it would be to describe an audition for *America's Got Talent* that even Tom Waits would dismiss as obscure — until you hear the vinyl for the first time. The head track, "Lodestone Blues," sounds dichotomously like a stadium jam and a street-side croon, and his new hit "Upon Choking" sounds eerily similar.

It's near impossible to chart the course of Wick's career in a singular arc, and the closest we can come is to list his LP's chronologically, which is as useful as a list of births, marriages and deaths scribbled into a family Bible — punctuation suspended amidst missing letters.

Wick is an artist striving to assert his own identity to a fan-base teeming with more sectarian conflict than all of Palestine.

But if you go out and buy a copy of *Gravity Waltzes,* make sure you also grab a copy of *Orange*, or maybe a release by an even less celebrated artist. You can always say you are buying it for a friend. If you're admitting you like him at this point, you might as well admit he's over. Either purchase all his albums or choose just one. And you better know everything about this living, breathing, inimitable contradiction before he either fades out or sells out.

I'm being burlesque.

After the initial interview with Wick I experienced something akin to decompression sickness. He had—I think—asked me to design the cover art for his upcoming album, one that he told me would be unlike any other before it. I had told him—I think—that I would agree to it. I was disoriented by the experience of meeting him to the extent that I didn't really know what had just happened. It was something I had to keep to myself, but I found it difficult to refrain from articulating my anxieties about the whole situation. I didn't know where to start. I could have just doodled some sketches of the motor, but then I couldn't tell if it was some sort of test, as if doing the one thing he seemed to be asking me was the one thing I shouldn't do. These anxieties seemed to be my subconscious telling me that I did indeed want to work with Wick, and that maybe something deeper bothered me.

I distracted myself with physical activity; I played squash with Joey one afternoon. Joey was a formidable squash opponent, in that he was not a formidable opponent, because I was not a formidable squash opponent. Neither of us were very good, and it did not matter, because we could each alternate between taking aggressive shots and laughing at either completely missing a hit or becoming the ball's next target. It was a chaotically pleasant form of stress relief. You could not get angry in a game with Joey. He would hit the ball with a deceitfully athletic determination, and then laugh at the outcome, no matter what, because it was all nonsense. We both decided to go pro.

"I saw this interview the other day," I told him as we took a water break. "I've decided I hate most interviews."

"Contrived?" he said, exhausted and mellow.

"Yeah," I said. "But then the interviewee either gives a series of bland answers or tries to act all punctilious."

"Who was it?"

"Sedgwick," I said, pausing first as if I had to remember something I had read somewhere.

"Sedgwick's really slipping," said Joey, hanging his head as if someone was losing a battle with cancer.

"Yeah," I said. "But everything's slipping, I suppose." I fanned myself with my shirt. "Entropy."

I didn't know why I couldn't just tell Joey that I had met with Wick, because Joey would have handled it better than anyone. I imagined he would have said "cool" with a bright and happy face, and then moved on to something else, his opinion of me not changing either way. Maybe a part of me feared such a response, and hoped he would parade the entire town into my full recognition. But the nature of the setup with Wick seemed like a well-kept secret that I had no right to let out. A pressure was swelling. I could only muffle it with squash, but it still hung around.

"I guess I'm just down about everything lately," I said.

"Why?" Joey turned his head toward me, happy to be selected as a recipient of whatever swelling burden I had to let out.

"It's like this...Cartesian Anxiety," I said. "Yeah."

Joey thought for a moment. "You're looking for something certain that can't be proven?"

I chugged water from my bottle to prepare for what I know would end up as a lengthy oration. "Well, I think maybe it's only about the future, you know."

"Like what'll happen to you? Where you'll be in ten years? Neil, what's plaguing you?"

"No, no, I mean about the future in general. I have no idea where I'll be in ten years. No promo. But I know I'll be more enlightened."

Joey laughed at this. I laughed too.

"It's a bit materialistic," I said. "But it's a material world. We can't help but access a certain model of the universe, and we can't escape from it. I want to escape from it, but I would have to leave my body to do it. Maybe in the future we will be able to leave our body. We'll be able to escape the imposed structure and emulate something closer to chaos."

Joey grinned. "Neil, I would love to see you emulate chaos."

"I am chaos," I said with my chest puffed out. I knew half of what I said had been only peripheral to what was eating me, but it was something I had thought of recently. "It would be nice just to have some certainty—about the world around us. Maybe just for twenty-four hours. Yeah, I could get a lot done and figured out in twenty-four hours."

"You need to go to a therapist and see what he can do about your Cartesian Anxiety," said Joey.

I took a gulp of water. "But if I reach true transcendence, all I need is like, a nanosecond."

"Neil, you could get a lot done in a nanosecond." Joey was the most sincere encourager.

"I need to go back and read more Heidegger," I said.

Joey postured himself as if in meditation, and addressed me in his bright, soft tone. "Just pick one thing in the world that is completely material and vain. Just one thing that fades. Commit yourself completely to it. Guilt free. Worry free."

"Mmm," I said, stroking my chin. "Something material and vain."

Apparently we both had thought of something vaguely base and perverted at once, and laughed.

"But really," said Joey. "One thing that has a chance of slipping through your fingers. Find that and pursue it. Subject yourself to that and live in the moment, in pursuit of it."

I turned my head. "Wait, what's your one thing?"

"Saving the human race."

"That's a little...non-material," I said.

"Fair enough," he said. "But that's my advice. I'm no guru. Go focus on your material object. Your material, losable object."

"Okay," I said, knocking the back of my head against the wall. "I will...tomorrow... perhaps."

I considered that I might have been homesick, and that this latent sentimentality happened to coincide with a rather auspicious job offer, instead of during those years of college. This often does not happen until the move to a large city, that permanent detachment from home. So I hung out with Tab for a day. We went to Las Paletas and reminisced over artisan popsicles, her idea. I cooled myself with a frozen avocado on a stick and laughed with her about the time she dropped her cafeteria plate in high school and thought it was the end of the world, about the time I stole her first pair of earrings as a kid, and about her father's goatee. Caraway the terrier came with us. We fed him a three dollar frozen granola bar.

I confessed to her that I was not interested in Kenna, which she didn't mind to hear. Apparently she had fixed us up merely as a joke. She couldn't stop laughing as she said it, laughing like I had bubblegum stuck in my hair.

"I know she has no interest in me either," I said. "But she keeps calling me and wanting to hang out."

"Maybe she's using you," said Tab. "It's like she's a collector. She has more Facebook friends than everyone at our old high school does combined. She likes to pull guys around on a string just for the connection. She's saving you for something."

"That's what I feel like," I said. "She's waiting around for me to break out on the scene. Not even, you know, to hook up with me or anything, but just be able to parade me around once I do. Like she owns me."

"I'm sorry," said Tab.

"Don't be," I said. "I doubt she will jump me or anything. Just pester me. You don't have to worry about finding me a soul mate. I'm sure I can repulse Kenna if I need to. I am pretty asexual, despite my irresistible prowess."

She laughed a little too hard at that one.

"Relationships overall are defined differently now," she said. "Don't you think?"

"In several ways," I said. "Be specific."

It wasn't often Tab would become so verbose, so I listened as if the combination of a dog, a popsicle, and a cousin had set the mood for her to perform the rare feat of reflective exposition.

"Well, I think part of it's digital media? But with a lot of my friends—the ones who aren't married—relationships are so short. Think about all the places you can meet, and it can go wrong, because you're asking for drama. College, work, a friend of a friend—"

I elbowed her in reference to Kenna. "A friend of a friend."

"Ha! Right. Everyone has these expectations for failure. Like, it seemed like before we had romantic expectations, and then we found real relationships. But now, everyone has such low expectations that they don't even put work into beginning relationships?"

Whenever Tab was prone to exposition, it was sequenced in a most inquisitive fashion. It is much safer, after all, to frame your theories in the form of a question.

"Are you arguing the theory of technological dependence?" I asked. "Because I remember when you had that online relationship that didn't work out."

"What?" said Tab, then remembered, for a moment gazing fondly into the distance and then blushing. "Oh. Yeah. I guess that would be a good example? It's easier to keep the the thing maintained through media, but we've gotten so used to it that face-to-face time can kill it."

"They used to just call it being shy," I said. "Like how everybody always said you used to be shy."

Tab rolled her eyes at a repugnant adjective she had heard time and time again.

"Or they're socially cautious. Some people are worried others will think they're just as two-dimensional as their profile. It's easier to be mysterious."

"To be inscrutable and reticent," I said.

"You and your words, Neil."

It sounded like half compliment and half ridicule, so I puffed my chest out and lowered my voice in satirical gallantry. "Why thank you, my lady."

"I didn't drag my feet around with relationships," she said. "I waited for Virgil. I mean, Mom and Dad were kind of surprised by him, but they didn't congratulate me like I thought they would after waiting for so long. Like, you know how we grew up with everyone talking about saving yourself for marriage?"

"Do I ever," I said. "I'm saving myself for when I reach my sultry prime."

"Ha! But you know, they never talked about saving, like, your personality or independence. It was always, you know, about sex."

"Sex," I said. "It's probably overrated."

Tab blushed, impressed that I had apparently not embarked on any escapades, but still somewhat ashamed of the topic in the presence of a family member.

"But, anyway," she continued, "it was always about that, never about saving yourself for just being ready in general. Like, too many of my friends were ready too soon? Just because they had found someone and wanted to sleep with them without the guilt?"

"I'm forever a bachelor," I said proudly.

"Don't be too sure," she said. "Mom has said it's my duty to find you a wife out here."

The pit of my stomach, cold and refreshed from the gourmet popsicle, became queasy.

"I feel pimped," I said.

Tab's laughter indulged my ironically egotistical prerogative for self-deprecation. I could not express any discomfort with the world without her making light of it in a fashion I was compelled to share. I let her do the sharing.

It wasn't homesickness I was feeling. The malaise was more abstruse. So I took to a more common recourse. I imbibed. When I say I imbibed, I mean I imbibed with friends, because drinking alone is, other than being irresponsible, rather drab and depressing. I am not a connoisseur of beers, but I am friends with some. I am not one to go into such a stupor that I cannot adequately rationalize.

Julius was hosting a brew party at his apartment out past the mass transit portion of the city, past the "NO PROMO" sign above the abandoned rails. His was the promise of free samples of a new batch of craft beer he made with Swedish hops. With every pass of a bottle he gripped your shoulder and told you the proud story of his brew, half of which you knew was a joke. At least, I hoped it was. He barked with the conscientiousness of a man who had spent all his focus and study on a craft and yet feigned having no idea what he was doing.

"I use a rusty pewter kettle for the process." The entire narration came with an indulgent smile beaming from under his vast beard. "I brew for forty minutes exactly and cool the wort as soon as I see the first bubble. I leave the yeast in my spice cabinet to gather a brazenly surprising array of flavors. The first time I brewed I used a tiny fermenter—runoff went all over the kitchen! I scooped up the froth and put it back in. I noticed the distinct flavoring of the organic floor cleaner my ex wife left behind. So I used the ingredients to tinker with the recipe. She's not getting a single check for that one! The word's best inventions are discovered completely by accident. Drink up!"

Everyone treated him to their laughter, assured he was mostly joking about the entire process. I could tell nobody there was an expert on brewing, and anything he said sounded brilliant, either in jest or in genius. At one point he put an arm around me and whispered loud into my ear.

"I sometimes treat the mash kettle like Wonka's liquor pot. Who knows what ended up in that brew?"

There came from him a most uproarious bellow I had not yet seen, and I sprayed the heavy beer from my nose.

The beer, if you must know, was orangish-red and smelled like raw, caramelized hops right out of the vacuum-sealed bag. It had an almost leathery top note, and a pungent dichotomy of sharpness and sweetness retained its form throughout every sip. The lingering malt ran down my throat and settled in the crevices of my mouth in raw floods like spiced sawdust, a sappy, resin flavor tinted with mango forming a confusing aftertaste. I cannot describe it without making it sound horrible, but it was a novelty to say the least, a beer that redefined the meaning of the word "robust" in ways most store shelves would refuse to carry. I didn't feel the least bit ashamed that I had designed his label for him at a discount price, something with a stock likeness to Trader Joe's product marketing.

Jules was wearing a gold-button Confederate frock coat the whole time. When it came time to replenish the ice bucket he took an iron pick to a brick of solid ice the size of a human torso, chipping large, uneven chunks all over the counter, some of them falling into the bucket, some of them ending up on the floor, where they were kicked around like soccer balls out onto the patio. I think everyone came more for the showmanship than for the beer. I asked him if he did kids' parties.

"My lifelong dream is to open up a theater pub here in Nashville," he said. "Not film theater. But stage theater."

"For kids?" I asked.

His laugh told me he was in love with the idea. "Ha! For kids!"

I brought Frenchy with me to the party. She stayed mostly on the patio smoking with whoever was out there. When she was inside she kept getting hit on by a guy with an old rangefinder camera who was in love with the way her cap fell over her ears. I didn't blame him. He kept taking snaps of her and playing around with the focus, lecturing about the importance of negative space and depth awareness. She listened for the attention, but grew bored with him quickly, I think. It wasn't a date, so I didn't feel any more jealous than I should have. Anyone can snap photos of raw moments. The still camera is the lazy man's guitar.

Amanda had showed up at the party, and hit on several of the guys. When she finally focused on one, who had already been enthralled by another girl, she proceeded to transform herself into a bisexual for the duration of the party, just to see if the gentleman she had concerned herself with would become jealous of her faux flirtation with the other girls. This was a counterproductive measure, and Cline, who had showed up with her, accosted her concerning the embarrassing charade, until a skirmish of a slap-fight erupted between the two. Julius, after laughing at the pair, announced that they had "displaced the mirth" by nearly erupting into pugilism, and they did not occupy the same room for the rest of the night. I promised myself that I would never share an apartment with them. Frenchy dismissed it, and said they fought like a brother and sister.

I was more pleased by the music than the beer — David Wax Museum live recordings, early Avett Brothers, Gogol Bordello — the latter of which spurred some clumsy, lively dancing. A Sedgwick song crept in there somewhere, and in a light buzz I mentioned to a girl that Sedgwick was "getting me to do one of his album covers." She just nodded and said it was cool. Either she didn't know who he was, didn't believe me, didn't hear me, or didn't care. Maybe it was none of those. I wasn't trying to get laid; I was pretty sure she was into women anyway. I just felt I had to tell somebody.

If you've been to one party you've been to them all. Every discerning and tasteful person has at least one moment where they want to get outside and either smoke or catch a breath of fresh air. Someone is ragging on their Republican father, someone is preaching about mono-culturing to two other people, someone is asking who's party this is anyway. Someone is placing bop jazz somewhere on a scale between Charley Parker and Miles Davis, and you realize you're the only person in the room that knows the guy doesn't have an opinion of his own. At some point either you find interest in a girl who turns out to be gay, or a guy who's gay finds interest in you and you have to find a kind way to let him down. It's about that time you begin to want that smoke or breath of fresh air.

After an hour Jules went around and took names of anyone willing to buy a case of his new brew. We had all become drenched in the zeitgeist of agreement that it was a horrible brew, and for this very reason we were all compelled to buy several cases of it. After all, where else would we find it, and when else would it ever taste the same again? I know I would not be the only one to even save a bottle, and I wasn't even a collector. Jules reveled in his evening.

"Your beard is cute," Frenchy said to him, without any elaboration or context.

"I thought about shaving the beard for this occasion and just going with the mustache," he said to us. "But the last time I did that I looked like an 1890's German strongman."

He pantomimed the lifting of a heavy barbell, forcing me to picture him in black spandex, and again he laughed so contagiously that we spilled our beers, which made him laugh louder still. We all found ourselves drooling.

By the end of the evening I knew I was stalling. I felt like I needed to get to work on Wick's new stuff and to let the word out. It would have been advantageous to my career, to my societies of friends. I was letting overwrought anxieties hamper my motivation. Everyone here was moonlighting as an amateur something—exotic herb gardener, sustainable T-shirt manufacturer, artisan knitter, ceramic painter, digital music pioneer, organic dog treat baker. Guessing the next person's hobby was as unpredictable as snatching any of their iPods and hitting shuffle. Everyone was doing everything short of trying to sell a fringe product they had "really gotten into." I had just begun my career, and had brought nothing to show and tell but a cute *devochka* in a fur cap.

I would like to think that there is something meaningful throbbing beneath our romance with these patchwork trends of hobby-hunting, these bursts of enthusiasm, a bundled, democratic exchange of enlightenment that each human can contribute towards. We have become a breeding ground of peripheral weirdos, a species who used to be called "nerds" with such disdain we learned to survive by milking the cool out of our creative lore. In high school we would have never crossed the borders of the AV Club, the Chess team, or the Basket Weavers Club and found one another. But sometime between high school and college we permanently fled our philistine homelands and migrated to these underground utopias budding ever so triumphantly as distinct, esoteric spaces that transcended place and time. We have too much time on our hands. Anything can become a craft now, and it can crop up anywhere.

What was I going to do, sketch somebody? I could only talk about what I read. I didn't have to ferry Frenchy home because she maintained enough sobriety to ride her scooter. I warned her that while texting while scooting was not a crime, it was dangerous even before having a beer. I thought about heading home to read some Kerouac but fell asleep with a book on my chest.

7
"THE PORPOISE SONG"
feat. a significant increase in awkward tension

According to Hank Scott, the second most revealing moment in Country Music history was during the CMA awards ceremony of 1975, when "Silver Fox" Charlie Rose presented the Entertainer of the Year award to John Denver, and then subsequently burned the envelope. Clearly drunk, Rose already had the audience on their toes, a parody of himself and of alcoholic performers everywhere. The camera focused on the awkward faces of stars in rhinestones and slicked hair who hardly resembled their musical forefathers as he stumbled through his recollections of them. If clowns were included, Silver Fox was the "performer" of the evening.

Speculations arose concerning the rationale behind Charlie's behavior, if there was one. He had a suffering in his gut, after all, having just reached the peak (and end) of his career well after his hair had gone gray. Perhaps it was mere jealousy over this naive hippie from Colorado who was riding in to take his throne with Pop Country tunes. Were that the case, it would have been white noise against ongoing accusations that this and that artist wasn't Country enough, including Charlie and his Jazz migration. It could have been angst at the entire Country scene being flooded with Pop from Music Row, or perhaps just a publicity stunt or prank that his inebriated self imagined would be cute.

The motives of the Silver Fox didn't matter, because the moment opened a subtle door to a room of conversations that had been going on for a good while, and are still going on today. Somehow the Country scene had evolved into a pursuit of money and fame where the competition was over who was Country enough for an industry whose label executives seemed to be the only ones who knew what the crowd wanted. After all, he mused to himself about the award, "this is the most beautiful thing in the world, right here." People have been known to speak a truth when they're drunk. *In vino veritas*. Or rather, *in biber ex amino*.

I'm being mendacious.

I'd thought Sedgwick would either have me over to his studio or out to some other joint, not have me up to his apartment. He had me come up to his place at Velocity in the Gulch on 11th, a building that looked more like it housed MI6 rather than a host of bourgeois residents.

Wick was fully dressed, if that's the right word, in jeans and blue cotton shirt with a large V-neck that looked two sizes too big. He balanced himself in the doorway with a subtly optimistic relief I had shown up.

I had expected a studio flat, but walked into a spacious one room apartment, one furnished as if the guy had blown all his money on a polished condo and scoured a rummage sale for furniture. The bedroom wasn't really a room, but a space sectioned off with incomplete walls and no doors, the kitchen and living room blending into the hall. The tall, ample space with its smooth, rich, uniform tones all round the wall and ceiling were the only signs — besides the window view — that this place was high end, as if a hobo had been squatting unnoticed.

As he led me into the living room and asked me if I wanted coffee or a shake, he couldn't once stand or sit still. He had a toothpick in his mouth that he constantly fiddled with, not like a good ol' boy trying to get free pie and a phone number from a waitress, but like a man desperately trying to trick his body into thinking he's still a smoker via some Freudian placebo. Compared to the day we met, he was less nervous, and more restless, as if he had mistaken our first meeting as a date and now I was suddenly his long-lost father, here to see he the new life he had built for himself.

In the hallway was an ironic, tacky poster for outlaw Country crooner Hoyt Murdock. Neil Young was playing in the kitchen — not the actual Neil Young, but an album. Actually, I wouldn't have been all that surprised if Neil Young in the flesh were playing in the kitchen. Wick went over to lower the volume and begin to fiddle with the computer. "This was actually a pretty cool gift," he said, fingering the edges of his iMac. "The, uh, the edges are rounded differently than most Macs. So it's like a custom mold. The angles are meant to be ultra-ergonomic."

He let me hold the Mac by the edges and lift it up and down in the air. I couldn't tell a difference. I felt incredibly disconcerted, like I had just wandered onto his property and he was too polite to shoo me away.

He brought over a copy of *Remembrance of Things Past* and handed it to me. "You like Proust?"

"I've been meaning get into it," I said.

"You can keep it," he said. "I don't get it at all."

You don't say those things. You don't tell someone you can't understand the reading. You tell them it's overwrought. You tell them it's boisterous. You tell them it's fallacious. But what you don't say is that you don't get it. I sensed an immediate, and somewhat alarming, streak of honesty.

Sedgwick went to the kitchen counter, took the final sips of a breakfast shake, and then poured it in the sink. He closed his eyes, then held a finger in the air. "Have you ever wondered why ice floats?"

"Well," I said, "it's a density thing."

"I know, I know," he said. "But just thinking about it. Ice. Floating. On water. Ice is water. I guess it's all about adaptation. It's how we float. We have to alter our density."

"Right," I said, idly brushing my jeans and looking around the hall. I saw a pair of very masculine legs sticking out from under the covers in the bedroom. There was a rumor I had only heard once about Wick and, granted, he was somewhat gender ambiguous, though not in the Steven Tyler kind of way. I asked only out of curiosity, because the opportunity had arrived.

"So, uh, the guy in your bed over there?"

Sedgwick shook his head. "Yeah, that's Sean's bed. He's always in his bed, sleeping or programming, or something. He's like an internet security wizard something. I forget what he does. I told him you were coming over, so it's all cool."

"You share the place with him?"

"You kidding? No, he's letting me crash here. I probably have a FICO score of 2. No, I've got so much equipment my apartment is just for storage. I don't want people trying to find me, so I'm never there. Plus I'd feel like a hoarder if I was. Sean's cool with it. He hates daylight, so this ends up being my 'room' when I'm around."

I looked down on the sofa, which had no distinct imprint of a body periodically stretching itself out, but only cushions defeated and sunken by perhaps endless and nameless previous owners and their acquaintances. The table in front of it was only an oblong sheet of glass held up by hardbacks of various sizes, meticulously stacked in perfect equilibrium like the masonry of Machu Picchu. On the table was a juniper banzai saturated with green, by far the most refined furnishing in the room, as if it were stolen from Xanadu in order to equalize the *feng shui* of an otherwise drab living space. I wondered what other homes Wick either partially owned or frequented, the lengths to which he avoided being anchored down to a singular place.

The blue bike near the door had to belong to him as well. Everything else tied together in the cheap, tacky knot of either a software programmer with no eye for decoration, or an artist with a deliberate eye for bargain mismatching.

"You don't *really* live here," I said.

"No, just cook, clean and compose a little. Here, we can talk where I sleep. It's also where I do my thinking."

"Where do you sleep?"

"The sky lounge. It's like my one guilty pleasure. It's kinda midtown, but it's totally deck if go up there alone. Roof of the world, man."

We are hermit crabs who squeeze into dissatisfactory shells with one another, time after time. We cannot bear to live in a singular space for too long. We are restless. If we do not have the funds to hitch across Europe, the luxury of following jobs from city to city, or the taste to merely rearrange our furniture and break out the seasonal pillow covers, we train ourselves to believe we are not actually residing anywhere in particular.

Many in my lot are amateur, aspiring gypsies, eager to withstand a lack of permanent residence as if it is a form of fasting, shifting through transitional districts until we feel we are encompassing more than a plot of land—we are everywhere at once. Our grandparents' grandparents were attached to plots of land, and we in no sense reject such a value, especially among oppressed minorities whose communal land ownership are exploited by corporate interests, but we ourselves do not feel a right to claim a land, and so we opt for a residential limbo. We do not form communities intentionally, it seems, but find ourselves corralled into them by our shared interests, ghettoizing ourselves wherever there is cheap housing, expensive coffee, and a pioneering scene.

Living in a house is conventional, yet pragmatic. Rent is slavery, yet freedom. To be vulnerable to eviction is to prove to oneself that flexibility reigns in the growing soul, that mobility is the key to survival, just as volumes of zombie literature has taught us. We want to sympathize with the immigrants, because our education, either through reading, viewing, or actual travel, has taught us that all vulnerable people experience the plights of transition through inhospitable barriers, either voluntarily or involuntarily, and that exposing oneself to possibility of immediate dispossession or even homelessness is a pilgrimage as holy as attending to any geographical location. It is both a guilty shame and a humble privilege to call upon a friend to allow us to crash at their place and, like a true vagabond, we find it difficult at times to even want to abjure the benefits thereof.

We see not a promise of a good home and a big yard; we see a horizon dominated by a stale middle class trench we may never want to climb out of, and have already spoken out against. The ones out there building the houses are building too many, too fast, too horridly. The prospect of owning one makes us feel too hungry, and even when we do own a habitat we habitually shape it into undocumented communal housing, or furnish it lightly. The most frightening thing can be the compunction to settle. For the time being, we dwell.

I'm being deprecatory.

The sky lounge was a place Sedgwick didn't belong, and that might have been why he only went up there when nobody else was, as if at some hour of the night some other resident threw lavish parties that left no trace the next morning, and after all the tenants had gone to work, Wick came to lay under the canopy and watch the sun conquer the skyline of the buildings where they toiled. We didn't occupy this resort space as if we owned it, but as if we had busted the padlock and crept up to it. We bypassed the fine weatherproof couches and claimed the roof's edge, him treating me to a breath of fresh air he himself seemed to need to carry our business further. He eyed an ambiguous part of the town, his face protected by dark wayfarers and a white Panama hat.

"So let me get this straight," he said. "You're into the music, right? I just didn't want to drag you into this kicking and screaming. I apologize for the contrived set up. I wanted to make sure you weren't like a crazy fan. You never want to surround yourself with people who might worship you."

"Hey, we're both trying to make a living," I joked, trying to lighten an unnecessarily solemn mood.

"Look, I'll be real," he said. "You sketch. So you tell me if you get this." He squirmed in place as if jealous of some other man's house miles away. "You got this guy over here who's got his own farm. Grew up on the farm. All he knows is farming. Every day is the same. Gets up, eats bacon, rides his tractor, sows his oats, goes to bed. Mundane life, right?"

I shrugged, because you don't disagree with a client. "I wouldn't want it."

"But here's the thing," he said, balling up some abstract struggle and weighing it in his hand. "At the end of the day, he can sit down, and he can put on his plate whatever it is that's out there in his field. The fruit of his labor is sitting right there in his G— d— plate right before his very eyes. He's shaped it; He's let it shape itself. Even God shaped it. And it sustains him and nourishes him. He can hold it in his hands like that."

"And it withers away," I said.

"And it withers away." We spotted some great bird shooting across the sky, as if to cue him to complete his musing. "And see, that is a true artist. What if we picked the wrong thing?"

"I don't know," I said. "I mean I feel pretty nourished. Then again, I do feel hungry a lot. It's very back-and-forth."

My attempts at spinning levity only deflected his drilling for deep diamonds in the empty air before us.

"You know what the first truly frustrating and challenging words were that our generation ever read?"

I shrugged. "Kafka?"

He exhaled. "Our princess is in another castle."

"Yeah," I said, straining to agree. "I get it. Because it was interactive. It was actually your story too."

"It's like the feeling every time you complete a song."

"Maybe we are more like farmers," I said. "I need to sow some more wild oats."

He stared me down as if to shame me for my verbal frivolity, and then looked away, dismissive. "Do yourself a favor and never create anything."

He wasn't laughing, but he wasn't taking himself too seriously. It was something else he was grasping at. I was almost envious at his sincerity, as if I had won a "breakfast with the prince" contest only to walk in on a captive sovereign who wanted desperately to climb out and join me in the bazaar instead. This wasn't self-mockery. This was boundless, flustered enthusiasm. I was the only audience, and he was in plain clothes.

"So in this new album," he said, "I'm taking a different approach. With most of my material, I sit down and I just start out with the sound, the sound comes first. Then I start singing and something comes out. If I've been thinking or reading about it, it comes out. If it's good, I keep it; if it's not I don't. It kind of grows from there."

"I'm taking notes," I said, listening.

He sighed. "I swear, sometimes I'll be on stage and when I walk off I'm thinking 'Holy F—! Did I just play a show?' I want to be more conscious of a song when I'm playing it. And to do that, I've got to be more conscious about the writing."

I drummed my hands on the plaster edge. "I don't know if I can help you with the writing."

"Just hear me out," he said, twisting the soggy toothpick and then throwing it off the balcony. "I want to say what I want to say, lyrically speaking. I can't remember the last time I had a human conversation with someone I can trust—outside of talking about music."

He was trying his best to establish trust, and I admired him for not accentuating the process with typical formalities or merely treating me out to lunch at some posh restaurant. After meeting Bruce Fey, I had expected something of the like. Without actually wanting to admit it, Sedgwick really was trying to reach out from the bars of some bastion and touch a human hand.

"So," I said, now trying to help him jog his effort at expressing the concept behind his new album. "Is there a story behind this project? Or is it more of a concept record? I know we talked about the motor thing. I did some sketches—"

"That was really just an initial process," he said. "I don't think I want that on the cover. I don't want to look pretentious or anything. I can't stand it when artists just put some random sh— on the cover and make it like a guessing game so somebody can say they were the first to figure it out."

"Well they won't recognize me, that's for sure," I said.

"I guess—" he began. "I guess these songs are all dealing with the specters I've had ever since moving here. The past is very present in the songs I'm writing. I'm sorry. That wasn't a pun."

"What pun?" I said, unable to hide my grin.

He continued, straining to be honest before me. "I knew I was meant to come here, but why? One thing I've actually tried to avoid is singing about past relationships, because nobody wants to hear that. But I could be wrong. Nobody wants to hear the fiction. They want you to articulate the real pain. That's what they relate to."

"Maybe you should design the cover yourself," I said. "I mean, not to banish myself into obsolescence."

"The thing is," he said, "I've been dealing with other peoples' struggles. Real and imagined. I think it's time I deal with my own. Pair my own work with my own life. I mean, without being autobiographical or self-indulgent.

Put something out people can relate to, not just admire. I'm tired of being admired. I'd rather be hated for being naked than admired for a masquerade."

"Do you feel like you're wearing masks?" I said. "I'm not talking about as a cover design thing. Just—do you really think your work is reflected in that way?"

"I don't know," said Wick, anxiously pushing himself back and forth on the balcony, as if he was about to attempt a record-breaking jump. "Ever listen to Nirvana?"

"I had a period," I said. "Kinda don't these days."

"Man they make you feel real. You know?"

"Yeah."

And now Sedgwick finally faced me, and I knew he was about to get real about whatever it was he wanted to discuss, that maybe it wasn't even about the album art.

"There was something else I wanted to ask you about. I'll get to it later. I just want to make sure that you get me. I don't want you to get the impression that I'm out to make a name for myself. In the business, they make your name for you. If only one person in the world listened to my music and loved it, I'd still be happy. I'm not in this for any reason other than what I love most. I think I just need help this time. I mean, you're a part of it, and I've assembled a few people. But I want to make it a personal experience for everyone. I want you to be able to put your heart and soul into it too. I want everyone to collaborate like we're not making a cent off of it."

"I can fulfill your request," I said, then added facetiously, "but I do have bills to pay."

He went on as if ignoring my interjection. "I just hate feeling like I don't have time for normal people and I end up putting them at a distance, putting fans at a distance. But you just get so disconnected—I almost don't care if they hate the new record."

"I'm sure I'll have an opinion about it," I said. "Maybe you should just record it and get it over with."

"I plan on it," he said. "I plan on it. I think I'll have you up on the day I record it. I'm just glad I can get to know you and stuff."

"Yeah," I said. "Your work is pretty decent." I had meant to say something about him, detached from his work, but despite the face he had begun to show me in the smoke I still felt I was only glancing at a mirror image from afar. I still saw the man who made all those albums, played all those shows, and seemed to drift in and out of conversations.

"I've got tickets to some shows I can't make it to," he said to me. "You want some tickets? They're for a bunch of groups. I know you just moved here, probably want to see more."

"Nah, man," I said. "Don't make me steal it off you."

"Won't hurt," he said. "When I really want to get into a show I go. Some of the tickets are promotional anyway. I sponsor new performers. Come on. It'll give you some time to soak up the city. Give you plenty to sit on before we start collaborating."

"Sure," I said. You can't say no to free shows. You can only say they sucked after you go.

I scanned the horizon of the city for some visual inspiration to apprehend me in the wake of our dialogue. To a great many people every city looks the same. Were it not for the AT&T monstrosity, I could probably say that certain angles of this cityscape are no exception. Sedgwick had made it here, and if a guy like Sedgwick could make it, maybe I could make it. I could wait to work on his project when he was ready. I had other clients, anyway.

*　　　*　　　*

Over the next month I managed to find some good work, enough to keep me going, at any rate. I re-designed a menu for a delicatessen who wanted sketches rather than photos of their food. I helped design a hand-drawn font with a niche book publisher who ran a boutique. There was an imaginatively sectioned map of the human brain, a treasure map, a series of pointing fingers—all for websites. There were several banners. I even did some work with Microsoft. I slowly began to build my portfolio, and was for the first time tempted to apply to a firm. I had ignored phone calls from the Community Church about their design, until I finally sent in a sample matching exactly what they told me they had in mind. The next thing I knew I had been given a check without additional communication, not even a thanks. I felt used, but I felt paid.

For a while I foolishly chose to meet various expenditures with overdrawn student loan money, until my income became more stable. I took Wick's advice and saw other shows, both on and not on his charity. It was one of the reasons I hit Nashville and I couldn't miss out. I got a little carried away and nearly maxed out my week's budget. For the near entirety of a month I must have subsisted on meals consisting of takeout Chinese food with Sriracha and Arizona tea. I would sometimes splurge on coconut water. I felt a little dispirited.

I've determined that hunger is the phenomenon that delineates an artist's integrity. Some who work merely wish to hit the scene. The truly creative have an unhealthy work ethic, not motivated by deadlines, but by passion for the art itself. We starve for the ideas and their manifestation. The starving artist is starving not because he cannot afford to eat, but because he cannot afford to quit working on a pursuit regardless of the supply of bread. His or her bread is the work. A steady flow of capital is nothing without the threat of inspiration. Risk is paramount because it is the ward against stagnation, in which we cannibalize our own work, recycling as an ouroboros would its own tail. If we barely make rent, we are then reminded of the need to pursue the next great gig, because we are only as credible as our last accomplishment, and our last accomplishment must make us hungry for the next. You cannot dare be satisfied with a single thing you do. When you are satisfied, you have broken your fast.

Creative or uncreative—I do not know which I am. There is no point in asking. Neither have I said anything that has not already been said.

Joey came to the rescue by splitting rent with me. I say split, but since I took him in partially out of pity, he didn't quite exactly pay an even portion. He had softly requested that he crash at my place for a few days, and a few days turned in to a couple weeks. He felt so guilty he offered some rent money, as much as he could afford. His most premium contribution was that he cheered me up, expending his casual aura of illumination. He was in between jobs, having misplaced the motivation to continue his marketing job. "I was tired of working with those tools," he said. When I was tired of working and he was tired of searching for work, we would head out to a park and play shuttlecock with Sam and Sam.

I felt settled in Nashville, somewhat. It did have this energy, this enthusiasm about itself. I could even live with the energy of the tourists and the instant cowboys and the odorous drunks who stumble out in the street in any city and spoil the night with repugnance. I entertained myself with the thought of places I had yet to go, places I could go and be at only once, never to be judged, because to try anything once is a novelty, no matter how trashy or cliché. On occasion I would begin to feel misanthropic, and after Joey moved in I could not attribute it to living alone. Even if I did not eat alone I felt it, and sometimes wanted to eat alone when I wasn't, a young and emerging laborer in the twilight of one of thousands of cities, vainly striving against the depression of being small in a town that does not know you, does not care, but whose hospitalities almost convince you that it is glad to have you stay. It wasn't particular to Nashville, and it wasn't particular to me.

On innumerable nights I joined the flocks who stood outside doors with hands in their pockets. I was never the type to indulge myself in the public sharing of atrocious lists of shows I'd seen, but this manifest is of some relevance to the narrative. You have to get an impression of Sedgwick from all valid angles, and a panorama of bands he played with, played after, endorsed or expressed indifference toward is, I feel, crucial. It was with these bands that fans could claim to know whatever they felt important to let us know they knew about the value of Sedgwick's work or, if they didn't, merely clutch their beers with the labels facing out and roll their terrible eyes:

Chesterfield Deluxe
The Sufis
Him and Her
    (I got photos with "Him," but not "Her," which
    made me melancholy)
Codeine Velvet Club
    (Broke up in 2010; you can't see them any more)
Donnel Jeffrey and the Carter Clan Brass Band

Vilde Chaya
Beirut
> (Everyone there just had to talk of how they
> wanted to visit Europe—that or scoff at the band
> that wasn't quite Neutral Milk Hotel)

The Inscape
Tall Boy Plunger and the Cornstalkers
> (Actually it was just Tall Boy's solo act)

Tobin
Jeff Mangum
> (With Neutral Milk Hotel and O.T.C.)

The Shins
> (Or might have been Marr with Modest Mouse)

Morrissey
> (Flipped out and socked a roadie for having
> hamburger breath; also got away with wearing his
> own band merch)

L.E.D. Sweeney
Rubble Puddle
> (They had a raw edginess about them I found rare)

Sylvester Churchill
Picasso Trigger
Olivia Tremor Control
> (Personally asked me for a recording of
> my dreams)

Deer Tick
Deer Hunter
Devendra Obi Banhart
> (Broke his wrist boarding: show and cancelled)

The Stone Roses
MGMT
Whitebait
> (Their guitarist was a septuagenarian)

The Mink Coats

Wavves

Pomplamoose

> (And their fans, sadly)

Edward Sharpe and the Magnetic Zeroes

Polecat

Menomena

The Mark Summers Incident

> (With Conchrite-Canada)

Gulag Lazy River

> (Or as you know them, GLR)

Fondle Orchid

> (I remain an avid fan of their music videos)

Yuck

The Catlips

Dandy-Walker Epidemic

Radiohead

> (Played "The Boney King of Nowhere" and "Rhinestone Cowboy," both of which made me giggle)

Dr. Brony and the Liver Transplant Specialists

Ariel Pink's Haunted Graffitti

Molly Parden

Local Natives

Ferret Garden

> (Where a drunken cop accosted a fan)

Donovan Frankenferter

Duckweed

The Young Quincies

> (They had broken up three times already)

DJ Cake Batter

> (Before his untimely suicide)

Black Keys

> (Their emulation of The White Stripes was juvenile and base; it was like a musical palette swap)

Airborne Toxic Event
    (Who offended me with their self-described
    "captivating blend of literate, visceral indie rock
    and propulsive, anthemic choruses")
The Avett Bros.
She Walks in Squalor
Wilco

There were also art shows, restaurants, films. I would not adhere exclusively to the music scene. The Tomato Arts Fest was delightful. I attended with Tab and Virg. There was a little bit of everything there, and it was in the most perfect neighborhood. Art shows sent me into a meditative regretfulness over the path I chose to take my own work. My doodling and designing supplied me with income, so I could not complain. There were ways of blending into a scene, and there always would be, doors that fluttered open and shut at a moment's notice, like they sometimes do with relationships. You're sitting in a coffee shop one day, someone strolls in, and by the time you finish your cup your entire paradigm of the world has been altered permanently, or at least for that afternoon.

I went along with with Tabitha and Kenna to have coffee at Fido in Hillsboro—yes, the one that used to be a pet shop and still has a monkey on the sign. I ordered an iced milk bone, per Tab's recommendation. I felt odd saying the words, and made her laugh when they stumbled out of my mouth, as if I was the first person to feel odd saying "I'll have the iced *milk bone*." It was a product of my repressed upbringing that I have remained supremely conscious of sexual innuendo. At least I didn't try ordering a frothy monkey.

The place was usually busy, in part because of the location and food quality, but also in part because of the celebrity frequenters. Kenna was elated over the possibility of spotting Taylor Swift, whom she was eager to snap of a photo of. However, on this morning it was unusually vacant, probably because of the rain. There were only a few other tables filled with people murmuring and sipping at a low volume. Rain is typically favorable weather for coffee sipping, but with difficult parking, some would rather sip at home.

The intimacy worked to our advantage. Tab was not a fan of large crowds, and Kenna's loud baritone had to be offensive to most bystanders. It was one of Tab's favorite places, which she reminded me with a winking emoticon when she invited me to go, and I worried she was up to romancing me toward Kenna again, just for kicks. I could see why it matched her taste. It was classy, pricey, took itself seriously without being smug. The staff I could tell were used to a warm crowd whose warmness they returned, except for today, when the crowd was absent. Cheerful blends were stacked on the shelf like a home pantry, and the brick wrestled and flirted against the faux stucco of the walls. If someone had brought in a date on this day everything might have felt both drowsy and enchanting. The three of us were by the window, the patter of rain a blanket keeping us from wanting to get up from our chairs to do anything. For a coffee place, it felt anything but bubbly.

We were going on about some idle news or another when one of the staff set out a stool and a mike.

"That's funny," said Kenna. "I didn't know they did live music here. Sure picked a sh—y of a day for it."

Tab's wrinkled furrow echoed the same sentiments.

"It's a treat," I said. "Just for us. I guess this means we can't sneak out without tipping."

"I don't have any change," said Kenna.

There was a stool and a mike, and that was it. From the way the staff bustled about, this seemed to almost be a last minute change of plans they didn't quite understand.

"If this is Taylor Swift I'm gonna sh— my pants," said Kenna. "We are like the only ones here."

The performer stepped out from the back room and into the shady corner not with a guitar, but an hourglass dulcimer. He wore a black fedora and a matching vest, with a plaid shirt and a mismatching plaid scarf.

"Is he seriously gonna play that thing?" said Kenna. "Did he hitchhike here? He looks like a fairy Tom Petty."

Tab tried not to laugh out loud, but did.

When he mounted the stool, I recognized him immediately from his hair, and tried to discern what kind of message he was trying to send me. I momentarily suspected I had become a target of his affections and he could not articulate himself to me.

"I like dulcimer music," said Tab, resting her chin on her palm in anticipation.

"Hey folks," the performer said to nobody in particular. The few other patrons in the coffee shop continued their conversation, but their eyes flicked to him and back. Most of their backs were to him anyway. "I'm just here to play a few pieces. How's the brew?"

Nobody said anything. The dulcimerist laughed nervously, as if he had dreamed for this moment and was tickled to behold the faces of listeners.

Tabitha winced in embarrassment on behalf of the guy on the stool, and said under her breath, "When's he gonna start? It's really quiet in here."

The man on the stool lightly strummed his dulcimer, checking the tuning. "I used to play out on that corner over there," he said softly, gesturing outside. "Right under that tree. Can't right now, 'cause, you know, it's raining."

He fiddled with the dulcimer some more and grinned with excitement.

"Wait, is that—" Kenna stopped herself, and then sprung upright in her chair. "D—! I think it is. That is Sedgwick on that f—ing stool!"

"Who?" said Tab, straining at the face in the shadow of the corner of the room.

"Whoah," I said, feigning discovery. "What's *he* doing here? Did he, like, reserve this place?"

Sedgwick leaned into the mike, looking up from his exotic instrument. "Kinda miss just bein' able to come in here and just explore music with a small crowd who doesn't know me. It's just nice to have that rare and darling risk of failure, just that complete surrender before a room of people. On days like this I can reclaim it, if only for an hour."

Nobody seemed to be willingly paying attention but the three of us, our eyebrows turned, each confused in their own way.

"I have got to Instagram this," said Kenna, scrambling through her iPhone. "Neil, write down what he just said. This is too good to miss."

From the minute he sat down Sedgwick had oscillated between resolve and hesitation, as he had with everything he'd said since I met him. He took deep breaths and adjusted his instrument. Then, he began to play his song. The picking came first, and for a good half-minute, with some familiar tune that wasn't one of his own but wasn't immediately recognizable. He had gone pale, and a generous beam of light fractured into color somewhere between the rain-empty sky and the window, hitting his glasses with a murky rainbow, casting him like a stained glass saint having emerged from a long, monastic isolation. His face looked different now, and he could have been anybody else until this moment, like his face had just become remolded by his own performance, imitating a ghost or gargoyle.

It was a soothing tune. I leaned back, now that the irritating silence had been smothered. Kenna was capturing it all on her iPhone like it was a wardrobe malfunction worthy of tabloid journalism. Tab was ever so slightly tilting her head back and forth as she leaned forward, legs crossed, her brown leather poor boy hat covering her eyes. Then I saw her mouth drop a little, and her head cock to the side. This happened just as Wick began to sing the lyrics to the song, which turned out to be Eric Clapton's hit, "Layla," slowly and desperately crawling his way through an arrangement much more like Clapton's famous *Unplugged* performance than his studio recording. In this rendition, only a trickling dulcimer supplied the melody, and Sedgwick's voice was a plaintive falsetto.

Tabitha gave a startled gasp of laughter. Kenna and I perked up, because in such a quiet room with such a quiet song, her laughter was noticed. It was a laugh of disbelief at something she saw, or knew upon seeing. She murmured something I couldn't hear, and some connection had just been made in the room that escaped me.

Kenna must have recognized what this meant, because she looked up from her iPhone at Sedgwick, over to Tabitha, then back at Sedgwick in shock. I was oblivious still to the exact nature of this serendipitous connection, but I began to grasp the fundamental nature of it, one that perfectly explained Sedgwick's sudden appearance. Two things I knew: Sedgwick had attached himself so uncannily to me, and Tabitha had always been a fan of Eric Clapton.

The awkwardness was horribly intolerable.
Kenna dropped her iPhone.
"F— me holy sh—!"
Well I guess Cupid is no longer an archer.

8

"3 ROUNDS AND A SOUND"
feat. retroactive exposition

Have you read the ending passage of *Grapes of Wrath*? When Rose of Sharon lifts her shirt and bares her breast to the old man dying of hunger? She says, "You got to," and he does, because he's got to. She smiles mysteriously. It's very uncomfortable, because it's taboo, and you're left at the end of the book with that uncomfortable feeling, and that uncomfortable silence that follows.

Or there is that moment in *Requiem for a Dream* where Marion meets the pimp and he calls her "Maid Marion." The lens focuses on his very large, black mouth as he says the words, and it is very uncomfortable — that large mouth insinuating sexuality and dominance, as well as the exploitation of our middle class fears of a black man having his way with a white woman, compounded with our shame and guilt at having such fear. And then the very degrading scenes that follow. It's like having that feeling while watching that film with someone else beside you in the room.

This communicates something akin to the excruciation I began to feel after that moment in Fido's. I may have given the impression that the awkwardness ended abruptly after, that we all just got up and left the coffee shop immediately. The discomfort only began to deepen after that first song. Sedgwick finished his set by covering two more classics that surveyed Tabitha's surviving tastes in classic rock music—"Stairway to Heaven" and "More Than A Feeling"—during which time Tabitha and Kenna whispered to each other incredulously about this ghost across the room. It was no secret he had spotted and recognized them, but the one secret that burdened me was that I too had already met Sedgwick. Somehow I was being manipulated into reforming a bridge. I suspected he had used his connection with me to somehow spot her once again, knew we were showing up at this coffeehouse at this hour. And yet I felt obligated to keep my mouth shut about it. He was trying very hard.

If you were not already aware, Clapton based "Layla" off of a surviving text by 12th century Persian author Nizami Ganjavi titled *Layla and Majnun*, in which a moon princess is forced to marry a prince she does not love, helplessly forsaking her true love, Majnun, who descends into madness as a result of his permanent loss of his hope of love. To complicate even further the composition of the song, George Harrison's wife, Pattie Boyd, divorced him and left him for Clapton, who was deeply in love with her around the time of the song's formation. Sedgwick's allusion was uncannily contrived.

When he finished there was a trifle of applause and he approached us with patient surprise. He exchanged a hug with Tab, who examined him closely as if he could not be the same old friend she had once known from somewhere. She was quiet with shock, but her eyes were wide like open windows. Kenna was the ecstatic one, unable to contain the inner hype of realizing that this old flame of Tabitha's was now an established indie performer in the heart of Music City, whom she was meeting face-to-face, yet not for the first time. He greeted me as if we had never spoken before. It was a silent agreement not to speak of our business together, one I reluctantly held, one that confirmed for me that this was no happenstance. There was an affirmation that he should meet up with her again, to catch up, with an additional invitation to a concert, which they both accepted. This was the most he could accomplish in our presence in such a space and in such an hour. It would have been rude, after all, to approach this one girl from his past while Kenna and I sat idly by, and it would have been rude of us to dismiss ourselves and leave them alone.

All three of us had known him before, and it made no sense that I was the first to recognize him, especially considering that Kenna had followed his career quite obsessively. Of course, having heard his name several times, neither of these girls ever once made the connection previously. It is an all too common motif, after all, for a professional performer to brand themselves an alias.

There is no way Chance Merritt would have ever become Garrett Sedgwick, not without at least going to college and finding himself. I knew how Tabitha was in each of her phases growing up, and Kenna didn't need to explain that to me. She fancied herself an old soul, and avoided flirtation with boys because they were less mature, even the dreamy ones. As far as I knew, she never seriously dated anyone until she met Virgil. But Kenna had shared with her summer trips to a three week Christian retreat out at some camp, and it was there that

Tabitha met a boy who, in the words of Kenna, "knocked her completely flat."

"But here's the craziest thing," said Kenna. "It wasn't just his name that was different. Like, you wouldn't recognize him, either, Neil. Chance was a f—ing country bumpkin. I mean all he played and liked was Country. Like Top 40 radio Country. Cowboy boots and hat and everything, walking around that camp like a f—ing stud. But he was straight off the farm. And he would have called a kid queer for dressing like he did back at Fido just now."

Tabitha was smitten as she never had been before, but word of it didn't reach her family at home. She had some reputation to keep up with and didn't want them to know that she had broken her unspoken vow of high class breeding in order to hook up with some farm boy with a guitar and a charming smile. She wouldn't dare mention that she had fallen for a boy her age who was simple and pedestrian. She wouldn't dare walk hand in hand with a boy so unpolished. Somehow a window had opened, and they were inseparable for the remaining duration of the retreat.

"He was a complete dumb f— too," said Kenna. "She didn't really see it until after camp, when they started calling each other and chatting online. He thought the names of pasta were based on how they were cooked, and when she had to tell him it was the name for the shape of the noodles, she couldn't stand it. She'd roll her eyes all the time when talking about him. It's no wonder they broke up."

"Why'd they hook up in the first place?" I asked.

"She thought he was a complete gentleman. He was hot, dressed like a grown man, smelled like a grown man. And she was in that Country phase, remember that Country phase? We were both in it. I got her into it, and it was just in time for him to come along and sweep her up. Once she was away from the smell and touch of him the honeymoon phase of that relationship totally flat-lined. Now he's a f—in' Indie Rock god. She could have married that guy. Sh—, Ryan. This is cracked up."

Tab had outgrown her phase, both in regards to Country music and Chance Merritt. She went to college, eventually came back with Virg, and before we knew it they had spoken their vows and were moving to Nashville.

And upon hearing this my paradigm began to dreadfully shift, because what these two girls assumed to be coincidence I knew to be the desperate machinations of a relentlessly immature youth. The musical craft into which he had flung himself had not been born of its own addictive passion, but of a very hormonal love. This changed everything about Sedgwick; this changed everything about everything. He was now unmasked, solidified in my consciousness out of the nebulous cloud that was his polarizing mythos. Fans would be shaken if it were made known to them that his concerts were given in hopes that one attendee would show, would grow a familiar interest in him, and discover him in his new element. After five albums and countless venues, Tabitha failed to show, but her graphic designer cousin showed up not a moment too soon.

A true gentleman, the new Chance Merritt masquerading as Sedgwick was not one to storm the castle. Nonetheless, it was all a bit contrived, and I couldn't get out of it. I was exhausted from ruminating on the whole instigation. I wanted to go home and read some Heller.

*   *   *

There was one rite of passage I had yet to undergo since moving to Nashville, but I had only lived there a few months before passing through it. I was never offended at not being invited to weddings, and most of my friends either would never marry, were married when I met them, or had already married and divorced when I met them. I feel I'm like many people when I say that my experience is summed up in two parts: one being the listening to short, sappy sermons on the meaning of love taken from an ancient Bible passage and reworked into middle-class values; the other being the consuming of food, wine and dance. We don't remember much about the couple, what they said, what we said to them, or even what we gave them. After about ten years, weddings have all run together, and any more we attend will run together still. Our postmodern consumerist economy ethic constructs most of what such a day becomes, and if there is anything meaningful in these ceremonies, such meaning is drowned in the lavish preparations and expenditures of an orgiastic and ephemeral celebration enjoyed not at all by the family and only halfway by the guests.

Kenna invited me to go with her to a wedding shoot for the sole purpose of gossiping further about Sedgwick and Tabitha. My reluctant curiosity compelled me to attend. Kenna would not be gossiping about a bridezilla, a cheating groom, a clash of clans, a drunken best man, or a controlling mother-of-the-bride. She did, however, complain about the boutonnieres being too bright for natural lighting. That and the tablecloths not matching the ties.

"Whatever," she said. "It's not my wedding, right?"

This she said about many a thing at the wedding. Kenna was a cynic about these occasions, but an opportunist nonetheless. There are photographers who grow more enchanted with the institution of marriage after every shoot, and there are those who find another reason for themselves not to marry after every shoot. Kenna was apt at faking the emotional investment of the shoots. It wasn't the couple themselves she captured, but the aesthetics. She fed off them, a promotional artist for a killer industry. Killer dress and killer boots. Hung lanterns and pebbled vases. The rustic, rented farmhouse juxtaposed against rakish, rented suits. The white gown against tan white skin under the floral arch. Hair done up, undone and done up again to resignation before the impossibility of perfection. Towering cakes, towering gifts, and towering tents over tables laden with layers and layers of cloth and burlap and moss and petals. Bubbles blown through the gauntlet to the stretch limousine. I just felt overwhelmed.

Kenna snapped and snapped, taunting the couple and their party for sweet, proud shots. In between locations, waiting on the bride to carry her heavy dress across the field, Kenna reminisced further about the Fido surprise.

"I just want to know when he turned into Garrett Sedgwick," she said in frustration. "Never told us about that. But you know, Tab stopped talking with him like right when she went to college."

"When she met Virg?" I said.

"No, no, remember, she didn't at least bring him home 'til like Junior year? That's when I met him."

"It was college," I said. "It was academia. You said Chance wasn't cut out for college. Tabitha wouldn't dare let a guy date her who couldn't even get in."

"So what did he do? Fake his transcript and come up with a new name? Nothing shows up. I even looked it up on Wikipedia. Just a short bit about how he grew up a Nashville native—yeah right—but nobody remembers him until like five years ago."

"Well, it is Wikipedia," I said with authoritative flippancy. "The definitive go-to."

"It was like he just crawled out of a drain pipe and on the sidewalk with a guitar."

"He crawled out of Alabama. Put that on Wikipedia. Word for word."

When the DJ arrived at the farmhouse to set up for the reception, Kenna recalled the missing piece she had been searching for. Chance didn't just take a guitar to school, to family gatherings, and to teen retreats—he had put an album out.

"He had this little CD," she said. "He probably sold like twenty copies of it."

"Was it drenching with banality?" I asked.

"It was the worst," she said. "Even had this goofy picture of him on the cover with his cowboy hat all tilted down. I mean I can see why Tab thought it was cute when he sang right next to her. But even when she was in to him she didn't play the album. Everyone bought it out of charity. He had a friend with some studio he borrowed for a couple days and did mostly cover songs of Randy Jackson and Garth Brooks. He sounded worse on a mic and scrambled the worst backup players. D— it, if I can get a copy of that old CD! Sh—! I probably threw it out! Can you imagine the talk it would stir?"

"Wait, wait," I said. "So his name was already out? That's why he did it? He thought his career was already cemented? With a selling-albums-out-the-back-of-the-trunk release?"

"Neil, he wasn't even known outside his county," she said.

"Maybe that was why," I said. "A prophet not even welcome in his own town, because that's where his starter material emerged from."

"You're taking this way too deep," she said.

I persisted, at the risk of giving away my postulation and its insinuation concerning Wick's motivations. "If Tab rejected him because of his background, even his identity, maybe that's what he felt after his CD didn't sell. Maybe he just threw his whole self into becoming something that would astonish everybody. He fled to Nashville and just breathed everything in until he's this completely different guy. Don't tell me you were the same person in high school."

Kenna grew somber for a moment. She had pried some additional history from Tabitha after the encounter at Fido, but hadn't had time to meaningfully assemble it until now. "He did spend a huge chunk of his own money on that record. His dad even took some out of savings. I remember. Tab said he almost cried when he told her how much he lost on it. His dad owned a hardware store that never did well after they put a Home Depot in."

"Did he think he'd make it big?"

"Huge," said Kenna. "His parents did, too. Or they supported him because he thought he would. I think he thought it was his only shot at anything. They couldn't afford college, or he didn't make the grades even if he could. They pressured him to go to technical school, but they entertained this dream of his where he'd hit Nashville and be a Country star. He even told Tab he was going on American Idol."

"And she laughed?"

"She laughed."

"But I mean he was cocky, too. A bunch of girls were all over him. But Tab didn't show it. She wasn't as easy, so her pursued her."

"So he humbles himself," I said, recounting a story neither of us were witness to. "He reinvents himself. He completely switches genre, becomes literate, gets a haircut—"

"Gets a d— makeover. Why? So he can prove everybody wrong?"

"Or prove it to himself," I said, resisting the temptation to bring Tabitha back into the story.

"I still can't believe it," said Kenna. "The same guy that used to walk around that retreat with a G— d— toothpick in his mouth, wearing shirts too small for his arms, pronouncing words wrong and talking about his truck, and somehow impressing Tabitha enough to make her— Sh—! Neil, what if he did it all for her?"

My stomach hardened, but it wasn't like I had given it away myself. "I doubt that," I said. "It seems contrived for him to go through all this just for Tab. I'm sure she was one of many influences in his great reform. You know, Ryan Adams started out doing Alternative Country."

"Yeah," she said, the idea fading from her eyes like a dying spark. "It would be crazy as H—, though. Tab would freak out. I wonder if she ever told Virg about the whole Chance thing. Doesn't that make it weird, that they got married, but didn't *really* get married? What if Chance knew that?"

Had I known the couple, I might have remembered something from the ceremony. I tried to imagine what Tabitha's wedding would have been like if she had had one, and then I ended up alternating between imagining Virgil Davis or Chance Merritt up there. Depending on the groom, and the time in her life, such a ceremony would have been entirely different. I considered the reasons she had explained to me, or rather, the reasons she had explained were not reasons they had not had a wedding. It wasn't money. It wasn't drama. It wasn't feminism. Well, it might have been a percentage of those things, but as far as being a revealing action, it wasn't anything but a complicated, suffocated desire to escape from the mediocrity of an institution taken for granted.

When there is nothing else to do, a couple fond enough of one another is bound to seriously consider the nuptial sublimation of their relationship, even if they find marriage in itself to be in decline for viable reasons—the divorce of their parents, the end of promising careers, the burden of children, the domestic conflict, the financial toll, the religious guilt, the sexism inherent in the worn practice. If a marriage in itself cannot be avoided, then it is the norms of a wedding that are shunned. Out of a very primal cognitive dissonance emerges the desire to both engage in a time-worn tradition and challenge that time-worn tradition. They cannot resist the urge to have a wedding, to solidify in an expressly permanent sense their commitment to one another, and yet they very well resist the conventional definition of what a wedding itself is.

This demurral often manifests itself in a wedding that gives more attention to theme than to pomp and circumstance. Attendees appear and realize the couple was serious about everyone bringing a walking cane and a monocle, donating to an animal shelter in lieu of gifts, choosing an abandoned equine slaughterhouse as a venue, or the bride sporting a faux mustache in all her photographs. To form a whimsical and radical wedding is to take ownership of it like no generation has before, to defy the industry of ceramic marriages that continually roll off the press and remain on the domestic shelf, stagnant and fragile, on the edge of shattering in the lightest of quakes.

Especially for those of us whose parents married too young and can't stand one another, we either cope with the trauma by making the same exact naive mistake, or by fighting against "marriage" until we turn thirty, sworn to find ourselves before we pledge ourselves soul mates. The option to either spend lavishly on a single day or to save up for a house or car or small business loan is taken in a cynically practical direction. A shared investment in easily dividable futures is less regrettable than a shared splurge on ceremony. Given that compatibility seems to have been established through the practice of cohabitation, it is not the moving into a place forever that we are celebrating, but a moving into yet another space together.

A wedding becomes a novelty in itself. Even the girls—and I deserve any accusative flak from feminist criticism for this—do not seem to plan weddings any more, or at least admit that they do, until they have found their soul mate. When commitment is imminent, an obnoxious, Herculean task is set before us. We must craft the most trendy, personalized wedding experience the world has ever witnessed. We have seen enough brides walk down the aisle and be told afterwards, "you look so pretty." We now want to prance on the lawn and hear them say, "I love what they're doing with the whole marriage thing, totally rethinking the experience of being wedded—so edgy." It is not so much a wedding as it is an interactive art project commenting on the lack of sincere, sustainable marriages, a subversive cry screaming to be articulated in a world of rehearsed rituals. Marriage for us is not the glorious beginning of life together, but an adorable accessory to it.

I'm being acrimonious.

At the reception I met up with Greg Dickey and Mason Leary, who knew the couple getting hitched. Greg had brought a date with him, not Shelly from the night at the Wick concert, but a different girl named Bryce. Greg openly admitted that part of the reason things hadn't worked out with Shelly was because he talked too much about Cameron around her, which he defended on the basis that Cameron's name only came up as a reference point and not as the subject of a regretful dirge. However, as he brought up this very argument, he began to digress into the subject of Cameron again, and already Bryce was growing tired. Her mouth had a permanent smirk that remained even when hey eyes frowned at Greg.

He defended himself. "I'm only saying that with Cameron I knew that if she ever married, she would be in trouble, and I realized that today."

"How do you just know that?" said Bryce, raising a defiant hand. "How do you know the alternative future of this girl?"

"I'm only saying it's a prediction," Greg said defensively. "It was the way she talked about marriage. We went to a wedding together once, and she just kept going on and on about how she wanted to do things differently if she ever got married, but when I started asking her about what kind of man she thought she would marry, everything was based off of her own tastes and her own preferences. She didn't talk about virtues or how godly she wanted her husband to be—"

"Maybe she didn't know what kind of question you were asking," said Bryce. "You were at a wedding, not a church."

"But, see, that's the thing," said Greg. "I'm sorry, I'm going to get on my soapbox for just a minute."

Bryce threw up her hands. "Okay, you get on your soapbox. I'm going to talk to those people."

Clearly Bryce had had enough of Greg for the day, and was willing to even let him alone with someone she just met. I didn't want to hear Greg on his soapbox any more than she did. As she walked away, Greg turned to look at her, and then whispered to me with large, ecstatic mouth movements, "She likes to make out a lot. Like, A LOT." He then laughed exhaustively.

"Sounds like a keeper," I said. "Well, so what's your soapbox?"

"So, I'm not saying Cameron is entirely guilty of this," he said, closing his eyes as if he had said the name of a dead grandmother. "I'm not saying anything like that, and maybe she's matured more since we dated. I know I have. But I have my finger on why divorce is so common with our generation. And this is just my theory. But I think when you have all these people our age who grew up in our churches and gave up on our authentic Christianity we give up on moral standards and place our own personal feelings first. So you become more lax with how you define and value marriage, just like you do with anything you decry because it's an institution."

"You could also blame the church doctrines," I said. "Maybe the dogmatic teachings about marriage aren't relevant to real life."

"I'm going to have to seriously disagree with you on that," said Greg. "I mean, I know a lot of people go overboard with their 'doctrine! doctrine! doctrine!' stuff. But I think it's a strong spiritual value to look at a marriage in trouble and say 'we made a pledge and we're going to make it through this.'"

"Maybe," I said. "I'm not one for commitment."

"Yeah," said Greg. "But you're not looking to get married."

"No," I said. "Not in the least. I'm a perpetual bachelor by choice."

He shrugged.

I shrugged.

"But I think every generation faces it in their own way," said Greg. "We live in a culture of instant-gratification, right? We grew up with commercials, we gave birth to Twitter. I mean, the entire site is designed to communicate as few letters as possible."

"It's a convenient exercise in brevity," I said.

"Yeah, but when you see marriage as a convenient exercise in brevity, that's the problem. People don't have patience with each other any more."

"I'm losing my patience with you," I said, and although it was true, the way I laughed told him I was joking, and he unfortunately continued.

"If you marry impulsively—and believe me, I've seen several of my friends do that—then you're going to divorce impulsively. If you marry because you're lonely, or because you grew up conservative and you want to finally have sex, or just because it's the new thing for you to do, I won't be surprised if in four years you've broken up."

"Yeah. I'll concede to that." Once dogma was brought out of the picture, Greg was beginning to make sense to me.

"There's also adultery," he said, and at the sound of the word I cringed—that religious word blanketing the complexity of relationships seeking a resolve amidst the loneliness of a problematic relationship. "If the novelty of your new spouse wears off, you can just find that fresh feeling somewhere else, because you have to be happy. And right now you're not happy."

"It's a little preachy," I said.

"People need preachy," said Greg. "See, Neil, I know you're my friend, so I feel you can trust me to ask you this, but why do you feel sick at the very mention of something preachy? I mean, I know you haven't necessarily jumped off the atheist cliff, but do you think sometimes you're just cringing against things you were taught because it's too overwhelming and confrontational?"

I cringed as he said the word *cringe*. "I don't know if I can give a sufficient answer."

"I wish we could talk sometime," he said. "You know that I love you as a friend."

And although I could tell he meant it, I couldn't help but feel that through him as through a conduit the generation that raised us was speaking with that paternal condescension so distant that it cannot hope to find us in the waves that have carried us off. Maybe I want to be set adrift. Maybe I want to undulate and surge with the ocean for a while. Maybe I need to.

Mason Leary, in dark shades, approached the two of us, rescuing me from the soapbox. We chatted for a while about idle things, people who were there who we might have known and how they were doing, the music that was playing and whether we liked it, and I felt the conversation become one between just the two of them, but didn't know who else to float towards. Then Greg detached from us to go and join Bryce, and instantly, as if there only to bring me a coded message, Mason pointedly asked me a direct question.

"So that whole Sedgwick thing at Fido. Crazy, right?"

"What?" I said, and giggled.

Mason must have been one of the few people in the shop, and I formed a vague memory of him with some girl sitting at a table on the other side of the room, though mostly based on suggestion.

"There was like nobody there," he said. "Then he walked up to you and those other girls? Do y'all like know him or something?"

"Yeah," I said. "I, uh, I'm probably going to help him with his next album design."

"That's cool, man," said Mason, casually, and proceeded no further to question me or feed off the hype of my connection with Wick. At this point I felt a necessary urge to divulge to him the rest of the story, not because he had asked, but because he had not asked, and because this guy who was the first one to introduce me to Wick seemed inexplicably deserving of such a secret. Mason Leary, a guy no more enthusiastic or cynical than he had to be about anything, a guy I hardly knew, was immediately trustworthy of the complete knowledge of the cosmic predicament I had slid into.

"Yeah," I said. "It's kinda weird. I, uh, I think he has this thing for my cousin."

"No kidding."

"Yeah, apparently they, uh, dated in high school and he wanted to be a country singer. And he went to Nashville to get her back by forming a band, and things just got out of hand. And so, like, now I'm dragged into it."

"Welp. That's messed up, man."

"Yeah." I laughed uncomfortably.

Mason just stood there and shook his head. I couldn't see his eyes through his shades, couldn't read his thoughts. "Hope you get that worked out," he said.

And in the next moment we were both walking toward the same crowd to meet different people. I had just told the full, yet simplified secret of the love triangle that likely defined the very career of this underground musician, the shape I had been pulled into the middle of against my will. Mason and I, who had previously shared no more than a hundred or so words together, were now the only two people who had seen the breadth of Sedgwick's career and then become privy to the elucidation of his ambitious passage still enshrouded to all his fans and haters alike. He had shown me Wick the artist, and I had shown him Wick the dreamer, the pursuer, the poser. He didn't seem to care, other than to wish me luck in getting out of the mess. Part of me wondered if he even believed me; part of me didn't care if he believed me. It was something I had to get off my chest, and I was relieved to so do, because he was the one person I knew who would never mention it to anyone again.

It was as if the universe sent me this sangfroid individual upon which I could relay the summary of my latent anxiety, and all he gave me in return was a cool nod. It was a moment so inconsequential I was confident I could replicate again without prevarication. I had just been told it was possible to be cool without overanalyzing anything.

Kenna Rothchild ignored those who didn't perk their ears around her. Her gossip was the one thing I was disgusted with the most until it had to do with Sedgwick and Tabitha. Someone like Kenna could not bear to be without the power of knowing the immediate and the sensational, the power of dishing it out like mother's milk. If only to pay her back in kind for all that she had told me before, or because I had been infected by her urge to spill the news of other people, I told her after the wedding what I had just told to Mason.

"You're killing me," she said. "You weren't going to tell me any of this 'til now?"

"The cover illustration isn't a through deal yet," I said. "I didn't know if it was going to work out."

"Neil, you can trust me," she said.

"I don't know if I'd label you as a trustworthy person," I said, the word *label* like a smokescreen over my insult.

"What the f—, Neil!" She said it like she had been cheated out of a deal.

"I just mean I wouldn't count it among your top virtues."

If you were looking for another reason why I am single, look no longer.

"You can't hold out on me like that, Neil." Then I knew that she only saw me as a friend, which was a relief, because I could have only betrayed her so much by waiting so long to tell her. She almost pitied me to the point that she didn't take it as personally as she thought she deserved to.

"Why do you think I told you now?" I said. "I thought you'd like to be the first to know."

"Yeah," she said, somewhat appeased. "You can't just design an album cover for Wick and not tell me. I thought we were tight. Keep me in the loop next time."

"So you know what this means, right?" I said. "I mean, isn't it odd that he finds me in Nashville, and then finds her?"

"Are you serious?" she said. "No way. He probably has mad girls all over him. No way he came back for Tab."

"We'll see," I said. "It couldn't have happened fortuitously. He used me somehow."

"That would be insane if he did. In-sane."

"It would be problematic."

"Thanks, Neil. Glad you told me. Does anybody else know this?"

"I haven't told Tabitha, if that's what you're wondering."

"I can't believe it. I can't keep this a secret. You're killing me."

"You got to," I said. "For Tabitha's sake. That's why you're the only one I told."

She technically wasn't the first to know. I told Mason Leary because he sincerely took Wick's music for what it was and didn't build a temple around it. But depending on whether the songs and the crafted persona were all for show, or whether Wick had propelled himself into refinement with a single romantic goal, I couldn't make up my mind as to whether Chance Merritt was the most cultivated, most fabricated artist I had ever run in to.

"This is some serious James Gatz sh—," I said.

Kenna was clueless. "James who?"

"Nevermind," I said. "I'm being allusive."

9
"MY LITTLE JAPANESE CIGARETTE CASE"
feat. The Ryman

I was able to do more work again, having told two people about Sedgwick and Tab. Most everyone else was too busy to hang out with, too. Sam and Sam drove out to Burning Man for their three month wedding anniversary. Amanda had instigated some sort of drama with someone and constantly let everyone know that she didn't want to be talked to, which was her way of letting everyone know that she wanted to be talked to, but was a sound excuse for me take her at her word and not talk to her. Frenchy was at the beach with some guy. Cline was taking a summer course at Belmont. Jules was rehearsing for a role in a production of *I Hate Hamlet*. Joey was trying to find another job as well as another place to stay. He turned down two offers on account of their "no flip flops" policy, and Joey was an ardent believer in letting his feet breathe. He had found a nice apartment room to split on Craigslist, but cowered away when his potential roommate casually included in his bio that he was "also the living embodiment of the living god, Amon Ra."

"I don't know," I told him. "I think you should take it. What's there to lose?"

"Everything," he said. "Maybe I should tell him that I'm the Keymaster."

I completed a project involving a number of T-shirt designs within the span of a week, and was very pleased with myself.

In a week's time Sedgwick was playing the show he had invited all of us to, and I dreaded it. I felt obligated to attend, even with Kenna, Tabitha and Virgil all there. It was something I wanted to get over with.

Sedwgick hadn't sent me a single follow-up message after our meeting at Fido, as if it had never happened, and I began to see him as kind of a jerk. As if to make up for his lack of communication, he gave me a free ticket to see him at the Ryman—me and three other people. He reserved four seats for us on the middle edge of the balcony. He chose the venue for its excellent acoustics, intimate size, and vintage legacy, a move he no doubt made with Tabitha in mind. One could not just book a spot at the Ryman on a whim. This had either been calculated long ago, or done with well-connected desperation. Bruce Fey had to have something to do with it.

Wick would stand on a circle of wood and serenade Tab from below, hoping for roses. It was as if Virg wasn't part of the picture. If Virg didn't know about Tab's past with Chance before, he knew by that night. He saw the random meeting and the show invitation as he had every reason to, his wife catching up with an old, close friend who had now become a success and was happy to invite them. If he saw anything threatening about such a move, he showed no sign of it. Nonetheless, given Virgil's habit of being too busy to do anything, I didn't put it past him to show up with us just to counter any moves Sedgwick would make. He even wore his best bowtie.

"Garrison Keillor calls this place 'God's Own Listening Room,'" he said, gleefully glancing around the place. "Your friend Chance has done well for himself."

Kenna and I tried to humor him without giving away our hidden concerns for what would transpire after the concert. After about five texts from her within the first song, I turned my phone completely off.

As far as the rest of the room was concerned, what made this concert special was not a reunion with his first and only true love, but a reunion with his favorite band with whom he released his sophomoric LP and giving it the eponymous title *Al Jazari's Musical Automaton Band*. It was his most diverse band, and arguably his most diverse album, an album that, while reflecting a wide variety of Eastern influences, also resembled a concept album more than any other, even *Faraday*.

Maurice Spitzer said in *Mother Jones* that "as Sedgwick has become a frenetic crowd-pleaser with evocative lyricism devoid of affectation," he has "continually broken new ground performance-by-performance," and that *Al Jazari* "promises another long list of melodies that will refresh our hearts and minds." Overtly positive, it wasn't a popular review. "Although ambitious on the level of genius," said Julie Moon of *Under the Radar*, "this album is dark and uninviting. It's almost too intricate. His songs end mid-thought, and he strains to finish them elsewhere. It's almost like we have the first draft of a compilation of field notes from an expedition into a far off land. Some explorers will obsess over the record, but it unfurls too much musical scroll, too much imagery, too much reference."

When Sedgwick's fandom orgy of critics finally got around to telling us why *Al Jazari's Musical Automaton Band* is so fine, their consensus fragmented in disputation. *The Deli* called it "a keen meditation on the notion of possession in a relationship"; *Bearded* said it was "a collection of compositions about the agony of composing"; *Paste* claimed it was "Garrett Sedgwick's deep disclosure of his many haunts"; *Indie Artist* articulated the record as "Sedgwick's most profound excursion into the dichotomy that is authenticity and performance"; a host of cultural critics agreed with *Salon* contributor Derek Rustad's essay describing *Al Jazari* as an "an orientalist fantasy."

The album cover reflected such a fantasy, a geometric explosion of patterns thickly layered with images of mechanical peacocks surrounding fireworks over a lakeside palace, and on the back, an illustration of an elephant clock by fourteenth century polymath Badi'al-Zaman Abū al-'Izz ibn Ismā'īl ibn al-Razāz al-Jazarī, after whom the album was named. The booklet contained a small essay fleshing out a personal theory of musicianship:

"Trial and error are where the real heart of crafting honest music lies," reads one of the lines. "You can move up and down on a scale and measure the exact notes you want, but you have to engage in the process of discovery by pouring yourself into the instrument itself. That is where the composition comes to live, not on paper. We are all powered by water. We are all powered by the rush of life and creativity. Sometimes it is not we who are playing, but the greater force playing through us."

The release became too popular, and by the wrong people, or so the story goes. When a radio show interview grows heated after music critic Joe Daugherty postulates that there is nothing special about Grace Potter and the Nocturnals and that they would fade into obscurity, Brad

Stokely, the host, then taunts him by inventing a nonexistent band with which to trap the critic. Scribbled on a piece of paper nearby is *Al Jazari's Musical Automaton Band*, which Brad thinks is a joke, and when he mentions it to Daugherty, the critic responds that they are in his opinion "the best middle eastern pop fusion band to come along in ages," clearly betraying his unawareness of who the band really were. The exchange between the two witless conversant personalities is recorded, replicated, and shared for several weeks. When NPR does a feature on Sedgwick, they become so caught up in his interview that they run out of time to let him play his set. As an apology, they invite him to play his entire album live on the radio. He turns it down at first on principle that it amounts to pity promotion, even after the radio station begs and pleads, and a small group of fans angers the remainder of his fans by dressing all in orange—his favorite color and the name of his first EP—and posting pictures of themselves holding signs begging him to play the full album live on NPR. Embittered from the experience, Sedgwick pledged never to reunite with the band to play any song from the album again.

Then came the night he invited Tab, when he did indeed reunite with the old band and play, not the entire album, but enough songs to constitute a flagrant backpedalling against his rash vow. "The Majnun's Madness" and "Elephant Mahout" were outrageous hits that night, and Sedgwick made use of the space to focus on the softer melodies from across his albums, resonating a sound within the old chambers of the auditorium that was distantly wistful, as if he were paradoxically calling from the furthest distance and whispering up close all at once. It might have been Virgil's presence that formed around me an air of unease unlike before, because he had to be unaware of the audacity of Sedgwick's pursuit for his spouse, of the buried references in his songs that hung like riddles for Tabitha to unwind and wrap about her. Here were the same people in the crowd as always, with the same devout concentration, but it was the first time I was unable to enjoy any of it, only envying the other souls in the room for their blissful ignorance. Sedgwick played with shamanic tenacity. Every movement of every song was terminally spun from his soul. And everyone thought it was because of the band reunion, because of the Ryman, because Sedgwick was something like a divine gift.

But even Tab was witnessing this performance with such incredulity that she had yet to fall headfirst into the heart of it. There was no swoon, there was no sigh. Once you've seen a phenomenon from enough angles to produce your own disillusion, watching someone else experience it for the first time as anticlimactic without a taste of wonder can bring you into a state of supreme melancholy. But maybe there was something simmering within her, and in that case nobody would be able to tell.

"He's very impressive!" Virgil shouted to us in between songs, as Tabitha nodded her head in nonchalance. "I recognize that fiddler from She Walks in Squalor. Terrific band!"

Virgil seemed to be enjoying it more than Tabitha, who tepidly kept a befuddled eye on Wick for nearly the entire performance.

After the show we were able to head backstage to meet up with Sedgwick and his band. Kenna scurried about to take photos of herself with everyone who had held an instrument on that stage, or at least take selfies in front of them. She then began hitting on the drummer, some guy with annoying sideburns and a shiny black vest named

Dan. One of the roadies mistook me for Ben Folds, and she blushed and apologized when I corrected her. Bruce Fey entered with a forceful energy, chewing gum and looking around disdainfully at everyone. He took Sedgwick aside for a minute and the two of them argued discreetly about something hushed. He finally left Sedgwick alone and disappeared like a hired assassin who had come to a Carleone wedding.

"This is Tabitha, an old friend of mine," Wick said to his friends. "This is her cousin, Neil. Turns out he's a graphic designer. Remember I said I was looking for an illustrator? This is Virgil. He's got a doctorate in—what was it?"

"Oh, no doctorate yet," said Virg. "I'm working on my Masters in Theology."

It could have been Wick's nervousness and exhaustion after the show, but if anything had been deliberate, it would have been that Virg was introduced last, that he was introduced apart from Tabitha with myself in between them, severing any marital connection they had in the introduction, and that Wick had falsely introduced Virg as a PhD recipient, almost as if it gratified him to hear the guy admit he had only been working on his second Masters. It could have been my highly attuned paranoia on my part.

Kenna had been asked by the drummer to hang out, and she obliged, giving Tab a kind of wink that startled her. Wick snuck us out the back door and bypassed Tootsie's, where a host of fans would have been expecting Wick to show up for some sort of second encore. We continued down 5th toward the Music Garden, where we stopped for some street food being served from a Crepe a Diem truck. Some of the crowd had the same idea, but didn't seem to notice Wick after he had changed hats, or they were cool enough to let him alone with us.

"Here they come," said the vendor. "Hungry, hungry hipsters."

We strolled together, and Sedgwick had gotten what he wanted, because it didn't matter if Virgil was there, or if I was there. Chance Merritt was on a vicarious date with Tabitha Redding in the park in front of the Country Music Hall of Fame. Even on stage, he had been cartoonishly inching toward her all evening, halting within Virgil's eyesight. He had asked her what she thought of she show, and in her kindest manner she had told him that she loved it. He had forgotten the intricacies and subtleties of her voice, and couldn't have picked up on the patronizing tone with which she told him. If it had been any stranger's band, she might have been intrigued and momentarily infatuated, but she seemed more appalled than impressed by the mystic mesmerism of his new persona, his newly crafted self. She was still in a state of shock, and could say very little. Here and there she began to give me darting glances of worry, signals for me to devise a way of asserting that we were all tired and had to go home.

Virgil talked with his mouth full, something he rarely did, unable to finish swallowing a crepe before letting out his aggressively provocative thoughts.

"I think that one song—what was it called? 'Camshaft?' I thought the lyrics in that one had some particularly poignant moments."

"Thanks," said Wick, taking it humbly.

"I find that whole album *Al Jazari* quite fascinating. Why the name?"

"Honestly," said Wick, "it just came to me. It sounded inviting and warm, which is what I was looking for. The meaning kind of made itself when I began to record."

"Interesting, interesting," said Virg. "I figured it was a nod to the Islamic Golden age. I've found that in the West we do a great discredit to the contributions of Arabic and Islamic peoples to civilization."

If he had said it in an academic discourse I would have taken it at face value and acknowledged it, but dropping it in a late night conversation with a musician over his own work while eating crepes seemed inflated.

"Yeah," said Wick. "That went into a lot of it, too. Al Jazari is just a fascinating figure. Was he Turkish? Was he Persian? There's a lot of mystery there. But I see him as like the Da Vinci of his time and place. I was just moved by his description of this water-powered automata band — completely fake wooden performers that look real from a distance, powered by nothing but water. And the guests are so drunk they might actually be fooled. It's kind of a grand metaphor for the question of what makes an artist legitimate. Do we want our encounter to be real life? Or do we want to be fooled? Do we want to be given something that resembles life and is too clever to be real?"

Tab's eyes widened in wonder at this new articulated man she had never known.

"Ah," said Virgil, nodding patiently. "I see. What you said just then about the mystery aspect — It reminds me of the words of Edward Said about how we exploit the discourse of Orientalism in order to dominate, restructure, and give ourselves authority over the Orient."

"Yeah," said Wick. "I, uh — I ran in to some of that in the work of Rushdie. He sometimes explores how perceptions of tradition operate in the Middle East and how leaders are pressured by the West to conform to their own stereotypes. His stuff is a real breath of fresh air."

"Oh, Rushdie as a living critique of grand narratives from a Middle East perspective is unparalleled," said Virg, licking this fingers. "But what you said reminded me of this tremendous *HuffPost* article on how Western artists are still depicting the Orient as this alluring fantasy, even in a benign way—like the old notion of snake charmers, for example—to stereotype the East in order to satisfy our lust for the exotic."

Wick scratched his head anxiously. "Oh yeah? Sounds interesting."

Virgil continued, energetically. "Yeah, it's a real good read. Just talks about how even in the arts we take Turkish baths, Japanese Geishas, and Indian Yogis and combine them into a kaleidoscope of old, recycled eye candy for the West to colonize."

"Confirm our own hegemony," I added, if only to include another voice other than Virgil's eager outpouring and Wick's diffident mumble.

"Like *Aladdin*," said Wick.

Tabitha giggled as if this response would have been typical of Chance Merritt years ago.

"Like *Aladdin*," I repeated, and giggled with her. The light moment was ideal for changing subjects, but Virg continued his commentary as if he were finishing a presentation.

"Right, and so those same cultural misrepresentations to portray the East as neuter, irrational and impotent. The West is there to gain a fetishized experience on their own terms."

"Okay," said Wick. "Yeah, I'm getting you. Like Americans reading *The Kite Runner*."

Virgil finished his effortless spiel using stiff hand movements, gesticulating in firm contrast to his blithe tone. "So in essence the article was saying that the Western artist is himself emasculated, and seeks to colonize the Orient in order to reestablish potency. The exotic far away land is not a people but a part of the artist's quest, and the only reason he embarks on it is to define himself by contrasting himself against the Otherness of this unattainable maiden that is the East, or something the East is just a metaphor of. Essentially, he himself is suffering an identity crisis, and is romanticizing an objectified solution."

"Oh," said Wick, as if he had been dulled by being struck against a boulder.

"Take Up the White Man's Burden!" I shouted, but to no avail. The tension would not diffuse any slower than time and silence would allow.

Tab was reticent, blushing. Everybody was too embarrassed to say anything else, and nobody seemed to know that everybody felt the same, or that everybody knew why it was embarrassing. As our tongues picked at the last of the crepes in our teeth, we collaborated into an awkward silence in the cool of Music Garden that stretched too far. It seemed that all of us had one of two ideas in our head that we didn't want to share.

One possibility was that Virg had been his normal self and thus far monopolized the evening with the incessant echoing of some random chunk of literature in the presence of a guest and friend of his wife and cousin, that he had comically and inadvertently diluted any chance of glowing enchantment for Wick to sneak into the conversation.

The second possibility was that Virgil had begun to sniff out Sedgwick's grand scheme and in a matter of minutes dismantled his most beloved album with an academic critique.

The trouble was that I couldn't tell which of these was true, whether Virgil was so absorbed in his own studies that he couldn't spot an errant suitor right under his nose, or whether Virgil was so clever that he was able to erode the mystique of Chance Merritt's personal renaissance and render his long journey inert with the single e-journal reference. Was Virg gallantly defending the sanctity of his wife with the best tool he had? Not because he was a chauvinist, but because she preferred not to speak herself? At the time, I decided he was either a fool or a jerk, and I was almost rooting for Sedgwick.

In that evening, in that dimness lit by street lights absorbed by roses and daylilies, I strolled uneasily between Sedgwick's tender seduction, Virgil's equivocal foil, and Tabitha's tacit fatigue, unable to work up a dissolution of the oppressive discomfiture. Sedgwick, having dedicated an entire concert to the girl he still loved, now in the evening's remainder tried to draw her away from her man by a subtle thread. Tabitha must have known he was trying, but she could not say a thing to him, not in this unpleasant space. Whether Virgil had picked up on this was irrelevant. He had romanced Tabitha as easily as he had countless evenings since they met, and all Sedgwick could do was feed vicariously off the whatever charm still hung in the air.

It was the smell of dying flowers; it was the smell of stubborn desire. It was a beauty and three fools who stumbled more foolishly down Demonbreun Street than any drunk on Broadway, and the one fool who enjoyed the night was the one who was likely the most clueless, triumphant only through his careless absorption. I only remember walking until I could see the outline of the back of the "NO PROMO" billboard across the river, relieved that everyone had finally said goodnight and parted ways.

I'm being punctilious.

I read on *Slate* once that in the fifteenth century the act of rolling one's eyes signified not exasperation, contempt, or frustration, but passion. Eyes, like the tongue, were rolled in a fever of lust, or even in delicious flirtation. The one visual that lingered in our stroll after the Ryman was the way, multiple times, Tabitha rolled her eyes upward and sighed. This look of hers always stood out to me, and it was branded into my own retinas that night because of the alarm it brought me. Tabitha had an eye roll for every occasion; she was no ordinary girl.

During a moment of sexual ecstasy, it is often reported — and we see it often portrayed — that one partner, in particular the female, will roll back their eyes at the moment of climax. The eyes are not vital organs of sexual stimuli in women as they are in men, and turn inward into the self when a woman peaks, or so I've heard. This is a cause of resentment among men, who naturally feel rejected by a woman not merely closing her eyes, but turning them back to such a private space that the male feels used, his eye contact not reciprocated. An evolutionary explanation, and perhaps also a psychological explanation, is that the female is asserting her own role in both copulation and fertilization, ignoring the male partner and retreating into herself in this vulnerable moment of penetration in order to reestablish sovereignty over one's self. I am not trying to make you feel uncomfortable here.

Consider portraits of the saints, looking upward to the point that their eyes almost seem to be rolling backward. They are so taken in with spiritual ecstasy that they dare not face the fearful god who is their source of being, but rather retreat into the inner soul, making God in their own image, sketching him into the cathedral of the mind.

In a more rational world, we have evolved the rolling of the eyes to more brazenly express our intolerance, our fatigue, our scorn. But this mechanism still has its roots in pleasure. A teenager who rolls their eyes at adult authority revels in their own arrogance. A feisty debater, patiently waiting their turn, exults in the private victory of rolling their derisive eyes like a jab at their opponent. Anyone personally insulted, proud to gain attention and excited by the thrill of an attack, rolls their eyes vainly into the self, into the secret arsenal of rebuttal. We are Narcissus gazing into the reflection of our righteousness, our victimization, our rationality. This is not a gesture of open contempt; it is a gesture of private pleasure. Overwhelming, private pleasure. And this is what stings most when someone roll their eyes at you.

This is what makes adults feel disrespected, opponents cheated, aggressors maligned. It is not the displeasure conveyed, but the pleasure withheld. Seeing someone's eyes roll invites our envy, and thus our discontent. This is why men hate women, because they see women's eyes roll as they laugh and drink Starbucks and talk about YaYa Sisterhood novels with each other with their fashionable scarves. This is why women are stoned for showing more than their eyes. Men are discontent that we were never invited to own their pleasure.

Tabitha rolled her eyes the same way she had when she ate exquisite Italian food on her birthday, when she heard Frank Sinatra play at the grocer, when her parents called her strange for being sixteen and liking Audrey Hepburn movies, when Kenna bought her a poster of Brad Paisley. It was the one look of hers that could tell me why any guy could surprise himself with being enthralled by her. She rolled her eyes in the same way that night with us. She was uncomfortable, but somewhere in her cocoon she was experiencing a kind of secret pleasure at being pursued.

Wick wanted to be invited into that world, Virg was too occupied with talking to even peek at that world, and I, who had known Tab the longest, but not the most intimately, was curious to know which of them filled that world in those moments. Maybe she was just thrilled to have three strapping young men escort her through the park. Maybe it was the crepes. But when Sedgwick caught a glimpse of her upturned eyes through her intensely reserved smile, he must have known that she was probably off somewhere in a Tuscan villa, like a fantasy conjured in a dentist chair, and it flustered him to no end that he was not in there to accompany her in the splendor of such a vision.

But like I said, maybe it was just the crepes.

10
"CLASSY GIRLS"
feat. nostalgia revisited

It was me and Joey and we were at Barista Parlor with Sam and Sam. Sam had just gotten off work and hung up his apron, and we were waiting for Cline to get off in the next hour. Sam and Sam leaned against one another like posed corpses, too tired to even text, as if Burning Man had drained them of their blood. We entertained ourselves by supplying captions for the outfits around us, speaking in first person for our victims like shooting at wooden ducks at the fair.

"Look at his outfit," said Sam. "It's screaming out 'I am a Nineteenth Century lumberjack.'"

"'Or am I?'" said Samantha.

"'I am the first to ever fit into a pair of human jeans,'" I said of another guy. "'Nailed it.'"

"'I feel like a pro in my oversized, untied Vans,'" said Joey.

Samantha nodded to another in the corner. "'Truckers can wear earbuds too, you know.'"

Our game continued in rapid succession.

"'I am a f—in' pirate.'"

"'With a blog.'"

"Sh—! I forgot to take off my overalls before attending that flapper's wedding."

"'B in 1989, stopped buying my clothes in 1981.'"

"'Why, yes, my friend and I did get the memo that it was Beard and Suspenders Over a Collared Cotton Shirt Twin Day.'"

"Excuse me, am I in the wrong place? Where's the Judy Funnie doppelgänger contest."

"'My other uni is a fixie.'"

"'I'm-a just prop my bare feet up on this here rough edge wood table, 'cause I'm sheriff of this town.'"

Samantha's line made us all erupt in laughter, and half the room glanced in our direction like we were the resident pre-teens who had overspent our stay. A guy walked in wearing a Mickey Mouse T and a purple scarf with biker gloves and high heel boots.

"I got this one, I got this one," I said, but after a moment, my mind drew a blank. "Oh man, I'm stumped."

We laughed again, but with restraint, because we hated the looks we got. It wasn't like we stood out from the rest of them entirely.

We might have the money for cool, but we do not need it, because we have the cleverness for cool. Someone has stolen our cool, and so we are out to devour your cool and regurgitate it as meaningless.

We learned too much to feel so abject and precarious, and so we head to the thrift stores and rummage sales, not out of practicality, but out of protest. We dress from discarded and variable scenes and eras out of an aesthetic of recycled, disheveled, niche cultures. We are first-world fauxhemian scavengers engaged in performance the moment we open the closet, fetishizing the ironic wearing of any and all gear with exploitative abandon. Our headphones and goggle-esque specs are esoteric impedimenta, working to filter out the unwanted stimulations of the supra-terranian world. Yet our body language convincingly tells you we are listening to every bit of it. We'd rather spoil it for everyone.

I'm sure somewhere across the room someone was mocking me in my *"Te occidere possunt sed te edere non possunt nefas est"* tee.

Cline rounded the corner of the counter, stormed over to us, threw off his apron, and slouched beside us on a chair.

"I quit."

"What happened?" said Joey. "Tell us."

Cline adjusted his glasses and huffed. "Amanda's gotten like every third order wrong, she sucks at lattes, and she still works here. And I'm practically running things whenever it's my shift. I get no support."

"Aw, man," said Joey, reaching out to Cline as if to give him a soothing embrace. "You're not really gonna quit, are you? Hand in there, Cline. You're doing great."

Cline stood up and threw up his hands. "I can't—no. I just need five minutes to cool off, and I'm gonna go over there, and I'm gonna tell Antony that I'm quitting. I'm done working for that tool."

"Hey, man," I chimed. "You can't just toss around the word 'tool.' This isn't Starbucks."

"I know what a tool is," said Cline, "and my boss is a tool."

"I'd consider him more of a chump," I said.

"Yeah," said Joey. "He seems pretty chumpy."

"Chumpy," Samantha repeated. "That just sounds gross."

"Because it rhymes with lumpy," said Sam. "It's like chumpy and lumpy."

Antony, Cline's manager, approached and we dropped our conversation, although he didn't seem to have heard us. He did look kind of chumpy. It's hard to describe what that means.

"Hey Cline," he said. "You can have off tomorrow. I got someone to cover your shift."

"Cool," said Cline, nodding his head and rubbing his hair.

"Hey," Antony added. "You wanna hang out tonight?"

"Yeah, man."

"Cool."

"Cool."

Antony left us in complete silence, and we eyeballed each other until a shared release of laughter came over our corner.

"Man," said Joey. "You really showed him."

"Yeah," I said. "You put that fascist in his place, man!"

"Shut up," said Cline.

I did feel bad for him. He didn't want to be a barista any more than anybody our age who hadn't by now tried to grab more hours and practice forming milk leaves on the surfaces of cappuccinos. He treated it like a job to be proud of until it took too much from him.

Everyone is an artisan something, even while in transition jobs that have nothing to do with our career. We can't bear to choose just any coffee shop—no, we have to go home at the end of the day knowing that we didn't pour a single cup of mere coffee, but hand crafted each and every mug with intent and design.

We define our current employment not by what we are, but by what we do, because we are not our occupations.

We do not say "I am a wood cutter," but "I do wood cuts." Not "I'm a videographer," but "I do videography work for small-budget projects." Not "I'm a software developer," but "I do software development work for companies." We say "companies" plural even if we are contracted with one and only one. I am not an enviro-friendly cleaning product sales rep. I do work with enviro-friendly cleaning products. This is no small nuance.

We avoid actually admitting that we have jobs, but rather insinuate that our hobbies happen to provide us money. We must have horizons, we must always have horizons. We shuffle to define ourselves by what we are against before we admit to having something as fogey as a mere job. We do not climb corporate ladders; we leap across stones and branch our like trees. We are productive children of the universe, and we are its caretakers. Our work must be so amorphous and flexible that we can blend into anything else at any given time, and whatever we do is giving something soulful back to the world. We must be niche pioneers; we do not listen to market trends, but market inspirations. Our work is a charity of the mind.

We adore the validity of the working class ethic, but are much more comfortable at a computer in an uncomfortable chair at a desk that does not look like a desk. We work with our minds because our minds are gifts, and with our minds we praise the sweating man, the sweating woman, the day laborer and the migrant laborer and the fort-hours-a-week wage laborer who wipe their brows in the sun and in the furnace and on skyscrapers and in crab boats. We will even dress like them. But our minds are far too precious to be expended on such tasks — unless as hobbies, perhaps. We are like the noble Greeks, who wouldn't dare perform manual labor, yet worshipped the gods of the trades thereof.

If I am ever anything assuredly then I just may spend the rest of my life doing it over and over again. If we ever feel we are merely pulling a lever, pushing a rock up a hill and letting it roll back down, we get antsy. And this is why we put ourselves in quotations, because in this way we can do anything, and we refuse to be pigeonholed, because we have spotted the horizon, the far horizon, the same horizon seen by everyone else — only we have seen it through a spyglass we found at a consignment shop and refinished by hand.

I'm being supercilious.

Chance Merritt found himself beating down the highway across the country, hitting up roadside bars for time on a stage or stool, as if hoping to be discovered by some talent scout in some unlikely hut of a town. He lived day-to-day in the awful, poetic work of staying on his feet. He spurned the invitations of cowgirls and cougars alike, allowing them to drink with him until he reluctantly uttered some remark that turned them away from a man too young to be bitter and hard. They couldn't know the turbulence of his yearning.

Chance had nearly given up after hitting Denver and being driven out by the competition. He had enrolled in vocational training for engine repair on the night he tottered into Country Rose Saloon and witnessed a performance of the late legend and one-time outlaw brawler Hoyt Murdock.

The Country star was in his seventies, and some had thought he'd already died. Murdock had amassed a colossal legacy of record upon respected record, a legacy chiseled into every monument of Country and Blues like his old wood-carved face. He was immortalized by the constance of his own tradition, a rare, untouchable *sensei* of a genre his own hands had pioneered and shaped as a member of a select and indisputable pantheon. Old men of the South whistled in reverence at the sound of his name, and old women pined for the days when he had come to their town, towered over their adoring faces and hands. Hoyt Murdock was a monolithic tableau anchored against the current of time, and his voice cracked prophetically from well preserved records cast in gold.

To this unknown boy, leaning against the back wall of the saloon, the ancient man and his ancient guitar were the restoring fountain of wisdom and purpose. For a minute he might have forgotten the name of that girl who drove him searching.

But the singer/songwriter up on that stool was not Hoyt Murdock. It couldn't have been, not with the sound coming from his lips and strings. It was an aberration Chance Merritt heard that night. A lifelong dream of his was to see this stock-still monument live, and there he was, dead and reanimated as something else, something hijacked, something phony. The song he played was not his own, the sound was not his own, the spirit was not his own. And worse still, the crowd was swallowing it with enormous glee.

He steps out from the crowd, he shouts at the man in a rage, a righteous heckler gone berserk. "It ain't you! It ain't Hoyt!" he cries. "They don't wanna hear none o that!" Shocked patrons try to hold back this bucking young drifter, but it takes several strong arms. "Where's Hoyt Murdock? Where's ol' Hoyt Murdock at! Anybody seen 'em!" And the star stops his playing and stares at this bold nobody from nowhere come to put him in his place. "How much they payin' you, Hoyt? Huh? What's the price on you! What'd you sell out for!" And before the crowd can take this boy outside the man climbs down off the stage and struts up to him and sees the lost frenzy in his eyes and he knows this ain't no punk with no respect, this is a glint of himself somewhere in those eyes and what does he do but he balls his knuckle and socks the kid in the face and somehow the crowd is in an uproar of applause and cheers at this old man beating this boy until he tells them all to "get 'em outta here" and they toss him out in the alley like a dog.

He doesn't crawl away. You can't crawl away like that, not because you're too sore, but because you're too down. Where is there to go? And Hoyt Murdock knows this, because he comes out into that alley drunk and cold and picks that boy up off the ground and brushes him off and says it was a necessary lickin', but it was he who needed it, not the young man. Says he was braver than him, but you can't tell anyone that in a hungry crowd. Says "Son you don't understand how this world works." Says "You ready for this road? You wanna walk it?" Reaches into his coat like to pull out a gun and pulls out a little black notebook and tosses it on the ground in front of the kid. "Here you go, kid. It's yours. I quit for good. H—, I quit long ago. Good luck and get the f— outta here."

And he rounds the corner and is gone, and nobody sees him again until his gin-soaked corpse is found in a hotel bathroom outside Oklahoma City.

"What was in the notebook?" I asked Wick as we stood again at the edge of the sky lounge, this time the night lights of the skyscrapers before us and the whipping wind assaulting our hair.

"It was all his songs," said Wick. "Or all the songs he'd never recorded. What was left."

"So it was like a blank check to plagiarize his work?"

"He never did anything with it. It was like he didn't care any more. I don't know whether he believed in me to carry on with his last gift or if he was just testing me with fraudulence."

And as Chance was telling me this story, his accent had regressed. I finally heard what must have been the real Chance Merritt, unadorned by what I had for so long thought to be the Garrett Sedgwick. Here was a man who could be both and still seem stripped of duplicity in either form, as if one man had split himself through mitosis and diverged into separate but equal paths. And yet nothing was more true than the fact that Chance Merritt had existed long before Garrett Sedgwick, and I was straining to accept the possibility that his transition was as natural and necessary as a caterpillar morphing into a battered moth.

"I didn't use a single one of his songs," said Wick. "I've held on to that songbook. I thought about it several times. I hit Nashville and I thought about it all the time. How I could just take his songs and make them mine. But I couldn't."

"Why not?" I said.

His dexterous hands shivered in his pockets. "I never earned it."

I was then surprised by the profane thought that if there was anything Chance Merritt had earned, it was the antiquated prospect of winning back the love of Tabitha Redding. Hardship and talent combined into this nearly inspiring grand narrative wherein he had every right to return. He had not sat on his haunches and coasted on the vehicle of his natural talent, but had allowed the world to drag him through the manure so that he could strive his way, fecund with raw experience, into the heart of a budding scene that would form a love-hate relationship with him forever. He had hit the streets, drifting from corner to corner like an orphan, painstakingly searching for the right moment for her to serendipitously bump into him.

"So all this," I said, finally confronting him with the current problem, "all this was for Tabitha."

"It started that way," he said, looking toward the ground and shaking his head. "I don't want to involve you in anything, but I know it's too late to say even that. And I know you don't understand and have every reason to tell me to f— off, because she's your cousin. But it's not like that."

"Not like what?" I said, raising my voice. "Are you trying to take her back or what? 'Cause all evidence points to that conclusion."

"I don't want to steal anything," he stammered. "All I want right now is to show her. I just wanted to show her where I was."

"So it's a revenge plot," I said. "Have you proven your point? You've really made her uncomfortable."

"Look, it's not revenge. I just—I want her to see, at any rate, that I can deserve her, even if I can't be with her."

"You want her to like your music, because if she likes your music then she likes you."

"She liked me then," he said. "She let me know it."

"It was her that changed," I said. "You can't help it if it was her that outgrew it."

But she hadn't outgrown him, not in his mind. She had merely grown into her own world sooner than he had into his, and they had only to catch up. He talked into the night about what happened between them, filling in the gaps that Kenna could not have been privy to. Sedgwick's evolution had to be full-circle, returning to his whole self as Chance Merritt. Only, the spell of time that such measures took had robbed her of him. It just wasn't fair.

He tells me what's fair. It's fair when he is playing for some girls on a fallen tree off to the side of some gravel path, and he spots this mysterious young woman pretending not to look at him as she walks down the path, whispering to her friend. The summer does wild things inside of young people, and he abandons the other pretty girls to walk over and speak to her. She pretends not to care, she pretends to be shy, but she would like nothing more than a good conversation that leads to trust and friendship and, at some certain moment, the holding of hands. There is a garden barred from everyone, and no matter how incompatible, once you know the entrance you feel it is your destiny and duty to court this beautiful space and tend to it.

She is a challenge, almost forbidden, but not in the sense of a reputation soiled, but by a chin held high with pride until it meets that which makes the face blush. But when he kisses her for the first time, and possibly too soon, at the end of their time walking together in cramped cabins under the stars, something clumsy in his kiss signals to her that he is not a prince. She closes up and gives him the first reason to doubt the everlastingness of their adolescent flame.

And when his immediate presence was gone, when his smile and strength and musk and voice were removed from her and from their initial walks among the rustic space of singing birds and whistling peers, she found him less and less majestic. But she could hardly express it, even in remote words easily sent instantly across the air. Even within the comforts of her own room she could not bear to tell him it was over for good, that he had become repugnant to her.

He once asked her, "Are we ever going to start talking again? Maybe if things change? If we change?"

"I don't know," she said back. It was only her terse words he received, brief and lacking the fullness of expression, words inadequate.

He asked, "I just want to know, just so I can know if it could ever be. Do you think we could ever light the fire again? We could hold each other by that fire again and it could burn just as hot?"

In juvenile sappiness he had alluded to the bonfire that hexed them together on that last night of the summer retreat, when the sensation of youth and spirituality drove dozens of others to renewal and repentance, and some to bonded friendships and romances. She could have told him the truth she knew, that it was a silly love manipulated by the engineering of whispering friends and bewitching outdoor lodges. But for whatever reason, she fed him words that he would hold like a fermata sustained by angelic pipes.

"Maybe...Perhaps."

It was a promise easy to throw out, a bone tossed to distract a ravenous dog or a paper kiss to appease a lustful admirer. It could have been true to her, it could have meant nothing to her. She could have rolled her eyes when she sent it. She had only hinted at another universe. For him, it was the only right future. It was the next best thing to Tab summoning the courage to tell him the incommunicable certainty, "I will love you again. Just you wait and see."

As he told me about it, he was being pretty schmaltzy.

*   *   *

"I want her to tell me if she meant it," he said.

"She might not remember she even said it," I said. "This is a new you she's met. You want her to love a guy that's not you?"

"It is me," he said, "just as much as she's the same her. We adapted. There's no reason why we can't adapt again."

"But she married!" I said.

He spastically flung his arms. "Then why didn't they have a wedding? Why is there no ring on her finger? Why don't her parents like him? Why does it seem like she's reluctant about this guy."

"They both swapped names," I said. "You could interpret that as a pretty final commitment."

"I just need to know," he said. "I need to know what's possible."

"You've proven to yourself what's possible," I said. "You've altered yourself completely."

"I've become who I am," he said, "because she was waiting for me to. She came into her own space and I came into mine. She's seen me *now*. I can be this for her; I've been this for everybody else."

"So it isn't really you," I said, looking this lost specimen up and down. "You've been holding a facade for half a decade."

"It's not a facade. It's become real. We grow to fit. We're water."

I felt anger, true anger as I spoke. "You can't just be somebody else, man."

He looked up and beyond himself like a felon on the run caught long enough to gaze out from a wanted poster.

"But I just have to," he said. "They're making me."

"Not everybody can be Jade and Alexander," I said.

He faced me doggedly as if I had challenged his right to breathe. "Why not?"

He must have waited on the corners of every bustling street in Nashville ever since he heard of the marriage, and the lack of a wedding that came with. He must have played and played until somebody noticed him. He was just like every fool with a guitar moving to attract women like bees, only he had set his eyes on one. He had inherited a chance to break the Nashville scene with the Hoyt Murdock playbook, but he chose to plunge his fingers into something strange and new, to expand himself and spread his emperor wings. The scene was his education. This know-nothing redneck had lighted himself a consuming fire, and instead of drawing out his cherished butterfly, he drew a skittish crowd of fire ants.

"We're recording next weekend," said Wick. "If you want to stop by, I mean. If you're still interested in the album work."

"I don't know if I'll be in the mood for it," I said. I was feeling miserably misanthropic. I really needed to go home and read some Froer.

11
"THE YEAH YEAH YEAH SONG"
feat. an enduring abundance of turtles

Tab didn't want to talk about any of it. After the night of the concert and the talk with Wick I had to bring it up to her, against my better judgement. I wanted to gauge her feelings for Wick and possibly warn her. I realized this may have been what Wick wanted me to do, and the last thing I wanted to do was become a pawn in some affair. I was already wrapped up in the drama. I just wanted to figure out what to avoid next. I avoided asking Kenna, and she had ceased harassing me after hooking up with Wick's drummer. She must have found the next rung on her social ladder. The only thing Tab wanted to tell me was her reasons for breaking up with Chance.

"He was just so...uncouth."

"What do you mean?" I asked her.

She sighed. "He just—he chewed tobacco then. I could smell it when he kissed me. It was gross."

"That was it?"

"No. I mean, it was other things. I think he just couldn't grow up. I guess he finally did."

"What are your feelings on it?"

"I'm happy for him. I—I can't believe it's him, though."

And I couldn't ask her if she'd get back with him, not even for myself to know. I didn't really want to know. I just wanted to navigate out of this queasy spot where nobody knew what was happening next. Virg still showed no obvious sign of awareness or naivety. After the concert he had tweeted, "Caught up with an old friend tonight at a Sedgwick show. So nice to catch up with old friends and hear good music." This could have been Virg unaware of Wick's plot, or it could have been Virg stamping his confidence and ownership into the social media sphere, segregating Wick into the space of "an old friend" of Tab's who vicariously was a friend of his as well, claiming Wick's music as merely "good" as a way of establishing its mediocrity. Sometimes I read too much into things.

I had the opportunity to ask him myself at Beer Church, but I didn't take it. Julius invited me to go with him to this novel experience, a combination of the "there will be free beer" impulse and the "hey, what if we totally went there?" impulse. Because Virg was studying religion, and because I initially wanted some excuse to milk him of his opinion on the Sedgwick situation in order to allay my anxieties, I invited him along. He also invited both his friends Obadiah and Philip, whom I had met at the picnic months before, and we arrived at a congregation of eight meeting in a bar downtown in the mid-afternoon.

The beer was bad, and the conversation both conceptual and cowardly, as if there was an unspoken ban on pedantic certainty, and if anyone strayed into the territory of certainty they would be ignored. Although I would have been the first to critique and deconstruct religious tradition, I felt that the "church" moniker was somewhat mendacious.

This we had in common, that we had all been given some upbringing and become too educated to not rise out of it, enlightened revolutionaries in a cellar below the fortress of the monarchy, who yet feared the impending revolution we all anticipated and, rather than shouting in a beer hall, we fed each other on half-baked mumbles of Apophatic Theology and washed it down with alcohol. On one end was Virg, who had half a beer, and on the other, Jules, who had five, and in the middle I drank slowly and tried to piece together what was no more decent or orderly than the ramblings of a story-telling, front porch preacher who had now spent his retirement hopping around from graduate course to graduate course in the liberal arts. It was a suspended space that half of us would not have been caught dead in had we not somehow drifted there on that afternoon, for various reasons. Virg would not have expected me to willingly attend a "church," let alone invite him, and I would not have expected him, being the husband of Tab, to agree to such an offer. "I think it's important to understand the experience," he told me. "It's a very revealing counterculture." He was here as an observer of what he called "interactive transformance art."

Virgil set the tone of the hour with questions directed at the first year of Pope Francis, an unusual topic, considering nobody there was Catholic, but a relevant one, because everyone was talking about Pope Francis. He reigned in with an almost aggressive sense of paternal guidance.

"He's definitely opening a once-closed door of conversation," Virg said of the Pope. "'Who am I to judge?' It's a bold opening statement. I look forward to the exciting things that will be coming out of the Vatican in coming years. Converting the Papacy itself to the hermeneutic of reform."

"Dogma, dogma, dogma," said Jules, already on his second beer within ten minutes. "Orthodoxy, orthodoxy, orthodoxy."

"I have to say I love the irony," said Obie, gesturing dramatically. "He comes from the 'inner circle' and he totally slammed the 'inner circle.' Part the waters, priests. You are fallible. The only certainty is God."

I interjected. "Didn't the Pope say something about denying absolute truth?"

"I think certainty is a false image," said Philip. "It's our ultimate false idol. It's provisional. It's flimsy." He had a new look on his face, one of wan suspicion.

"So what's under it all?" I said. "What's behind the curtain?"

"Oh, don't peek behind the curtain," said Obie. "You might see what God really is. Then we'll have to actually start living according to what we've seen."

"What if when Jesus died," I said, "that was God telling us that there's nothing behind the curtain?"

"It's like a magic trick," said Jules. "It's a long con, and we want to believe we're not being conned."

"Or people want to be conned," said Philip, matter-of-factly. "They want to suspend their belief—or more accurately, suspend their doubt."

"Well, that's what's difficult about language as symbol for communicating divine truth," said Virg with carefulness. "It takes a certain crafted literacy to accurately communicate a divine truth, or a divine mystery. But Christ broke it down in parables, earthly comparisons of heavenly ideas so that even the illiterate could access—"

"Or maybe it just takes a good magician," said another guy, one of the "church" hosts.

"I am reflecting what is unutterable within the circle," said Jules, raising his glass. "What Chesterton called the 'divine discontent.'"

"I don't want to be one to breed discontent," said Obie. "Don't be bitter, but be outraged. We've got to be a church of the outraged. As the folk saying goes, 'If you're not outraged, you're not paying attention.'"

"Does anyone know where that quote came from?" I asked.

"Does anyone know where God came from?" said Philip. If anyone was drinking bitter beer in the room, it was Philip.

"Our conceptions of God are filtered through our earthly paradigms," said Virg.

"So you want to define faith as being against faithfulness?" I said. "You're deconstructing faith? Then what?"

"Exactly," said Philip. "Then what? Just turtles all the way down."

"What's that from?" said another one of the hosts.

"Bertrand Russel," said Philip, shuffling on his stool like a pitcher at the mound. "He was giving this lecture on the sun at the center of the solar system. And his lady tells him that it's not true, that the earth is held up by a turtle. He asks her what it's standing on, and she said another turtle. So then he asks her again."

"And she says it's turtles all the way down," I said.

"Turtles all the way down," he repeated.

"The anecdote reveals a lot about scientific ignorance," said Virg, "but I think it builds a straw man case against a created cosmos. I mean, I see your point. If you want to expand on the myth as metaphor, I think the point can be made that the turtle is swimming. The earth is suspended. This is science and faith at work."

"But it's hard to escape the paradigm," I said. "If there's a soul driving your body, what's driving the soul?"

"Desire," said Jules. "Are we embodied? Is there a homunculus in this skull?" He knocked on his head with a smile.

"What's in the homunculus?" I said.

"Homunculi all the way down," said Philip. "We like the idea of having a will. How do we know we have any volition? How do we know we're in a purposeful universe?"

"Now let's not just toss up philosophy cheaply," said Virg. "I think it's more rational to ask questions we are intent on answering."

"I think we live in a universe of wills," said another host. "I think we try to bend the universe to our will, and that's the struggle."

An innuendo came to me, and the utterance came out of me anticlimactically. "I'm trying to get the universe to bend to my will."

Everyone seemed to almost acknowledge the insinuation, but not, and we all exchanged glances of eyes locking with one another. Then Jules burst out with his trademark Christmas laughter and we all guffawed over our beers. There were no prayers, there were no songs, there was no liturgy. It was like we had all been locked into a studio with a blank slate and warring notions of epistemology at our heels, forced with the challenge of painting a brand new world. We couldn't do it, and instead there was beer to imbibe.

There are churches out there trying to win us kids back. One kind is too dumb to convince me and too vindictive to care anyway. The other is trying desperately to attract me, but doesn't know me at all. This time I saw something that was a new kind of low.

Virg drove us home, having hardly sipped his beer. "You know, wine has a long history in the liturgy of the church," he said, almost to himself, "but that just wasn't going anywhere."

"It was bad beer," I said. "Not much potential there."

He shook his head. "They lacked direction. They just didn't have any direction."

"They need it just as much as our fundamentalist brethren," said Obie.

After dropping Philip and Obie off, Virg grew serious and tapped the steering wheel rapidly. It came to me then that I had meant to possibly bring up the whole Sedgwick thing, but didn't know how to, and it seemed like a faint buzz might would open him up, so I waited.

"It's just harsh," he said aloud. "Lucy said Philip just woke up one morning and said he didn't believe in God anymore."

"Turtles all the way down," I said.

He hook his head. "I just thought this would amount to a last ditch effort to get him to open up and talk about it.

"I don't know if it had the effect you desired," I said.

His forehead scowled with worry. "Now I'm not sure what to do at the moment. It's an unfortunate thing to think about. The error of it."

"Yeah," I said, just to say something. Maybe he had forgotten that I was in a similar place. Maybe he was trying to revive me as well as Philip.

"I read this gorgeous piece by Marilyn Robinson the other day," he said with a faint smile. "It's very apropos for our generation. 'To err is human; to err catastrophically is definitely human.'"

"Yeah," I said. "Definitely. Human all the way down."

And here again I couldn't tell if the loss of his friend's faith was the only consuming thought he had, distracting him reading into the Sedgwick situation, or if this admission of helplessness was merely a projection of a deeper worry that his wife was being pursued by the "old friend" with a guitar and a new look, and he couldn't figure how to ask me about it. It wasn't my place to ask. Nothing got resolved.

We don't want anything resolved, because resolution makes the future perish and urges us to take actions we can't afford to regret. We believe ourselves a balanced crowd of romantic idealists tempered by scintillating cynicism that spurs a will for genuine belief. When we meet together we concur that our roots were not genuine, and we are glad to have severed the connection. We live by sight, not by faith. We reach only for promises within grasp of our vision; we are too clever to search anywhere else.

After I got home I hung out with Joey. We listened to his copy of *Jesus Christ Superstar* on vinyl while I worked and he went job hunting online, both of us stalling in our endeavors. I told him about the absurdity of beer church and got to talking out our own theology.

"I don't feel I have to jump on the bandwagon of belief in something just to image a place to go when I die," he said.

"Yeah," I joined him. "I feel pretty sure God is so infinitely beyond my comprehension that he would completely understand my incredulity."

"I guess that's where faith—where *foma*—gets brought into the picture," he said. "I don't believe there's a purpose in slavery and genocide. If you assign purpose to one person's life you invalidate it to billions of others. It makes more sense for there to be no purpose."

"That's pretty bleak," I said.

"Yeah." he said. "But that's what harmless lies are for. You've got to be happy somehow."

That was about as far as we got, and then we listened to the radio interview. Wick went on air with Brad Stokely, whom he had previously refused to speak with again, about his upcoming album, which he had previously refused to speak about. Both of these refusals were an obvious publicity stunt, and Stokely seemed willing to play along. You can find the transcript online:

Brad Stokely: [With a well-practiced enthusiasm] So, believe it or not, sitting across from me is Garrett Sedgwick, premiere success story and one of the hardest working performers on the Indie scene! He's got a new album he's set to record in two days. Nothing known about it yet. No word about the band. This project is top secret. So Garrett, let's see, not only is it your sixth EP in five years, but it's also your second in a span of eight months.

Garrett Sedgwick: [As if he had just woken up] Yeah.

BS: Why so much secrecy? Is this the last one? You gonna call it quits?

GS: You're referring to the tweets? Yeah, I'd hit a rough patch, creatively. And I decided that if I couldn't create what I'd been creating, if it wasn't just the same, it'd be better to just drop out.

BS: I hear, I hear. So, it's two days 'til recording time. Who've you got in your lineup?

GS: Still not entirely sure, and I don't wanna throw any names out, because I'm still in talks with several guys who might show up. I don't wanna spoil anything.

BS: So, who's reuniting? Hymists? The Follies? Gargamel? Nothing like that?

GS: [silence]

BS: All right. That's cool. No promo. Okay, so fans are really gearing up for this one. Hopes are pretty high. Every time you come out with a new record we keep wondering, 'is he just playin' around or is this his real voice comin' out?'"

GS: I imagine at this point anyone would be excited to try a new thing. I have a short attention span. I guess my fans do too. They won't have to wait too long for this one.

BS: They're getting tired of the over-hype these days. Songs leaking, streaming live—but you're not planning on anything like that? No surprises like that?

GS: No surprises. I mean, I can't control if something's a surprise for you, you know? But I'm keeping this one close to the chest this time.

BS: I see. This one inspired by a new relationship or something?

GS: That would be oversimplifying things a bit. I had a lot of people in mind when I composed this one. It does have a special dedication feel to it. I've got a lot of people to thank for their presence in my lives. I don't wanna just give a shout out or something at some awards ceremony. I want to craft something living for them, you know. Something that lasts.

BS: Wick, you're one of those artists—

GS: Please stop with the whole "Wick" thing.

BS: [a pause] Okay? Sure. So, you're one of those artists who really seem to have a sort of cult following. Words like "prodigy" and "prophet" get tossed around.

GS: Yeah, I've never felt like that. I don't have the time for keeping up with who's following what. Music criticism has just turned into this by idol polishing genre.

BS: You seem to be free of any pretension for someone who's fan-base is rife with pretension. The things you're in to—it comes out in your music, but is it in your life?

GS: No, it's me. I don't know why you'd want to question that.

BS: Well, on your latest album you did include a dozen photos of yourself sitting in a vast collection of upholstered chairs.

GS: The chairs are a thing. I love the chairs. At first it was the Victorian stuff, but I threw a lot of those out and now it's Gustav Stickley. He's just got his own aesthetic — but, you know, I get hungry for something and I get into it. Besides music, I don't think I've ever had a steady hobby. I just lock on to a style or a book I found or collecting something and it pulls me in — don't really care if it's trending or not. If some little hipster wants to eat right outta my hand, that's his deal. I'm a Gemini, so I'm like a jack of all trades, master of none. My one concern right now is that I'll leave behind just a bunch of attempts, nothing substantial.

BS: But you've carved out some pretty substantial territory. How has the help of a major label manager contributed to your success?

GS: Look, I've said it plenty of times before. I'm not on a major label, never will be. I've had tools watching over my back, trying to squeeze me dry. Signing on a dotted line so I can have my career defined by how many spins I get on a station like this one? Lookin' over my shoulder at the charts and being told what my next record should sound like? No, that's some MTV sh—. It's not happening.

BS: Not even with Bruce Fey? People are talkin', man.

GS: Different topic.

BS: Fair enough. [a pause] So why Nashville?

GS: Why not? If you're gonna fail, fail here. Why does anybody come to Nashville?

BS: Everybody includes fans. Do you never get tired of the crowd?

GS: You can't surround yourself with people that worship you. I learned that from one of my mentors years ago. It changes you into something. You either start to believe something you're not or you flip out and alienate your fans.

BS: Has it changed you?

GS: [silence, shuffling]

BS: So what's at the heart of a performance, then? For Garrett Sedgwick, what moves your music? Is that a fair question.

GS: [a pause] Tunnel vision. I was at this restaurant once. It was a sushi place. The chef was a sushi master. Every move he made was calculated and concentrated all on the present piece of sushi he was crafting. I mean I was just engrossed in it. He made every piece like it was his last. He didn't know anything else in life, almost like an Olympic athlete, but there was no medal at stake. It was just being wrapped up in it for its own sake. He serves me this piece, and I watched every movement, every cut, every roll every brush stroke. And then he watches me eat it. And I don't know anything about sushi, I just know it's delicious. But he's searching my eyes, because it's his goal to please me. His definition of perfection is based on what I think. And that's a lot of pressure, on both of us, because he's so obsessed. Every piece of sushi he's crafted has led up to this moment, and I have to be pleased. But it's not about me, because I'm just there as a measure of how he excels at his craft. I'm just a consumer. And he's striving to be something he can't ever achieve, but for him to even feed off the dream, I have to come in and sit on the stool and eat from his plate.

BS: [a pause]. Wow. [a pause]. Uh, so you're saying your audience is just there to consume for your sake?

GS: It's a f—in' metaphor, man.

BS: Hey, you can't say that word on the air at this hour, man.

GS: [Voice raising] Well, it's—you claim you're here to promote me and you completely misconstrued everything I say—

BS: You said it yourself, man. You've got tunnel vision, and you're so focused on the art that puts food on your table that you don't even pay attention to the fans who pay to see you. That's pretty off-putting, man. You spend half a decade growing your own fan base without major label help and then turn around and bump them off as just something that pays the bills? Who are you doing this for if not for them?

GS: That's not—you don't understand the context. I write the music for their listening. That's how I walk on the stage, that's how I walk into a studio.

BS: But do you care about them?

GS: [Defensive] Why would you even ask that? On the radio? What is this? An interrogation?

BS: [Apologetic] No need to take it the wrong way, man.

GS: [Frantic] No, no. Do you see me probing into your life and questioning your commitment to your listeners? Hey all you f—ers! Does Brad Stokely know you by name? Has he taken any listener polls? Does he park his little radio van in the park and feed you pigeons?

BS: Where's this comin' from, man?

GS: Go ahead and air this. Air the whole thing. This is what we do. Jim Morrisson yanked his d—out to his fans and they still worship him. These days you say one hotheaded thing in an interview or a tweet and everybody goes ape sh—.

BS: It's just the scene, man. Chill. It's just an inter—

GS: [Voice growing distant.] No. I'm done. I'm out. Forget it...

BS: [muffled, distant communication] Well, that pretty much wraps it up with Garrett Sedgwick. He'll be recording in a few days. We can expect the album to be an early fall release. Wow. Some artists. Sometimes they speak in a different tongue.

"That was really bad," said Joey.

"That was horrible," I said.

"That was probably the coolest thing I've heard all day."

"I kinda feel bad for him. That was unpleasant."

"He completely derailed it."

"Yes. A veritable derailment."

"Is there a way off the Sedgwick train?"

I could have mentioned Sedgwick's added pressure of confronting the culmination of his five-year search for a lost romance, but I didn't. Instead I tramped in the philosophy of performance artistry.

"Maybe you just reach a point where you have no choice but to alienate your fans. Disenfranchise them. He said it. You can't surround yourself with people who worship you."

"Maybe that's how God sees it," said Joey. "Maybe that's why he seems so distant."

I banged the back of my head against the couch. "Yeah, like the disciples, man."

Joey propped his bare, grass-stained feet on the edge of his armrest and looked up at the ceiling dreamily.

"So is it better to burn our or fade away?"

"You can always join the twenty-seven club," I said. "Become a martyr without a cause."

"But really," he said. "Is it better to hit rock bottom and release all the energy given you, or to taper off and drift away?"

"Yeah!" I marveled at his tantalizing predicament. "Of course, supposing the two are mutually exclusive. I mean, I'd love to do both."

"Neil," he said. "I wouldn't put it past you to reach Nirvana and try to become a god."

"I feel it's the next stage," I said, tapping my stomach with the symbolism of hunger. "If I do, you can be in my trinity."

"Who's the third?"

"I feel like we need a woman."

"Yeah. That would really balance things out."

Whether he was beginning to burn out or fade away, Sedgwick was beginning to crack, and nobody knew the fullness of the reason but himself. I couldn't even tell, with so many forces pulling at him, past and present. Either Tab had not been responding to him, or she had, and it wasn't a positive reception. He was trying to live in two worlds. This interview, especially if Tab had heard it, didn't fare well for either of his two worlds.

12
"BACKDRIFTS"
feat. *Flatland* folded

People were still talking about the interview at Ugly Mugs the following night. One of Amanda's friends had formed a new band and was laying his first gig. I brought Joey and Frenchy with me and invited Sam and Sam. Only Sam came, after he and Samantha had some sort of argument. It was odd seeing only one of them without the other.

I sat down next to Sam on a gray couch so comfortable we were both sucked into its depths, and I knew I would be there until someone pulled me out at the end of the evening. We arrived early and played Scrabble—Sam and Joey and Frenchy and I—circumventing the game's original intent by awarding double points for spelling foul words, a proof that we were all still repressed from our upbringings.

Amanda was slinking about the place in a pair of non-prescription glasses I knew she had just bought, and her hair had that purposeful "I haven't showered in days, but I have treated my hair" look. She looked cute and annoying at the same time, because it was a new look for her but I knew it wasn't her.

Greg Dickey showed up with Hank Scott and a new girl named Anna. Greg had just bought a copy of *Flatland* for the girl and was trying to explain the premise to her, convinced she would like it. But she got hung up on the bit about the men being shapes and the women being lines.

"It's complete chauvinism," she told him.

"It's a satire," he said.

"But you said it was a treatise on space and dimensions," she said. "He's using a sexist allegory."

"It's both," said Greg. "It's about how hard it is for us to escape our paradigms of epistemology. It works on multiple levels."

"He could have given more consideration to clarifying that," said Anna. "He was writing in the Victorian era."

I interrupted. "I'll agree with her, because it is a little condescending. But even the points in Lineland are lustrous points."

"I'm glad someone here tonight agrees with me."

"But the symbolism is a little uninspiring," I said. "I mean, lines are a phallic symbol. It would be more typical for the men to be lines and the women to be circles. So maybe he was actually subverting the sexist paradigm."

"Or just using math to represent the way Victorians demeaned women," said Greg. "Which he was against."

"I still think it was a good point," she said. She didn't recognize her accidental pun.

"Well," I said, rolling my eyes facetiously, "every point I make is a lustrous point."

Greg protested. "Are you flirting with my date?"

I placed my hands on the back of my head. "I'm just being the omniscient god of my Pointland."

"That's very solipsist," he said.

"Very solipsist," I said. "But I accept it as my own conception. I am pretty satisfied with myself. I am the cosmos."

I felt like the cosmos, or at least a stationary collapsing star within it, people orbiting around my couch and occasionally falling in. Across from me, Joey nearly looked like he had been shoved back-first into the crevice, his body contorted so that the soles of his feet nearly pointed at the ceiling. Not a moment after Greg and his date walked off to get coffee, Amanda took the spot beside me that Sam had left when he managed to escape, and I found I was unable to escape Amanda. After a quick "hey" she picked up the copy of *Flatland* and thumbed through it, her leg bouncing with arousal from caffeine and society. She asked me what it was about, and I gave her the shortest summary I could, as she nodded and rapidly fired verbal affirmations. I managed to be as boring as I could, which only seemed to pull her in further. When I stopped completely, she began to look about the room for other stray gents, and I remained silent until the awkwardness was too much for the both of us.

I'm being capitulatory.

While seated I eavesdropped on a conversation Hank was having with someone about the absurdity of music lovers engaging in free peer-to-peer file sharing while simultaneously decrying the poor taste in music made possible by an industry of big labels preying on starving artists. Joey was now lost in reading Greg's copy of *Flatland* and might as well have fallen asleep. I didn't want any coffee, and I didn't want to get up. I also didn't want to think about Sedgwick and Tab, but Sam asked me if I heard the interview. I was so sick with it that I resorted to asking Sam about Samantha, which I didn't want to do, because I hate to pry.

"We just had a huge fight," he said at first, scratching his arm furiously like a rash had broken out.

"You guys fight?"

"Well, it's been happening since we got back from Burning Man."

Joey perked up. "Burning Man? Thought you guys had a great time. I wanted to go."

Sam, deflated, leaned over, as if about to regurgitate. "We had a great time. But it was like we didn't have to have it around each other. And then when we got back, it was like our lives are just too normal, you know? Like, she's not exciting any more. Is that weird? Is that weird to say?"

"No," said Joey. "People get used to each other."

"None of you met somebody else out there?" I said.

"No," he said. "We were around each other the whole time. But it was weird. I didn't really think of her the whole time. She was right next to me."

"Maybe it's a post honeymoon blues thing," said Joey.

"You've just returned from a liminal space," I said.

"Yeah," said Sam. "It just feels weird. Like, she's always like 'hey, let's try this new place.' And like now that's stopped. Now I feel like we're just there and we're cheating ourselves out of something. Like we ran out of things to do together or things to say. It's weird to explain."

"You don't have to explain it," said Joey. "Just crash with us tonight."

"Yeah," I said. "We'll be like a trinity."

And I looked at Sam, and he didn't look familiar at all, because I hadn't met Sam without Samantha, because they were Sam and Sam as long as I'd known them. I was now sitting beside a fraction, and we were both being pulled into the oblivion of the couch, and I wanted to tell him, "see you on the other side, man," as we both allowed the nether fabric to engulf us.

The band started up. Amanda's friend was some guy with a huge chin in a tight white button up and a skinny tie. His music sounded like Weezer, only less confident and with the lyrical depth of *The Green Album*, and I couldn't stand him. But I was too lethargic to move. Sam picked up the copy of *Flatland* and flipped through it before putting it down and getting up to hang with some other friends he spotted. Joey fell into his near sleep in which his eyes are closed and he is just meditating in neutral awareness.

Frenchy had been talking to some guy, a close talker of the sort that somehow backs you into a corner. She found herself up against the couch and gave every sign of disinterest, to no avail. She hopped up and sat on the top of the couch, glancing down at me as the guy continued talking. The start of a new song gave her opportunity to direct his attention to the stage, enough time to furtively inch herself around and over the top of the couch, until both legs were over the front, and slowly slide down into the seat beside me. In that lighting, and over the soft material of the couch, she bedazzled me with the ease of her nonchalant seductiveness, of her covert movement, which was not too coquettish. I said "hey." I didn't care that she was using me as a cover to avoid the close talker. She picked up the copy of *Flatland* and began to flip through it idly. We talked about the band and how much we hated it. Eventually, her smallness escaped the vacuum of the couch, and she wandered off.

I had picked up *Flatland* and flipped to one of my favorite passages when Greg finally remembered to come back over and get it.

"Do you want to borrow it?" he asked. "I don't think Anna is going to read it. Now I have buyer's remorse."

"I've read it," I said. "You didn't convince her."

"She's super sensitive about that," he said. "Kind of like Shelly, but not as bad."

"She knew it's a satire," I said.

Greg's eyes bulged. "I know. I know. But she said it didn't make it any better. Like how the women all have shrill voices. When I told her about that she said it moved beyond class satire and into misogyny. She said 'you can't just grossly stereotype an entire gender or class in a story and then just pull the "satire" card.' She thinks it's too ambiguous. Like you have to be mocking something in particular."

He quoted her in a shrill voice, and I could not contain my laughter.

His eyes rolled as he huffed. "But she really sounds like that! You're with me, right? You liked the book. You get it, right?"

"Maybe. I don't know."

"But she was proving a point I get out of the book, too."

I was still crippled by the comfort of the couch.

"It's very logical," he continued. "But the characters have emotions—at least as much as shapes can have. And they struggle to expand their paradigm. So it applies to relationships too. You have a rational side and an emotional side. Now, I know it sounds reductive, but guys tend to be more logic-oriented and girls more heart-oriented."

"You better get this out while Anna's not beside you," I said.

"Right. Oh, goodness—If she heard that she would go off. But whichever one you are, you have to mix it up some. If you're relying too much on logic, you have to listen to your heart. It's cliché, but it's true. And if you're too emotional, you have to weigh the logic of the situation. And so even if the relationship doesn't work out, because you couldn't match up, you'll still leave the relationship in a better state than you were."

"It's very elementary," I said.

"But it's applicable. When I took psychology my professor told me that men are more driven to see the world in hierarchies."

"Hegemonized hierarchies."

"Right. And women are more associated and more relationship based."

"But look at all the exceptions?"

"Name them."

"Angela Davis. Chris Carraba."

Greg Shuddered. "I hate Dashboard. But yes, those are exceptions. Like I said, it's just a trend."

"I wouldn't call myself a terribly emotional person."

"Right, and so back to binaries. Whether you're driven emotionally or logically, you're always making subconscious decisions about whether or not to take it to another level. If you're going to keep it going or quit."

"Love versus effort," I said simply.

"Well," he said, "even more broad than that."

"You said 'broad,'" I joked.

"She didn't hear it. But there are a lot of scales we use. But we're always weighing in on that decision, and we are using our 'heart' and our 'head' on some level. If you don't reach it, then one of you came to the conclusion that the effort wasn't worth the potential for love."

"Are you going to take it to another level with Anna? I feel like it's unfair for her not to be part of this conversation."

"I probably won't. I mean, she's cool, but neither of us seem to be at the point where the effort is there. Which is okay. Don't get me wrong—she's cool and everything, and she's a great friend. But like with Cameron—"

I searched the room for Frenchy. If I could lock eyes on her, I thought, I could signal her to come over here and interrupt Greg—

"It's just a staple of humanity that God gave us all a freedom of choice, and as adults we all understand that privilege, but if we act immature, we deny it. I mean if I held a gun to your head right now, you would still have a choice in doing whatever I told you to do—"

The gun-to-my-head thing was sounding very appealing—

"We are altruistic, but we want to be with someone else. If you poll everyone on Earth, that will be the general consensus—"

I wanted to be alone—

"And you can't fathom all the dynamics of a relationship, because we want it to be complicated. We even go after the things that we don't want. We actually begin to deify what we want in our hearts. I saw a little bit of that with Cameron, because she wanted to craft this relationship according to her own dictates. Like she bought me this Arabian kaffiyeh one time and she wanted me to wear it because she thought it looked chic. But it wasn't me and it wasn't even the style around here. And she got mad at me. She got *mad* at me—"

Joey was asleep, and I was envious —

"We want to fly to Jupiter, or just get the hot girl, but not everyone can be an astronaut. It's not realistic, if you calculate the energy and distance it takes."

Anna arrived, in time to drag Greg away so that the seat next to me would remain empty. Greg stood up, taking his copy of *Flatland*.

"I was just telling Neil about relationship goals."

She flinched. "You have goals already? I thought we were just hanging out. That's awkward."

"You guys are just hanging out?" said Hank, appearing to beside them. Now they all stood over me, and the couch eerily beckoned them to stay. I crept my hands out on either side of me as it to claim the empty cushions.

"No, no," said Greg. "I was talking about how we are constantly making the small decision to advance or retreat in a relationship. Mostly based on personal preferences."

"Like how you always talk about your ex-girlfriends," said Anna.

Hank laughed and patted him on the shoulder.

"I do not!" Greg shouted, causing Anna to let out a snorting giggle.

"Or like how you snort when you laugh," said Greg. "At some point I'll make the decision of whether I want to be with a girl who snorts."

"Seems pretty trivial to me," said Anna.

"People are trivial," said Hank.

"But it can be as serious as looking at someone's bad history," said Greg. "It's all what you make of it."

"But," said Anna, "if you are with a person, then you've already reached the goal of being with the person. So is your goal to stay with them forever?"

Greg sighed, his eyes checking the top of his skull. "But you're subconsciously weighing out the decision to stay dedicated to it. And that's the goal, to make a complete dedication."

Hank hummed the opening of "Here Comes the Bride."

"Or," I said, "what if you like two people at the same time? Then your efforts are bifurcated."

Greg huffed. "You just wanted to say 'bifurcated.'"

"Even the trivial things can have a great effect," said Anna. "If you hate my snort, we probably won't work out."

Hank jumped in. "Hey, bring it back to basics, man. It's just a matter of risk over reward."

Greg's eyes widened. "Hey! That's like a chart I made once."

Hank clapped his hands. "Or, or—what if you looked at it this way? Maybe it's not about finding someone who's quirks annoy us the least. Maybe it's about us making ourselves a more likable creature."

"What's more likable," said Anna, "is not spending five minutes making fun of me because I snort."

"I can overlook that," said Greg. "Eventually, I just want to find a significant other who can help me get through my own distractions and love me through it," said Greg.

"Sappy," said Hank, "but good."

"I think I just need a girl who's decent at copulation," I muttered.

It worked. Everyone felt so awkward they said goodbye and left.

I now had loner's remorse. I tried to conjure the motions of Frenchy over the couch toward me, and bend the light so she stayed. I craved a connection, but it wasn't with Frenchy in particular. It was with just about anybody, but nobody in particular. Eventually, the band called it a night and Joey woke up.

"I'm feeling a subtle yet persistent *vin-dit*," I told Joey. "I'm yearning for a *karass*."

"Are you sure it's not just a *granfalloon*?" he said, rubbing the cowlick in his hair.

"I think Amanda is a total *sin-wat*."

"She is something of a *sin-wat*" he said. "She does have some *sin-wat*-ish traits. I wouldn't tell her she's a *sin-wat*."

We both decided to head home, bring Sam with us, and talk about Vonnegut.

On the day of recording, Sedgwick had spent the previous day in his own stuffy apartment, listening to no music whatsoever, trying to purge himself of any influences, to touch *Tabula Rasa*. In the studio, I met the musicians he would be performing with, not necessarily a band, as most of the tracks would consist of two or three accompanying instruments. They were assembled mostly from his previous bands, and there were a couple others picked out from elsewhere. They had three days to record anywhere between ten to sixteen songs. This is the NaNoRiMo of music recording; this is the Alamo; this is Tour de France.

On accompanying guitar and other stringed instruments were the fifty-something Joni Mitchell type woman and the cowboy who looked like a white supremacist militia member who had renounced his cause and gone soft. Their names were Bette and Craig. There was Jackson, the Stevie Ray Vaughan clone, who played just about everything on guitar. There was a cellist with coke bottle glasses named Kirk and the girl in cutoff jean shorts who went by Myra was there to sing backup and a couple duets, as well as provide parts for flute and tambourine. And these were just the regulars. Dan the drummer from Al Jazari was there too, and I was surprised he didn't bring Kenna along. I could provide a list of the instruments they played, but it would be superfluous and distracting. They assembled like some diversely contrived team in a bad heist movie, and when finished they would all have a smoke while asking one another where they're each headed next, only to likely never see one another in person again.

The practice begins at 10:00 am on Monday, with Sedgwick scribbling furiously at his writing pad in between practice takes, wearing dark glasses. The tempo alters between speeds, with false start after false start, and he abandons one song for another, for hours unable to make it through a single take. The makeshift band cautiously eyes one another with patient, silent frustration, doubting the stunted process. For a couple takes of a song, Sedgwick tries singing an entire chorus to the accompaniment of the cello and a kalimba, but drops it altogether. The bafflers are swapped in and out several times, the whole crew unable to determine whether they want the instruments to bleed or not.

"Remember Parkinson's Law!" Myra cries out. "Work expands so as to fill the time available for its completion!"

"Remember the Law of Diminishing Return!" preaches Jackson.

"Miles Davis did *Kind of Blue* in five days," says Wick, shaking his hair like a wet dog.

"Yeah but he only had five songs," says Dan.

Only Kirk the cellist with cataracts never says a word.

Bruce Fey hovers behind the glass of the recording room like a cop inspecting a lineup.

Well into midnight now, and only one song has been successfully recorded. Three hours are spent on a second song, Sedgwick halting and beginning again. "It's off...it's just off." He puts down his guitar, rubs his scowling forehead, and declares, "It's slipping away. The song's slipping way, y'all." He chastises himself, he chastises the band. "Let's just play it through this time. Every part. I don't care if it's sh—. Don't decorate it. Just play the notes." When a coherent, fully formed tune emerges and comes to a close, Sedgwick forgets the last verse altogether and chucks his guitar across the room. He repents, "The song stopped speaking to me." He goes to a booth, sings the song to himself while everyone gossips about whether or not he's using. "Straight edge," says Jackson. "Wick ain't trippin' nothin' but the G— D— voice of Gabriel." He emerges, plays the song, records it, and everyone releases a long breath. Later, after he hears the take, he removes it from the final list and it ends up in a vault somewhere.

It's early morning, and I've dozed off and woken up again. Sedgwick already plugged up and plugged out for the only song in which he intends to play anything electric, only to reject the electric version altogether. The Salvation Army brass band has already come in to record their bit and left. Bruce Fey has disappeared from behind the window. Sedgwick is the only one who hasn't left the studio for so much as a toilet break, despite nearly emptying his entire jug of oolong tea. He begins to cough, and either the second-hand smoke has gotten to him or because he has not given himself a break, but either way it has altered his voice from the morning before. The bafflers have come down for good, and Sedgwick suddenly seems to have gained a stark clairvoyance that pushes him like a hostage into each take. Still, the recording is not without need of polishing, even in this late stage. But songs continue through to the end more often than not, even in a rough take, and after a good minute everyone is breaking into smiles with one another, climbers who had reached the top of a cliff.

"Get it on!" sounds off Craig at the beginning of every new take. "This one's too flawless to be good," jokes Sedgwick after a perfect take. "Maybe we should do it again to get a rough cut." Nobody knows wether to laugh, not even him. He does it one more time, throwing the kalimba in last minute. "Get it on!" says Craig. They burn through another one, and Bette dominates with her guitar countermelody. "I am so gonna get laid with this one," she says. "Get it on!"

The spontaneous, woven string of moments out of time and space comes to an end sometime around late afternoon Tuesday. Vision and revision lay to rest songs aborted prematurely and postmaturely, and Phoenix-like some have come up to claim a space with the living. Riddle upon riddle of lyrical prosody rises like incense from the burning of midnight oil in this studio, and now everyone begins to pack up their instruments. Sedgwick has disassociated himself from the curse of a heart too heavy to articulate poetry, and molded an album both dialectical and sentimental. He's reworked and abandoned enough lyrics to fill a short novel. Everyone in the studio is given permission to leave, a small reward for the feat of having pulled off a full record in less than three days, after having never played all together before. I've done some pencil sketches along the way, but will have to show them to him later. He says he's going to spend another day in the studio hearing the album again, arranging the songs in the order he wants, mulling over whether to include a couple surplus solo songs he had done in his apartment, and going through the motions of mastering, which he refuses to adulterate with digital alterations. There will be no paid publicity for this one. Word of mouth has done enough. He thanks me for coming, and I leave a room like a pilgrim from a shrine. I bum a cigarette from Jackson, my first one in weeks.

I go home and fall asleep reading Kerouac.

13
"SHE FELL AWAY"
feat. the inevitable surfacing of intangible woes

Everyone thinks they're Orpheus, every charlatan on the fountain steps with a guitar. Anyone can play guitar. Sedgwick wanted Tab to be the first one to hear the record. A couple weeks had gone by before he came to me with a copy he had made before the master was cut. He wanted Tab to hear it, but wasn't sure if he wanted to be present when she did. After much wavering, he wanted me there at Tab's place, some sort of cushion against the tyranny of two people alone with something to say to one another, a third party at a time when Virg was not home. Tab would have made me come, anyway. I supposed that would be the plan once she heard the record, once she heard him as if for the first time, or something like that.

I came with him, and when they saw each other in the door they both smiled bashfully. I stepped aside and let them hug, holding the record like a neglected shield-bearer.

"I am happy to see you," she said with a bravery of voice. I almost suspected that her previous silence had only been due to Virgil's presence, that she would open up to Sedgwick in these moments alone, and I would find myself in a deeper dilemma.

Sedgwick, hands on his hips and mouth twitching back and forth, strolled over to the Capiello poster in the dining room.

"Is this a real painting?"

Tab winced. So did I.

"We got it at Hobby Lobby," she said. "They have several."

"Oh. Well, it looks real in this light. It's very pretty."

Sedgwick studied the poster, moving his hands around the frame and eyeing it up and down, but only to avoid looking directly at Tab. The poster might as well have fallen to the floor and cracked.

"Still can't believe it's been so long," he said, a reference of one kind veiling another.

Tabitha had gone into the kitchen to fetch tea she had made. Sedgwick shot me a glance as if to signal some prearranged course of action, but I only knew to sit in the living room chair. He sat down beside me and let out a breath. He sat stiffly. He had quickly passed from the awe of seeing her face again to the embarrassment of traipsing ever closer to a moment he had so intensely prepared for.

We sipped tea for a few minutes and traded pointless information about the day, and I felt what I imagined high end escorts felt as they sipped wine before they engaged in the old in-out, in-out with a flabby businessman. I knew I was supposed to leave the room and go do something, but Tab shot me a look of unspoken command that I was not to leave the room. Sedgwick leaned forward a bit and bounced in his chair.

"So I had a guy let me borrow some studio time. I've got a new little record coming out, if you want to hear it. I—um, I kinda made it for you. I mean, with you in mind."

Tab put her hand to her face and looked away at the Capiello poster. I could not read anything except that she was flattered and nervous. She nodded that she would hear it, and we all three walked over to the turntable by the window. He took the record out of its sleeve and fingered the edge like a sword-smith. He turned to the window as if his next cue was written on the glass.

"I used to play on every corner hoping you'd walk by and find me again."

He said it as cooly as it could be said, expecting her to be the next to share that she had a secret collection of his music and clippings under her bed. Instead, she stiffened like she had swallowed something disagreeable before a prince. I ached on her behalf.

He handed the record to me and leaned against the window in the most confident pose he could, that old cowboy returning to his body. I placed the record on the spindle and backed away from the bomb, leaving Tab to disarm it.

"Go ahead," said Sedgwick.

She moved the needle and placed it on the record.

What came out was what I had heard in the studio, but it is always different as it comes from the grooves and through a speaker. I had chosen not to describe it before so that you could hear it for the first time as Tab did. It was an acoustic guitar with a rhythm bass, that first song. And then, Sedgwick's affected moan of a voice, a new voice, one he had never even experimented with before that night in the studio. It had a weathered timbre, with a deep sweetness within. It sounded how Dylan must have when the public first heard *John Wesley Harding* without that Okie beat inflection he'd inherited from Woody. It sounded like an impersonation. It sounded like a relic.

Tab tucked her chin and let out a low, quaking laugh. It was her laugh for when Caraway the dog chased his own tail. It was her laugh for when Kenna would cuss so crassly in public. It was her laugh for when I had gotten chewing gum stuck in my hair as a kid.

"It's so goofy," she said.

She had told him she was embarrassed of him, and he heard it clearly. He saw her eyes roll, not look at him but roll into her skull, away from him, with faint derision. She thought of him as nothing more than a curiosity.

Sedgwick was rigid. He bit his lip.

I was enthralled with the recording but now the record became disquieting, ruined for me. Sedgwick jerked the needle up.

"You don't have to listen to it now," he said.

Tab came to a sudden awareness of Sedgwick's own shame. "No, I wasn't—"

"No," he said. "No, it's just—I wanted you to know. I wanted you to appreciate, that's all."

They were both silent for too long. I gulped.

"You guys wanna listen to some Strokes?"

They didn't have to shake their heads. They had nothing more to say. Sedgwick pretended to get a text, and he left without giving Tab another hug, like he had just wet his pants. He had to have known that the encounter, the first time he could get her alone without Virgil, would be a complete fumble in the dark. His vigorous vision was no more real than her enduring love for him. He was not only a past embarrassment to her, but a present one as well. He had transgressed into territory beyond her, beyond the both of them, and was just as stolen away as she was. What a guy like Sedgwick can collect in his dreams, no spark or shower can mete out.

I'm being mawkish.

I stayed with Tab long enough for her to thank me for staying.

"He just—" she began to say. "He just tried too hard. It was like he didn't feel like he had to try with me when we met, but I thought he was. Now, it's just—"

"That you're married?" I said.

"Yes!" she said, as if I had solved a riddle. For a moment, this was not the primary reason she had turned Sedgwick down, not that she was taken, but that he had tried to take her the wrong way. It was unclear to me whether Virg was able to keep her by virtue of being wedded to her or by mesmerizing her with his intellect more than any guy with a guitar ever could.

"You could have just told him," I said. "You could have just told him up front. It was obvious. And you're married."

"I didn't know what he was intending," she said. "I didn't know. It's just too awkward. It's hard to know what you're supposed to say."

I couldn't blame her, not in the position she had been put in.

I went to see Sedgwick too, because I wanted to show him final drafts of my sketch ideas for the album. We met up at his real apartment later that night. It was a musty bottomless pit, part walk-in closet museum for an undefinable artist, part workshop for homemade electric science kits, part storage room for heavy, old-fashioned furniture. There was a bed by the window, and everything else was instruments, battery-powered junk, and the entire collection of velvet-covered upholstered chairs, the very same ones he had posed for pictures in as part of the booklet art for *Gravity Waltzes*, facetiously half-mocking his reputation as a "new king of Indie Rock." He had collected exotic instruments that had been used on various records, notably *Al Jazari*, and assorted other items from places he had toured overseas. One would expect a caged mogwai to be humming in a dark corner. Rudimentary Davy lamps and Faraday disks and cathode ray tubes and a vintage prototype electric motor were strewn about like an auction of Frankenstein's lab. The place was shut in and stuffy, waiting for someone to stumble in and discover it years later, like a steamer trunk full of the impassioned, folded poems of Emily Dickenson.

He didn't want the lights on. I bumped into the keys of a dusty piano making my way between the tightly spaced artifacts. He was splayed out in a chair, and in the shadow his stubble seemed like a full grown beard, one that gave him the stereotype of a hermit, or an alcoholic, or a hermetic alcoholic. I picked the Gustav Stickley beside him and sat down to listen.

"The look in her eyes," he said. "The look in her eyes was always so cultivated."

He had dropped a key just then. I didn't quite get it until then. She was cultivated. That was her charm to him. That was the damsel to his dulcimer that faded from his dream and refused to return to him, the glowing lantern he tucked away and searched for every night on street corners, cultivating himself into a performer of a different kind. His religion, his one talent, and his devotion to this refined girl were what drove him not only to play, but to live a hermetic, ascetic life of tortured creativity. He stopped dipping chew for her. He traveled where she had been, and even where she wished to go. She spoke

Spanish, and he learned Spanish folk tunes without knowing what they said. He studied Faraday because she had a scientific mind and electric motors were all he could decipher, at best. She would periodically fast from meat, and he had gone full vegan. But the music was central. His love for the art had preceded his love for her. His encounter with Hoyt Murdock gave him a kickstart, a motivation, as if the industry had shoved one artifact off the shelf and made room for one more to climb aboard.

"Maybe she liked the record," I said. "She did smile."

"She hated it," he said.

"Yeah, she hated it." I couldn't lie.

"Even if she hated me, that'd be better than this. She's just so — so unresponsive now. That's what burns me."

I reasoned with him. "She's moved on, man. She's married."

"I could never tell how real it was," he said. "Not from where I was sitting. You have to admit, because you knew her. Ten years ago Tab never would have thought that she would marry without a wedding,"

"I never thought a lot of things about myself ten years ago," I said.

He curled up in his chair, arms around his legs.

"Browning. The poet. He said that a man's reach has to exceed his grasp. What else is Heaven for?"

"I don't know if there is a Heaven," I said. "But it did drive you to make some pretty decent music. I'll tell you right now, it's good stuff. The new record. It's good too. Just throwing that out there."

"Part of me wonders if it was her I really wanted, or if I just wanted her approval. I couldn't even get that."

"That's a lot of work for one person," I said. "That's a lot of pressure on her. I mean, you could have just asked her to add you on Spotify."

No matter how much he drew her when they met, she grew too discriminatory too soon. He was to her the equivalent of a half-wit by the time she realized she did not love him. Without his guitar and ruddy looks he was too mortifying to her budding tastes. He had no sense to share with her the implications of culture and beauty as she saw them coming to her. It wasn't about refusing to marry a man who would watch football as she read herself to sleep; it was much deeper than that. She would always be more mature, had to find someone she could never be ashamed of while in the presence of the literate, the sophisticated. She fluttered off into college, and he felt like he had earned her. The gentleman that he was, he gave her time and space.

"You couldn't believe how excited I was when I found out she was living in Nashville, and the way I found out from a friend that she hadn't gotten married. It seemed like it was all coming together. I was afraid to contact her. She never actually broke it off with me, never said goodbye or that it was over. She just stopped talking to me. I wanted her to find me. I wanted her to stumble upon me, breathless. It had to be that way."

This wasn't the plan all along, to chase her down. This was not why he had wound up in Nashville. He sought his first love, and his first love was music. The transformation began not with the death of a relationship, but the death of a hero. The music he could lose himself in. He could write songs about her if he wanted. But he was a product of a culture he suddenly despised the moment he witnessed Hoyt Murdock up on stage with the dignity of a bear on a treadmill. The man gave him a gift. He showed Chance Merritt that a man could remake himself, for better or for worse. He gave him a book full of autographed lyricism as empty as a future yet to be filled. Chance made it to

Nashville, to the only scene that made sense. And there was Tab.

"I thought Virg was just some trophy husband," said Sedgwick. "Like she got with him to prove to herself daily that she was every bit the old soul she thought she was. I think I just had blurry vision."

"I think it'll last," I said, with just a hint of optimism. "If it's any consolation, Virg really seems to like your stuff. Maybe she'll come to like it too. If that's what you can settle for."

Garrett looked me in the eye, and it may have been for the first time that he looked at me, and not at himself thinking.

"When was the last time you had a moment where you felt you were part of something bigger?"

I couldn't think of one. But Garrett Sedgwick had one, and I listened.

"It was my birthday. I was in Egypt, during the Arab Spring, during the elections. Gathering music ideas for what would become *Al Jazari*. One day I was standing in Tahrir Square, protesters everywhere. There must have been thousands of them. Effegies everywhere, soldiers with shields, tanks, people crowding and marching. A whole 'nother world. You know, you see the pyramids, and then you see something like this, and it's real. And everyone's waiting for this big change. And it was a real revolution. We don't know what revolution is. We have no idea. It was just wrenching to feel the energy, man, like I was guilty for being foreign to it all. I felt welcome—I didn't feel American. But I was lost in it. And then everything just goes silent for an hour, and I can't understand what everyone is saying but I don't have to. And then there's this big stir, and everything just erupts and there are people falling on the ground, praying, people leaping in the air, dancing and sh—, and there was just this—just this massive outpouring of passion like you had never seen—it was impossible not to get caught up in it. And it was almost sad but really just sacred, that there were no news cameras around, no reporters, nobody to record this moment. And I was this lone American boy, but I felt connected to it all. And I knew when I got back home I wanted to do something deterministic, something fully deliberate."

His moment brings me to my moment, and I'm transported. I haven't thought back to El Tabernaculo since that night at Santa's Pub. I'm in Europe, on my semester abroad, because I want to be an artist, but more importantly to feel like an artist. The bar is small, the owner modest and generous. I'm with some friends who took the same semester ride. It's Easter. The place is full for Easter. It's my birthday. I've just turned twenty. I'm sitting in a chunky wooden chair with a beer and a plate of sausage, and all around me are images of saints and the dying Jesus. Wall-to-wall, every inch of the place, is a fractured mosaic of Messiahs and Marys and saints all pious and penitent and pierced, and I'm stuffing my face with sausage and giggling like a child. I'm not laughing at the agony, but at my discomfort with the agony, which is really my discomfort with the agony surrounding me as I munch on sausage and gulp down a beer in the twilight cusp of Semana Santa, and I'm cramped with the icons of horrific passion, and I sip and I chew and I glance from image to image of Jesus bearing the splintered wood and the thorny crown and Mary weeping blood and I am more uncomfortable than I've ever been when it comes over me that I don't care anymore because it doesn't mean anything, and it's so perverse it's transcendent, and maybe I'm meant to celebrate what has come over me, or come to terms with it, with ambling into a perverse bar like a living art installation, my experiment with the glut of indulgence under the barrage of religion, and it has no bearing, and when I emerge drunken into the Spanish night I am free, and every moment thereafter has a dreamlike quality of maudlin ecstasy until I wake up the next morning and the world has become so relevant unto itself, because I've let go of something I finally deemed profanely irrelevant. I've decided that maybe there's nothing behind the curtain, that it's just images all the way around, and they reference each other, and I have to make of it what I can. I hop on a train to Paris and begin reading Camus.

We were both silent for a moment, lost in our own meditations of greater things, and each of us might have been about to say something profound and consequential when my phone buzzed and it was Greg Dickey calling. I answered without even telling Wick. There was a roaring cheer in the background and his voice cut on and off.

"...at the concert! Do you hear it?"

"What?" I asked.

"Sigur Rós! S... Rós! Neil, it's beautiful! Ther...the song and ... rows back, and everybody's just crying and hugging each... 'nd I don't even know these people and I feel like I'm..."

"Greg. Greg, I'll have to call you back, man. It sounds awesome, man."

I hung up. The intimacy had diffused, and I pictured myself in this overwhelming moment where Greg was, where nobody was afraid to be human in a crowd and fall in love with a song, no matter how much gibberish the lyrics were. And I will shamelessly say that I felt a tear in my eye for no particular reason other than surprise. It was a connection, I will establish that. It was a yearning for connection. I am not one to cry, and if Wick was one to cry,

I didn't see him do it. But in the acoustic darkness I felt like I could almost smell his soul crying.

Wick asked me if I was all right, and I was. I was jealous of Greg being at the concert, but I was glad for him. I had no words for what I could have said other than to express my regret at not getting tickets for the concert.

I wanted to stay over at Wick's place, because I was tired. I felt bad leaving him alone in there, but there was only one bed and I couldn't stand to sleep in a chair. I told him I'd call him sometime, and we could hang out, and I felt surprisingly relieved, as if I was now free from any duties, and we could relate as human beings ought to.

"I really do like the sketches, by the way," he told me again. "But I think I'll just go with one. Not sure which one yet."

I suddenly felt like I owed him something more than consolation, a truth I could offer, because he had shared his most intimate pearls, and I'd answered an inconsequential phone call.

"Your fans are full of abandon," I blurted out. "They're caught in a cycle of careless vacillation."

"Oh really?" he said sleepily.

"They just—here's how it is. They break your heart and then retreat into the safety of their own criticism. They're too afraid to love you. And then they let the next wave of fans pick up the pieces, and scorn them for it. And it's just a cycle that will repeat itself, an eternal return."

"That's—I don't know how to take that. But it's feeling pretty true right now."

"I just wanted to get that out," I said. It was the only time I ever said anything real to him about his music, and it wasn't even about his music, but fans of his music. I wanted to do a sketch of him right then and there and show it to the public, to give them a peek into the tortures of his life, if only he would be understood. From outside his window you could get a peek of the "No Promo" sign spread above the East Nashville area. It beat having any ads invading your view of the skyline. Here I am, the ad illustrator, telling you this with words.

I'm being hypocritical.

The next day I got a text from Kenna. It read,
"Sh— I'm pregnant."
She made it sound like I had something to do with it. She didn't call me to tell me, but texted me. It felt imprudent. I couldn't be burdened with being the first one with such information.

HER: ur the first 2 know.

ME: why?

HER: because u r. f— wat do i DO

ME: i don't know. it wasn't me. i feel like you should call Tab or somebody.

HER: she'll just judge me u know that

ME: i don't know why you are telling me this

HER: you ditched me that night with Dan

ME: it felt like you ditched us

HER: i can't deal with this sh—

ME: maybe you should see a priest or something

HER: im not gonna see a f—ing priest!

There was no telling what emotions she was experiencing on the other end, or what she thought I was feeling on mine. I was oddly glad that it was only in text. It was the last message she gave me and I didn't hear from her again for another week. I was perturbed that she had ditched me the night she met Dan the drummer, even though I had no particularly desirous feelings toward her. It was the principle of the matter, that I felt used, and didn't grasp why I was responsible for her decisions. If she needed me for some emotional reason, I suspected she would have at least called. I didn't feel any more crass than she was being with me. I knew she was going to get an abortion, and I knew it was the kind of thing that would make a lot of people upset. Whoever else she told, I was one of few, and it was information I didn't feel the need to be privy to. I tried to forget about it.

Later, Tab called me and asked me what had been going on with Kenna. I told her I hadn't spoken with her in weeks. I received another call from her later, this time guilting me for not doing something. As with Sedgwick before, it had apparently become my responsibility to do something.

"She told me," I said. "She didn't say anything about telling you or not telling you."

"Why didn't she tell me about it, Neil? It's a pretty big deal."

"How the H— should I know? I figured she would have."

It was Kenna she was mad at. Kenna, for telling me and not her, for ditching her with Sedgwick, even though she had ditched Kenna. I had had enough of being the middle man in such petty communications.

"She told you for a reason," said Tab. "And you just told her to go see a priest and hung up."

"What else am I supposed to do? I had nothing to do with it. She got with that drummer."

"She had an abortion, Neil."

"I wasn't going to stop her. It's not my body. I mean, what am I doing to do? Resort to a chauvinistic, religious hegemony?"

She hesitated over the phone. I wanted to tell her that Kenna's decision not to tell Tab in due time meant something, and that was between the two of them. Too late in my entangling role in the lives of others, I told someone that I had nothing to do with an issue only they could work out. It was beyond me. I felt hated for it. I began to grow increasingly misanthropic.

I'm being indelicate.

I was able to forget about it after Sam moved in with Joey and me. He and Samantha had been fighting too often to occupy the same space. They weren't able to work anything out. They had seemed to have broken a record for the longest honeymoon phase ever, but whatever fumes it ran on had dissipated after Burning Man.

"We held out for a while," he said. "I mean, it was only a few months. But it seemed like a while."

"Well, to be fair," I told him, "I don't think she ever wanted to grow up." I had thought the same might be true about him, but I was looking him in the face when I said it, and couldn't complete the criticism.

"She only knew relationships as fun," he said. "Okay, we both did a little. Before we were married, like, when we were dating, we just let each other date around for a while. Just an open relationship thing. Then we wanted each other back, and then decided to get married."

"So you're trying it again?" said Joey.

"Yeah, separating. I think it'll do some good. I really don't care if she sees other people again. I just need go get out and do my own thing for a while."

Joey and I put our arms around him. "Yeah. We'll go do our own thing."

We did our own thing. We hung out, the three of us. Samantha had begun posting pics of her and her girls having the most outrageous fun in the wake of the split, and so we did the same. We rallied with Sam to compete whimsically for the right to have a good time against the mournful separation. We played shuttlecock. We went to Cheekwood. We went to store outlets and bought the most outrageous pairs of sunglasses we could find. We went around town asking people if we could take pictures of ourselves with their pets. We took a road trip out to Roswell, because we could. And all the while we posted twice as many pictures as Samantha. We were lackadaisical victors.

Sam and Sam were what Greg Dickey called a Manic Pixie Dream Couple. Perhaps you've heard of the Manic Pixie Dream Girl, the stock character in films so free spirited and whimsical that they are actually one dimensional, static avatars of happy-go-lucky innocence whose only purpose is to create a change in the lives of starkly depressed male protagonists. Greg developed the concept of the MPDC, a couple who exemplifies these traits. In a film they would exist until the end of the credit roll and beyond, able to sustain themselves on their carefree quirkiness for an alleged everlasting unto everlasting.

"In real life," said Greg, "they eventually have to mature. And if they don't, they usually don't last. These are the couples you'd think might last forever, but in actuality they're sometimes one of the first to go. People say, 'Oh, look, they're just in their own little world.' But that world comes crashing down if they don't adapt to the world around them."

They are only a concept, not just to everyone around them, but unto themselves as well. Each one has crafted their expectations around the high of falling in love young and vibrant, not around the commitment of loving through time and hardship.

"They're just as messed up as everybody else," Dickey said. "And you have to come to terms with that in a relationship. You can't assign the other person your happiness and blame them when it doesn't work out. You each have to cultivate the other person's happiness selflessly. That takes devotion. Otherwise you're just teaching the world how to be bubbly, and eventually you'll fail miserably. Bust."

In another month, a fourth joined us in my apartment. The circumstances weren't so pleasant. Jules had wrecked his bike out near Inglewood. A cop had found him and charged him with being drunk in public, but not before taking him to the hospital. We went to see him at his apartment, where he was recuperating from a neck injury. We laughed at his neck cast — we couldn't resist. He wasn't so bad off physically, but he was downcast. He might have been ashamed to have been unable to hold his liquor, but even Jules had to have had a reason to drink so much and try to bike home. Joey and Sam looked at him in a way that told me Jules had been doing more than just romping through the seas of rye. Jules had found a handle for the pains of his divorce and whatever else he was juggling. We just took it as a past-time. It wasn't a thing he could admit to us. But we took him in. It wasn't a good idea for him to live alone. It wasn't good for any of us.

Besides, now we totaled four, and could assign ourselves the four humors. But the truth was, we were all sanguinary and melancholic, this cabal of ours. We were all cynical optimists with a realistic outlook on apathy. We were an equation coming together, fearless of ending in a zero sum.

I never got to talk with Sedgwick much, except for the time he called me and let me know that the record was about to come out. For weeks he had been bugged by a new urge to write, rather than take his new songs on tour.

"I have this melodic line in my head that never resolves," he said over the phone. "And every time it ascends it just changes key again. It's kind of like…did you ever listen to *Pet Sounds*? It's like something from *Pet Sounds*."

"I think you should up your production value," I said in jest. He took it honestly and was probably too insulted to continue the conversation.

There wasn't anything else after that. There was only my final submission of the cover art for the record, which I didn't hear back from him about until a week later. In a single text message, he said to me, "clever work."

And just as easily as my direct communications with Sedgwick began to fade out, third-hand knowledge, fourth-hand, fifth-hand and additional-integer-hand sightings of him came to me in whispers and news releases and tweets and radio blips across the short span of a week.

It was late September. The undergrad students had flooded back into town, to Vandy and State and Belmont and Lipscomb. Hockey season was gearing up. Joey had gotten a job at some amorphous internet-based creative solution startup. Cline was still a barista, still stuck working with and living with Amanda. I'd made a decent sum on a cover for a regional magazine. And Garrett Sedgwick made the news.

Frenchy tweeted that she saw Sedgwick alone outside Tequila Cowboy, sporting a beard and stumbling about drunkenly. Another bystander posted eight consecutive photos of him wandering aimlessly about Church Street on Instagram. He made the daily news the following day when he was recognized post-incident as the smelly young vagrant who accosted the owner of a convenience store because he wouldn't lend him his glasses.

A day later Jules informed us that Sedgwick nearly ruined a performance of *Sweeney Todd* at the Repertory. Wick took pictures with his phone, and even lit a cigarette before being escorted out. On his way out the door, he called Sweeney Todd a "cannibal fag," and flipped off the entire audience.

The only arrest that came out of this was from his refusal to pay for his food at China Buffet. According to reports, he threw his fortune cookie at the waitress and told her he wouldn't eat at a place where the food wasn't Chinese and the cooks weren't American. When the cops showed up he laughed and said they didn't get it, that his explosion was a piece of "performance art" meant to be interpreted as a commentary on the ironies of consumption in our society. He spent a night in jail.

It this was all a publicity stunt, it wasn't drawing enough attention, not even the negative kind. Only his most devoted fans noticed, and they were all quizzical about this sudden binge. This was a new Sedgwick, and more than praise and disappointment, the reaction mostly that of curiosity.

His last recorded communication was a tweet of the following Georgy Zhukov quote: "If the nation only knew their hands dripped with innocent blood, it would have met them not with applause but with stones."

It was the next morning that Garrett Sedgwick's body was found in the Cumberland River, fully dressed and fully drowned.

14
"CHICKEN IN BLACK"
feat. release and critical reception

According to Hank Scott, the single most revealing moment in Country Music history was the moment Johnny Cash was banned from the Grand Ole Opry in 1965. Hank Williams had been banned before him, and died before ever returning, but the antics of Hank Williams never amounted to Cash smashing the footlights out on stage in a drunken rage. Cash was a wild foal before the crowd, and it became a major incident. He had already been arrested for possession of Daxedrine and Equanil, but he dared to show up at the Opry and lose it all because of a heckler and a bad mic. In the one great venue home to Country fans, Cash appeared and made a ruckus like none before, a drama that could not remain behind the curtain for long.

It wasn't so much the moment itself as what transpired afterward. He spiraled further into drug use, told the Fed to stick it after starting a forest fire, divorced his wife. He had his religious awakening, fixed himself up, and changed his image on the basis of what nobody doubted was a true spiritual crisis. When everyone else paraded in the masquerade of rhinestone, Cash remained "the man in black." He could not be ignored by the establishment that often sought to chain him, and became a champion of the battered, genius fringe.

When Cash returned to the Opry with his own show, Nashville was a true scene once again, however provincial. Throwback Country listeners, farmers, cowboys and churchgoers blended into the Ryman with hippies, college Joes and outlaws. And then Cash met Dylan.

The stage is a revealing place. Cash revealed he was the first of his kind in the 20th century. Beginning with his near career-shattering explosion on stage, Cash could have disappeared forever, and Country would have never gained its most enduringly authentic and influential performer — instead, the crowd that night witnessed a man too vast to be contained, an iconoclast against what a Country musician — or any musician, for that matter — could become.

"No more Garrett?" said Joey to me, on the day we heard the news. It was the only time I recalled having heard someone refer to him by only his first name. He said it like a child does when they first learn that animals can die. The context was doled out in portions over time.

"I thought he was one of them homeless," said the man who found Sedgwick bobbing up against the riverbank. "Didn't know he was a rock star. Very sad, either way."

A cocktail of drugs was found in his system, including alcohol and barbiturates. An artist who claimed to have met with him the day before used the words "depression" and "paranoia" in a later interview, reducing the complexities of Sedgwick's soul down to an amateur psychoanalysis.

The night before, Garrett Sedgwick was the one passenger on the General Jackson who didn't make it off, and the captain's log recorded a confirmed sighting of a passenger known by several young people by the name of "Wick" leaping off the side and swimming to shore. A policeman had been dispatched to apprehend the young fellow and take him. From the bits gathered from gossip, news reports, public posts, and my estimation of Sedgwick's state of being in those last hours, here is what I gathered to have occurred:

Around six thirty or so, Garret Sedgwick is hanging around the Grand Ole Opry, the one place he dreamed to play as a young man. Shortly thereafter, he sees the General Jackson preparing for a night cruise and thinks to himself, "why not?" He skips out on the dinner with all the old tourists on their anniversaries and hangs over the end of the deck, staring at the skyline of the departing city. He's riding an authentic paddlewheeler, a modern, diesel derivation of the steamboats of old now canonized like portraits in their own gilded legacy by the likes of Twain.

Eventually some young college kid recognizes him and points him out to his friends. Sedgwick removes all signs of brooding and playfully snaps photos with these carnivorous pests who have come to gawk at the unconventionality of this artist who, like them, was cruising down the river on a showboat, for no reason, other than the self-serving condescension of a self-groomed youth. They couldn't have been more excited if Bill Murray had shown up. He leads them in throwing firecrackers off the side of the ship until a crewman splits them up. Later, they break into a supply room and drink bootleg whiskey. When the old people have emerged from their dinner and populated the decks, Sedgwick and the little crowd of kids blend in with them and head to the sky deck to smoke. The band is playing Elvis Presley's "Suspicious Minds" atop the boat and Sedgwick is grinding against two girls. They can't believe this is happening, and they are snapping so many photos.

It's past ten, and the ship has already turned back and is heading back to port. The band has given a salute to the troops, and the patriotic balcony flags are flapping in the cool wind, draped secure against the rails. The crowned stacks are the first signal of the grand haul being returned. Sedgwick lifts himself up over the edge of the stern as if to throw himself into the cycle of the wheel before him. He tips himself over the side, somnambulating, limp, by accident or grace, and there is a thud before he hits the water and causes all the young kids to laugh.

Sedgwick is struggling to do backstrokes as the hip kids wave and chortle. The combination of high proof alcohol and the sound of the thud would have told a more sober crowd that the troubling way he swam was a cause for alarm, but instead they guffaw at the overwrought manner with which he flings his arms and legs against the water. They must really think he's a riot.

"We didn't know he was drowning for real," says one of the anonymous witnesses later. "We thought he was, like, trying to be transcendent."

A thousand passengers and not a soul there to save him. They will not anchor down until they came to port, and nobody calls up to the crew. If anybody sees him by the time they dock, he is hardly perceptible as even the shape of a person, and not even one flailing about. He's a rose floating down the river, and nobody can disturb him. Everyone disembarks and huddles into their coats as a heavy cold wind brushes early fall leaves over their heads and into the Cumberland. He drowns somewhere in front of Opry Mills. He is only twenty-seven.

It is kind of ironic. The ship was first christened the day he was born.

I didn't mind knowing Sedgwick in a way nobody else did, even after his death. Nobody knew to refer to me for any questions or remarks, and if I had wanted such attention, nobody would have believed me that we had become so connected for such a brief time. I didn't feel I deserved it.

Right after the news broke out, Bruce Fey contacted me. Actually, he came to my door. It was surprising, and I suspected he was going to deliver me some final words or keepsake he had been given charge of. But this man whom Sedgwick had reluctantly allowed into his professional life came only to settle the question of why he had become attached to such a musician in the first place. He stood there solemn and urgent, two moods mismatched like a coffin salesman with a golden Rolex.

"Look, let's just make this short," he said, as if under orders to carry out some task repugnant to his soul. "I think you know why I'm here. Did he give it to you?"

"No, what?" I asked.

"We can play games, but seriously, he's gone, man. I just wanna know if you have it."

He talked like he had years of practice cooking up crocodile tears, but at a moment's notice if he could summon the power of an army and a stamped warrant he would barge into my apartment and look for *it*, whatever it was.

"He seriously didn't give it to you, did he?"

"No," I said. "He didn't give me anything but a paycheck. What do you want?"

"Look, man," he said, with the condescension of a high school guidance counselor. "We're all shocked by what happened, right? We're all just trying to do our part to pick up the pieces. I don't think it's a good time for this any more than you do, but it's f—ing important that I know what he did with the notebook."

The black notebook, the one from Hoyt Murdock. A sufficient explanation as to the origins of Sedgwick's rise to underground stardom arose from none other than this dodgy clown. Either Sedgwick had gotten lucky after arriving on the scene, or the Murdock notebook was his ticket to the murky tunnels of anywhere.

"I don't have it," I said. "He never gave it to me."

"All right," he said, rolling his tongue in his mouth and shooting quick glances inside my apartment. "All right. I believe you, man. Just—If there's anything I can do—"

"You can leave," I said.

He put up his hands and turned to head out, but the look of some urge came over him, almost like he was going to knock me out and pilfer through my belongings. He aimed his hand like a five-barrel gun at me and grew red.

"You know, I don't know if he ever told you this or not, but I practically made Garrett Sedgwick, all right? He was nothing when he came to me."

I showed the disgust in my face. "Came to you?"

"Yeah, you know that little 'hobo on the sidewalk' routine he started out with? Running on his own steam? You know what he really did? He came to me with that notebook and you know what he did? He negotiated with me. He said he had the 'lost songbook of Hoyt Murdock' and he'd work out a deal with me over it. All I had to do was supply connections."

"That's an easy story," I said. "Why don't you go to his biographer with it? I'm sure it'll all come out."

"I set him up," said Fey, stabbing his chest with his hand. "His first gig in Nashville? His first record contribution? His first opener? I even bought him a new change of clothes because he smelled so bad."

"Well aren't you a saint," I muttered.

"The kid was off his rocker. He was trying to doom himself to fail—what with his little 'undiscovered' act. Picking the worst street corners to play at, using that name—'Sedgwick?' He begged me for a favor and every time he did something to screw himself over. Never failed."

"Sounds like you didn't make him after all," I said. "Sedgwick was bigger than you, or me, or himself. You think you know him better because he was desperate when he came to you? I know your business. You only deal with the desperate, the spoiled and the dying."

"Kids like you," he said. "You bite the hand that feeds you. You and him and everyone else. I wasted too much time on that kid. He could have been twice as much a hit."

"And twice the f—ing tool you are," I said.

"F— you," he said. I slammed the door. It was the only time I remember talking that way to a man nearly twice my age. I hated that sociopath. My scorn for him bled into a scorn for anybody and everybody. I was feeling incredibly misanthropic.

The notebook turned up, all right. It was listed among the possessions found on Sedgwick's body: one drenched black notebook containing soggy, illegible notations. It satisfied me that Bruce Fey and his record connections would never get it. Neither would anyone else. It was tragic and it was beautiful, it was poetic and it was abortive. Despite Bruce Fey's sickening yet believable spin, Sedgwick had ultimately gone against his impulse and refused to let the men in suits take control. He crafted himself more than they could. He had the opportunity to use every single one of Hoyt Murdock's unreleased songs, and never tell a soul they weren't his own, but he held it close for that one day when he could feel worthy. Now the songs were with him in oblivion, and in all their elegiac symbolism these unsung songs were laid to rest along with their last guardian, and one could imagine that the words and notes all bled into the Cumberland and rolled across the country that gave birth to Hoyt Murdock, Chance Merritt and every other musician once young and fervently pining for greater stages.

I'm being pretentious.

Tab didn't say a word to me after the news broke. I knew she knew only because I knew that Virg knew. The news might or might not have shown up on his news feed, but when it did he posted, "Sad to see the untimely death of a great artist." As to his not mentioning that Sedgwick was an acquaintance, this either could have been out of spite or decency. Maybe he saw no reason to mention he knew someone famous just because they died. Who needs to know?

When I asked Tab about it, she told me she was sad. I pressed her for more, because I wanted to be sure she wasn't torn up about it all. She grew stiff and defensive.

"What am I supposed to say?" she said, beginning to show tears, real tears. "It's horrible. He was a nice guy all his life. I hate that things were the way they were between us. I hate that the last time we talked it was so awkward and horrible."

My scorn for Bruce Fey and every other parasite out there had gotten to me. I found myself blaming Tab for his death. She didn't know the pressures of his career, didn't see him in the basement of his heart spinning new gold.

She couldn't have known how much it ate him up inside. On top of all this, she was married. Something in our culture must have shown Sedgwick that if their own relationship had dissolved so quickly and so easily, so could her marriage. I viewed Virgil as a charlatan half the time, but the truth was that he was a match for her, and he showed fidelity to her in every way. He flirted often with well-phrased speculations and commentaries, and against his devout faith these very notions had the potential to become mistresses, but in his love for Tabitha there was nothing phony or fleeting.

My proximity to Sedgwick had subconsciously moved me to feel that tearing Tab and Virg apart would be remotely fair and true. Even as a cousin I hadn't been protective enough. What was truthfully unfair was Tab being pressed by the overwrought signs of a boy bending over backwards to break her marriage bond. If she had any struggle to be expressive about her feelings, she had every reason to. Yet it would have been so easy for her to have simply told Chance that she had found a mate for life, that she meant every word of love for him, and that she hoped for the best for that handsome, talented, misunderstood boy she once loved years ago. Surely that would have been easy.

Sedgwick's funeral was more underground than he was. There were close friends who didn't even know where it was held or when. Since about twenty people showed up besides the family, and nobody was there to verify who wasn't, everyone spoke of it as if they had been there, as if it was something to have seen. I didn't go, so I didn't get to meet the family. Tab and Virg weren't there either. It was like one of those secret marriages people have, when afterwards it is announced in the paper that the family was invited to a "private ceremony." It was like one of those high school suicides where all the girls who picked on the freak begin to frequent the guidance counselor and cry at the candlelight vigil because they "just had no idea she was so lonely."

Another guy came to my door, one I didn't recognize until I saw the shrub he was carrying. "It's Sean," he said. He was the roommate whose face I never saw, the IT expert, or whatever. "Um, I think Garrett wanted you to have this." He handed me the banzai tree.

"Wait," I said, incredulous. "What do you mean he wanted me to?"

For a second I thought that the drowning was a hoax or part of an elaborate and premeditated suicide. But Sean's look of hesitancy told me that it was his own guess. The few things Sedgwick had kept at his place he was merely disposing of as gently as he could. I was mad at him at first, but his regretful face ran deeper than Bruce Fey's manufactured grief. Here was a guy short on expressive communication skills trying to cope with the belongings of a ghost in his apartment.

I kept the tree for a couple weeks, then gave it to Tab. I just told her I'd come across it and thought she would like it. It was the closest thing I could do to associate Sedgwick's five-year pursuit with some sort of consolation gift, as if to imagine that he would somehow live on in his own houseplant, an organic sentinel over her domestic life. I have to admit it was perverse, like I'd sold a lampshade made of human skin.

Later, Jackson invited me up to Sedgwick's apartment to pick out a chair. He had a copy of Sedgwick's keys and said that his parents took only a few things and called the rest of it junk. I went for the Gustav Stickley. It felt like a nice chair to sit and do sketches in.

As for the album art, I was one of the few to receive a review copy with the final printing, including my art. After much meditation, and alongside Sedgwick's scrutiny, I had rejected every solid idea for a single image — a homopolar engine, a single sushi roll, a salmon in a top hat, a cascade of chevrons, the face or figure of a girl faintly resembling Tab. Sedgwick was a self-induced iconoclast nobody understood and nobody deserved to see the true face of. True, nearly all of my drafts ended up as small doodles on the back cover next to the list of songs. But as for the cover itself, nothing else could be represented than that non-image that befuddled me until I made it Garret Sedgwick's and his only. On white, in bold, plain black stenciled letters, a single message was the face of the record:

NO PROMO

It was a reference everyone would know and yet nobody would know. No explanation for the "advertisement" ever arose, and it had disappeared shortly before the album release. It was an inside joke to anyone who had seen it, and a rumor would live on that Sedgwick was behind the ad, a long-term viral campaign for his own album, which would have been the only promotion given at all. At first I thought of going with the Gotham font for its strength, but it just felt too New York, too *GQ*. Garamond was flexible, but too plain. Although Baskerville had an effect of drawing the eye in and almost hypnotizing the mind, I went with a variation, Boudini, which was the same Nirvana used for their logo. I sketched the font by hand, stripping it of elegance. Officially, the album was sold with the listed title, *No Promo: The August Session*.

Here was Garrett Sedgwick, an elusive artist who had done everything he could to alienate his fans, and yet done all but risen past the edge of subterranean glory. He might have been laughing at us all. Some were even crude enough to postulate that he arranged his death in accordance with his album release, just to spite the scene and go out with a bang. Thereafter Garrett Sedgwick became great. *No Promo* became his bestselling album yet. When it came out, you'd never seen such an uproar. It was too hot to touch, but everybody was scrambling to touch it and appraise it, their nerves seared by the urgent hype of the tragedy and equally shocking genre reversal.

Nelson Peters of *Rolling Stone* declared that the "simplicity and openness of this last record trumps all his others. What seems like a romance with Folk Country in the first listen peels back in the second go-round to reveal what could very well be Sedgwick's mysterious roots." "Finally, an album that tells us Garret Sedgwick belongs here!" shouted Megan Weir of *The Contributor*. "Wick, you will be remembered in this town forever." In *the Daily Telegraph*, Erwin Thomas bid everyone to "treat this resonant, real record with reverence," risking ridicule with his profuse alliteration. Writing for *Nashville Scene*, Kirk Tuttle would have made Joyce blush with his opening sentence: "Anyone who suspects that either contemporary Country is no longer the real McCoy or that Indie Rock is too inflated with itself, the last will and testament of Garrett Sedgwick that is his posthumous album epitomizes the performer as outlier striving to earn respect from a crowd fatally disappointed by genuine music, a surprisingly old-school acoustic Folk Rock croon-fest that displays the late performer's idiomatic attention to the craft of songs, regardless of how the people will receive him."

After five years of closeted admiration cloaked in backhand insults directed toward his albums, *Pitchfork* displayed symptoms of amnesia by astonishingly praising *The August Session* with a rare score of 10 and prose brimming over with flawless adoration:

"No one has ever witnessed the creation of a supernova. No one. We will never be privileged to take in the explosion of a galaxy's sole protagonist as it radiates more than its weight in luminous ejecta of neutrinos and nuclea. Your corneas would be obliterated. He could have given us that, but we didn't deserve it.

Instead, Garrett Sedgwick was hunched over his guitar in pain, eyes rolling back into his closed lids, a conduit for a message from deep within the all-soul, etching into a spindle his ten songs like irrefutable commandments. Every word was a dying word, a Deuteronomy of the verse before it, preluding departure and the enormity of consequence. The critic in me mechanically catches the inspiration of the likes of Townes van Zandt. The human in me just weeps. Such a soundscape came into this world bastardized and alone, like the persona that has inexplicably wandered in and out of town to disseminate his revelation through six strings.

The previous perfidiousness of our beloved artist's preculminant achievements must attest to a cosmic anti-joke. His other releases, and maybe every other record to ever have been cut, is mere child's play. Dare to make a comparison? Apples and plastic. Establishing its genre is useless. The album is like Robert Burns' 'Comin' Through the Rye' as interpreted by Holden Caulfield— doomed to be misunderstood and misplaced, and all the better for it. These songs incomprehensibly make you want to take the Eucharist. Shakyamuni is said to have stepped down from his enlightenment to make way for Sedgwick's new album.

Hearing *The August Session* is to be equivocated with a man speaking to an ass who spoke to an angel because somehow it was the only way. If you listen close you can hear Garret Sedgwick grow despondent on his own iconography, melt himself down, and rise, Phoenix-like, more natural, more pure than we could have imagined him. In between stanzas are sighs you can only visualize. When you do, you will get chills that last for weeks.

Sedgwick takes his final bow with a cover of a lost Hoyt Murdock tune, embarking on a frontier from which he will never return. It begs the question of where this record came from, let alone where Wick was first born into the world. We are being treated to Benjamin Button, only in reverse. Aged, yet innocent; discomforting, yet allaying; impoverished, yet layered; textured, yet humble; visionary, yet sober. Every album you've ever heard will be scuttling to the rhythmic pulse of this one here. A distress signal of the soul emanates from the lips of this prophet like a new color out of Heaven. Garrett Sedgwick is the uncontested coolest carbon based human performer.

No Promo has done what no album previously could: In this spinning plate we hear a very profound and very captivating human message about seeking happiness. He gave us an event horizon from a telescope, and it's the closest thing to a sunset we blind mortals will ever see. It's an authentic record, though somewhat derivative of the "outlaw" Country of the 60's and mastered a little sloppily. It's a pretty decent listen."

Ok, well, nearly flawless adoration. I imagine that after the "publish" button was hit everyone put a mopey hand on each other's shoulders in resignation. Like the boy who cried wolf, the magazine spoke and nobody believed it was sincere. The 10.00 rating didn't help much either. For about a week #sh—fork trended across the Twittersphere.

"I call shenanigans on all these reviews," said Greg Dickey. "If that album had been released when he was alive, everybody would have just let out a big high-pitched 'Whaaaaaaat?' Like he was the first artist to ever break the mold? Shenanigans."

"I don't care," said Hank. "I love it. I would die in peace if I put out a record that real that sold that well. And that Hoyt Murdock song is legit. I want to know how he got the rights to that."

And yes, in case you didn't catch it in the review, Sedgwick couldn't help but take one song from the notebook of Hoyt Murdock and pay homage with it as his last and final track, giving the old timer full credit for the writing. The rest ran in inky streams out from his side pocket like water and blood, never to be heard.

I'm being pretentious again.

The news of death and the post-humous album eventually cascaded into obscurity. After Sedgwick's solo debut, *Orange*, was re-mastered and rereleased, purchases of the original lo-fi recording were made by those who "wanted to hear his early stuff, before he went and changed."

You can't question the integrity of a martyr. To a world who never knew his heart, Garrett Sedgwick was a martyr, his soul scourged by a bloodthirsty industry and treacherous followers.

Immediately after the news of his drowning, a comedian tweeted, "Sedgwick always was one to swim against the current. #irony."

This one received the worst backlash, but there were others. At a party I witnessed one guy announce his discovery that by default of his death, Sedgwick was "just like Buckley." Cline was there and lost it on the guy.

"Dude, shut the f— up!" he shouted in a severely crowded room. "Buckley wasn't on drugs when he drowned. Wick was on a bunch of sh—! He was so f—ed up! The two do not compare at all!"

They nearly broke into fisticuffs until we broke them up.

"Sedgwick didn't get the goodbye he deserved," Joey said to me later. "Warren Zevon got a better goodbye."

"It feels almost like a prank," I told him. It was hard not to tell people the story I was convinced Sedgwick didn't want me to tell. I also feared I would suffer from gossiper's guilt. I didn't want his narrative to draw attention to myself, especially if nobody believed it.

Although it would be followed by bottomless catalogues of recording anthologies and performance bootlegs assembled from the back of Sedgwick's proverbial closet, none of the songs on any album released before or after in any form matched the cohesion, sincerity, or genre-bending audacity of *No Promo*. His loss was his music's gain. Sedgwick's death was poured like a tonic over his work, and he was invincible. Suddenly nobody hated him anymore and everyone had always been a fan, even the ones who just discovered him.

He had said to me once, speaking of Cobain, "It's why you want to become an artist, so that when you die, they resurrect you." He never resurrected, never walked through the streets of Nashville afterward, never showed up at my door and had a long night's talk with me. I had my own stages of grief for this complicated dreamer tortured by the public eye. So many of them turned away from him just as so many others arrived. Where did they all come from? Where were they at when he needed them?

"Remember when Warhol invented the idea of fifteen minutes of fame?" I asked Joey.

"I don't remember if I was there, because I wasn't born yet," said Joey. "But yeah."

"I think we've truly reached the democratization of celebrity," I said. "Just look at what social media is capable of."

"Are you lamenting, Neil?"

"No. I'm accepting."

"You seem real down since the other day when Sedgwick died. I didn't know he was your Elvis."

"I prefer him being my Beatle," I said, because I had no other mechanism with which to mask my true connection to Chance Merritt.

"Don't let it get to you," said Joey, with comically melodramatic alarm. "Don't slip away from me, Neil."

"Here's an observation, though," I said. "People have always had fans nobody knows of. But through these latent outlets they can spot each other in their anonymity and gain their fifteen minutes. They can feed off celebrity and even replicate it. They expurgate their own opinions in the cloud, realtime, and because a few people clicked 'follow' just one time, they all feel like they have a following that validates their every thought."

"But what is the function of celebrity?" said Joey. "How much social capital does it hold?"

"It validates everything you say," I said. "Just look at your feed right now."

He looked at his feed. "Is this real life?"

I closed my laptop. "Oh well. It'll all be expunged in the annals."

Joey laughed. "Neil."

"What?"

"Annals."

I laughed.

I would be overexerting my insight if I assumed that somehow Sedgwick's martyrdom had somehow affected Joey. I would be conflating correlation and causation. I knew there were also the plights of Jules and Sam to factor in. But the fog that hung around after the incident seemed to hang around everything. It affected me. I clung to the *foma* that all these things were connected, because it pushed me to listen to Joey in his time of need, which blind-sided me even more than the drowning.

I went out playing squash with Joey one night. Joey was never one to exert himself, but on this evening he exerted himself. I was barely exerting myself, but I was beating Joey. I would serve and serve and the ball would ricochet and next thing I knew he was grunting and flinging his racket against the wall and pounding the wall, and no matter how hard he swung both he and the ball were trapped in the cube, and he whimpered through it swing after swing, and I was concerned for him, and finally he slumped against the wall and slid down to the floor as if a firing squad had done him in.

This was Joey like I had never seen him. I sat next to him. Everything we said would echo against the walls of the court.

"What's gotten to you?" I said. "Are you slouching toward misanthropy?"

"It's just *Zah-mah-ki-bo*," he said. "It's fated."

"What's the matter?"

He repeatedly nodded the back of his head against the wall. "I think I have to get out of here."

"You're not talking about the squash court," I said.

"I'm not talking about the squash court," he said. We sat in silence, until the silence echoed loudly.

"I miss her voice sometimes," he said. It was April, his ex.

"Are you thinking you want to get back together?"

"No. No, it wouldn't be the same. But I've lied to myself that I've gotten over it. The whole universe seems to be rather unfair lately. I saw this thing on the news about another drone bombing—I've been in a bad way all day. I don't feel like doing anything."

"So it's a bad day," I said. "It's not your fault. Allow things to happen to you."

"Things aren't happening," he said, slumping. "That's part of the problem. Neil, I've gotta commit to something. Otherwise it's suicide by tiny increments."

"That rings a bell. Who are you evoking?"

"Nick Hornby. *High Fidelity*."

"Oh."

"I've got to stop just appreciating things. I need to contribute now. It's about time I contributed because I figure I'm going to die."

"You're living in my apartment," I said. "That's a stellar contribution."

Joey broke a long gaze at nothing in particular that was hovering up in the ceiling somewhere. "You've ever had that thing happen to you where you repost a really good quote and then somebody mentions that the person who said it was a drunk or a philanderer or a slave-owner?"

"Sort of," I said. "That's why I don't repost quotes."

"As if even Hitler couldn't have said something inspiring," said Joey. "I can't stand those black-and-white people."

"Man," I said. "I didn't know you'd get yourself down over one guy on the internet."

"It just infuriated me," said Joey. "We're not making any progress. We're not learning from anything. Humanity's not learning anything. Is that us?"

Seeing Joey robbed of his usual self drove me to my own malaise. I had romanticized his outer serenity, avoiding the hints of an intangible melancholy brooding underneath. I'd always thought that in his moments of silence he was gazing innocently at some hovering glow none of us could see, but for all I knew he was gazing fearfully into the center of a confusing universe. There wasn't much I could think of to do for him. Even he had his limits when being harried by life. And because I could not help but connect this to Sedgwick, supposing that even I may have been a degree of separation between one mess and another, I fell into a deeper malaise. For the time being we went out for tea and talked. Then we went home and I told him to read some Salinger.

15
"SUN GREETS THE SKY"
feat. the coming of the narrative to an entropic close

I'm optimistic about the future. I feel like you have to be when you approach a dead end. Whenever I feel considerably misanthropic, I invest my thoughts in the prospect of futurism. As an artist, I've found that I have to believe in what I visualize, even if it is not yet here or statistically possible. At the hands of humanity, devastation is possible, but reality can crescendo upward to infinite improvements at an exponential rate. I need only adjust my paradigms to fit my will to power over my surroundings.

One day I woke up with a potent poignancy hanging over me like an eyeball, and I came to the dreadful realization that I was, with impenetrable snark, dwelling in a rebellious imperative of my own identity, assimilating it as a pastiche out of the refuse of discarded cultural abnormalities, and this tongue-in-cheek incarnation was true regardless of whether I denied it or accepted it. I have construed with all self-consciousness that I have scrutinized my way into an inevitably smug cave of self-deprecation for which there is no means of recourse.

You see, readers, why I have forced myself unscrupulously to remain optimistic.

When I told Tab how I'd been feeling, because as my cousin she could read it on my face, she suggested that I volunteer at a soup kitchen to regain my faith in humanity. It seemed like too simple a solution. It was kind of her not to invite me to her church, where I likely would have slipped further into despondency, with all the talk of an eternity forwarded to another time.

I'm almost thirty. I have another young eternity to ride out. I'm supposed to hook up with someone or remain lonely, unless I latch on to my entrepreneurial dream. I'm supposed to be too clever for dreams. We're supposed to paddle upstream, against the prevailing mood, delaying the delivery of the future until it is ours.

When we hit this age, our about this age, we are abruptly as young as we remember our parents being. We are those who do not cease to be teenagers until around the time we reach the age our parents were when we saw them in their god-like eminence of our earliest memories. We are as old as they were before they became imperfect to us, before we first rolled our eyes at them. We cannot help but delay the fulness of such adulthood. Straightway we cling to reckless immaturity.

Historically speaking, we are the culmination of generations who matured latently. By the time we have graduated college, give us about five more years, and we'll show you. We cannot commit to adolescence; we have grown past it. We cannot commit to adulthood; we have sworn never to emulate it. Our maturity is as ephemeral as the reality before us. We were those who took ourselves seriously when our peers assembled in frat houses and made fools of themselves. We obviate the onset of deliberate responsibility, and for this we believe we are ahead of the curve of generations. We will soon be ready to become something, as soon as we figure this and that out.

I consider myself an intelligent person. At this point in my life I can't become anything seriously.

I'm being obnoxious.

One of the reasons I was able to sustain my sanity through the malaise of that fall after the Sedgwick debacle was the knot of influences I was able to closely surround myself with. But before long Jules was leaving us. He wasn't meant for this town and he knew it. His plans were to move to Portland to find better venues for his beer crafting and theater work in that little village by the sea where nobody would mock his beard. We threw him a party. Joey and I played a duet of "Creep" on guitar with ironic attachment, and everyone laughed when we totally butchered the bridge in shaky falsetto. I hated the bridge anyway.

Jules slapped us all on our shoulders and smiled with the assurance that he would march to the ocean with a blithe and hearty song. I was in part jealous of him, because I would have loved to live in such a town and design my own dwelling on the edge of the coast and walk a dog up and down the beach strand in the mornings and do all my freelance work from home as I looked out at the Pacific. I was also in part worried for him, because he would be further from his home and away from the only friends who knew he had once wrecked his bike and wrecked himself after having too much beer. I wanted assurance he wasn't going to march headlong into the ocean itself.

The new trinity then became Joey, Sam, and myself, a trio of like-minded bachelors. We were one man down to play shuttlecock in the park, but a game of Scrabble with coffee would always do. Despite the interference on my work, I knew I needed roommates.

Not long after that Greg Dickey informed me that he was leaving the entire country to go to China. He was putting aside his current teaching career to pursue a ministry that involved the dual efforts of teaching the English language and teaching Christianity. He was thrilled to help the population learn the language skills necessary to gain mobility in a globalized world, but more thrilled to participate in the real purpose of the mission. "Church growth is actually really booming over there," he said. "The government kind of cracks down on baptisms and evangelists, but they allow citizens to openly practice faith. I really want the opportunity to encounter my beliefs in a different environment like that, and truly appreciate it for what it is, out of the whole 'Christian America' context where it's just taken for granted."

"If it's what you love doing," I said, "but it does sound a bit like propaganda being met with propaganda."

"See, that's the thing with our generation," he said, about to explode. "I don't mean to insult you, Neil, but what you said just demonstrates what really gets to me about the big crisis of our generation, is just this distrust and rejection of real religion."

I was a skeptic, and I was already used to Greg getting on his soapbox, so I humored him.

"We can't bear to see even the real thing," he said, "because it confronts us. We turn away from it. It's almost a visceral reaction, like an allergy. I grew up with so many people who had this wellspring of faith—just massive amounts of spiritual resources—and they were just apathetic about it. They never let it take root."

"I feel like you're talking about me," I said.

"If I am, I am," he said, touching my arm respectfully. "But I'm not going to hide it from you and cower away from it, because it's true for our generation as a whole. I have to go back to Cameron for this one."

"Yeah, Cameron. Who else?"

"Well, she's just a great example of this. You'd say black, she'd say white. You'd say up, she'd say down. It was like she didn't stop being a Christian because of an actual epiphany she had, but because it seemed too normal for her growing up, and so she didn't trust it. She didn't really want to examine herself. Truth wasn't even on her radar of interest."

"I don't have a radar of interest," I said, half mocking his metaphor. "Maybe I need to get one."

"I'm being serious here, Neil. I'm trying to be honest with you." Greg's eyes grew wide and his voice whiney in the way he always did when offended.

"Sorry," I said. "It's just I get annoyed by whenever Cameron comes up. She comes up a lot."

"I'm sorry. I just think of her a lot. Not in the unrequited way. I am over her. I really am. But I still love her, as a friend, and I don't care what guy she's with. It's just her soul."

"You paraded a lot of girls since her," I said. "Either you're a mack daddy or you're looking for a rebound."

"That's a sound observation," said Greg. "I think I'll go with the mack daddy option. But I have been trying too hard. Maybe not to get another girl, but I think I tried too hard to cultivate a perfect relationship with every girl since to make up for things going so sour with Cameron."

"Sometimes, man, sometimes you just gotta let go."

"I am finally letting go. I think China's gonna be good for me. I need to refresh myself as much as I want to help the people there. God isn't calling me to this because I've got it figured out. I'm being called in order to figure out more. I've got to step away from the dating scene and the fading faith I see around me."

"Sounds like you've grown pretty cynical."

"I have. And who hasn't? But I'm actually pretty hopeful. I think coming back I'll have more things figured out. From talking with others, I've gotten that people over there are more thankful, more sincere. If anything, I'm only bitter about our culture. I have no faith in our culture at all. It's like the song 'Rococo.' Have you heard 'Rococo'?"

"I have heard 'Rococo.'"

"We just build things up to burn them back down again. Faith is included. The way things keep going people will start to crave legitimate faith, where it's not born into you because you were just brought up in it and then you wander off, but you were wandering and you found it."

"I just hope you don't bully anybody into it," I said. "I hate propaganda."

"I wouldn't," said Greg, ever sensitive. "I want it to be legitimate for everybody. I want it to endure."

"You don't want anybody to end up like me?"

"You're a great guy, Neil. And I think you give me and everyone else a good reason to reexamine everything we're doing."

"When you come back," I told him, "I'll buy you four gramophones so you can listen to *Zaireeka* the way it was meant to be heard."

He laughed hard. "Thanks," he said, as if we had just finished a therapy session. "I needed this."

He hugged me strongly. I laughed.

I envied Greg's profuse optimism, however grounded in his questionable traditions of faith. I couldn't draw the excuse that he had been bought and sold into a priestly hegemony. He was critical. He shared my tastes in music. He judged me little. I would miss having him around.

Small town or large, people don't have to skip town to disappear from your lives. Frenchy met a guy, and they got pretty serious, so that train left town. I saw Kenna once, at a party. We didn't talk. We had nothing to say to each other, and the awkwardness of the severed line and the memories around it weren't worth the protocol of catching up. I was glad to see her alive and well. I worried for some time that she might have been sucked into a dimly lit world of cocaine and bourbon. This was a rare and prudentially conservative instinct, born as most conservative instincts are, out of some experience of cataclysm, be it war or plague or terror. Her abortifacient measures made me recall every warning I'd received in youth, as if by being a male in her life I had some responsibility to prevent or control her destiny. No guy would ever be good enough for her, because no guy could treat her as well as her iPhone.

Tab and Virg stayed in Nashville for a while, but I hardly saw them. Our lives were growing busier, and there was something about our connection to Sedgwick that smothered all our juvenile memories. I couldn't trouble Tab too much with reminiscence. Within a year, though, they both packed their bags and made the move to New York. Virg was finally accepted into a seminary and began work on his Doctorate. Tab would try and return to her law and language studies in some form or another. They would settle in that cosmopolitan metropolis they had longed for. There was boldness in them, although it was reserved by a desire to speak and act without rashness. You get around their kind and you sense that something is about to happen soon. I'm impressed by the conversions and dedicated acts of service they bring about. They were seeking an abundant life, and were on their way to finding it. The future held something for the likes of Tab and Virg, and whatever it was they would do next.

Caraway the dog died shortly thereafter. I know, I had meant to leave Tab and Virg on a strong note, but I figured readers would want to know. They made a big deal about it, posting this long thing on Facebook about the day they took the dog in and how special he was to them. It was a lot to invest in, compared to the loss of Chance Merritt. Maybe that's why it was worth mentioning.

My exposure to Chance Merritt made everything I was privy to seem less than triumphant. Even if Tab did share blame in Sedgwick's demise, she shared it as a particle in a roaring crowd of cold critics. Hers was only a failure to communicate to him the word "never," as if marrying someone wasn't shouting it enough. Virgil's knowledge of and attitude toward it all was inconsequential to his devotion to his wife. That paternal part of me had no fear for their survival as a couple. They loved each other, and they loved their new city. Every other word they breathed was a word of love for their new city, and hinted within it was a word of love they had pledged to one another. But not many people were lining up to play a song about that. There's no heartbreak in such a thing. But I suppose that makes up for the dead dog.

I experienced something akin to depression as I watched everyone move away from me. It had started with Jules and Greg, followed by Tab and Virg.

Eventually, even Joey was loosened from the cradle. He had been long subdued, and one day the glow returned to his face. He was once again excited with life, with the inner belief that freedom and transformation and self-realization were possible, and were out there somewhere.

"Neil," he said to me one morning as he sat on a chair by my bed. His angelic voice was restored. "Neil, I'm leaving."

"No, man. You can't." I begged him with a tone of mock sorrow, to hide the fact that I really was perturbed.

He smiled assuringly. "Yes. I'm leaving for Korea."

"But the war's over," I pleaded, yawning.

"War never ends," he said. "It's what makes us human, Neil. We could give up the whole war thing forever, but we won't. And so it goes. So I'm going to leave America, and go to Korea to teach kids there about English. And also about Dylan and Kerouac and Wes Anderson and Ghosbtbusters."

It almost felt like he was visiting me in a vision, not leaving my sight.

I sighed. "You're gonna change the world, man."

He smirked. "Maybe I'll just change a village."

"I suppose were were just a big *granfalloon*," I said. "Everybody's leaving me."

"Nobody knows what's going to happen to anybody," said Joey. "You still have Sam."

"For a while," I said. "I can manage."

"And when the apocalypse comes, I'll be looking for you. Make sure you have plenty of good records for the occasion."

We shared a healthy laugh, and then he quoted Vonnegut before he left.

"Harmless untruths make you brave and kind and healthy and happy."

He looked like an unadulterated beat poet, like a character written by a Salinger who had never seen war or pain. He pulled on his cap and coat and guitar, as if they were his only possessions, and he went out the door into the light. He was a glow in my apartment, and he left a fluorescent residue that would linger for some time, enough for me to figure things out for myself. He always had a keen mind. I didn't deserve to make him stick around and keep him from his next big venture. After he left I felt in the mood to read some Hunter S. Thompson, which didn't really help to allay my anxieties.

Some people stuck around. Sam remained with me for a long time, and we watched the Predators play regularly through the beginning of hockey season. Like any human we felt at odd times prone to bouts of random and needless violence. Hockey was a liberating release.

Cline moved in with us, much to our reluctance, after he could not stand living with Amanda and Frenchy any more. Frenchy and her new boyfriend would smoke together whenever he was over, and never bother to go outside. They had a party one night, and Cline wasn't in the mood to socialize. He was in bed trying to sleep when Amanda burst in, drunk, and laid on top of him. "F— me," she mumbled, over and over. "Get the f— off me," he kept telling her. The night ended with Cline exploding at everyone and pulling the plug on the music. Amanda accused him of assault after he shoved her into a wall.

Two days later he moved in with Sam and me. We felt we had downgraded. He knew he wasn't welcome. He managed to earn his keep when I accidentally deleted my entire digital music library and he helped me recover it. You never know how much you appreciate someone until a thing like that happens. First world compassion. Cline eventually re-enrolled at Belmont and found a new roommate.

I had cycled through so many roommates that I thought of selling all my things on Craigslist and moving to Denver. But I knew what such abandonment was like, and I didn't want to do it to Sam, not after what Samantha had done to him. So I stayed, because I was the one who had grown accustomed to living solo. When he was ready, he would go wherever he was bound to go next.

"I feel homesick," he told me once. "I don't know why."

"You miss your mom," I told him. "It's okay to miss your mom."

"It's an adventure to hop from one place to another," he said. "But when I got married I thought I'd put down some roots. Never happened."

"I wanna put down some roots," I said. "I'm not feeling very root-like. I'd like to become more rootesque."

That was me, always following the tangent of wordplay out of a somber conversation.

"I need a constant," said Sam. "I thought Samantha was my constant. Will you be my constant?"

"I will be your constant," I said, "but does that mean I have to sleep with you?"

It wouldn't be long before he would disentangle from me also. They were all disentangling from me. I imagined that all my friends from one end of the earth to the other were just across the room of some vast show, bumming around, and if we heard one another call out our names we would only have to rush over. We could all spend endless hours shooting the breeze and philosophizing and watching the skyline glow against the dark.

I was going to remain in Nashville, I knew it. It was more than just the music, although I could not put a proverbial finger on whatever the reason was. But where in Nashville, or perhaps the how in Nashville, was the greater question. Although I remained in the same town, I felt like I was on the verge of a drastic move, not the kind where you switch apartments, but like the kind where you smuggle across another border, marry and live in the sewer of another city.

I was doing an interview with a pair of real estate developers who had made some plans for a new neighborhood in upper East Nashville. Recently there had been talk of urbanization, of trains coming, of "new money" rolling in. It was a lucrative opportunity. I even wore my skinny tie for them.

"We want to brand our new community as luxury-casual," said one of them.

"Picture this," said the other. "Rustic revival. New buildings, but with old brick. Furniture matches the floors. Lampposts match the chandeliers."

"Yeah," said the first one, bouncing off the idea again. "Not so much French Eclectic. We don't want to come off as arrogant."

"No, no. Not that fancy. You know, more of a Scandinavian import meets Southern sensibilities. And everything is hardwood floors—"

"Right," I interjected. "Kind of a post-hipster, convincingly culture-conscious home environment for ultra yuppies who drink expensive coffee and have issues of *Kinfolk* and *Oxford American* on the table that they never actually read."

"Right," they said, with a little laugh. "You nailed it. Now imagine a whole downtown neighborhood eventually looking like that."

"Like kinda how I look today," I said. "I think I might turn into that."

They gave me this look like a couple asking a celebrity priest to marry them.

"We know. That's exactly why we called you."

I felt like squirming. I looked down at my business get-up. I usually worked at home, wearing something akin to a field cap I found at a rummage sale and a self-designed tee with the words "my metanarrative is better than yours." Here I was in one of several recent interviews I had done, bending over backwards not to look like some stooge in a tawdry suit. It has always been cooler to me, sexier to me, to look impoverished – there was something off-putting about stainless steel countertops stacked with Cuisinart appliances. I avoided girls who didn't study philosophy because they would want to eventually marry and we would spend our weekends looking for "some place nice to go and eat." I didn't want the terror of mortgage payments like my parents did. Surviving is expensive enough. I didn't want to heap additional anxieties over my being and doing. These tools were wooing me to do everything short of wear a logo on my shirt.

But who was I fooling? My Mac alone was worth over a thousand dollars. The cost of my coffee and my education together could sustain dozens of third world families. I'm not a class warrior, but I'm no careerist. I did have an occasional desire to settle down into a homestead from which all my domestic operations could be evenly distributed between myself, some fair *devochka*, and maybe even a child or two. I just didn't want to build a bourgeois philosophy out of sane living and good times with a dog by the fireplace and a white picket fence.

So far in my work I'd found that clients often had a false perception of their own brand. I had deliberately avoided developing my own visual identity through any design, but my inadvertent design had been my choice of clients in the course of these months. It wasn't pleasant to experience the apotheosis that I had been mistaken about my own image. I felt queasy about the prospect of working for them. I wasn't sure if I could be so obsequious.

In any career there is always this vague longing for arrival. I can't name a single intelligent person who can claim they have ever arrived anywhere. They're always anxious about how much longer they are going to be cool with themselves being wrapped up in whatever they're wrapped up in. We become fidgety, we grasp at constellations. If we can't make something with our own hands, we consult. We dare not settle for crunching numbers, pulling levers, and digging posts. We'll even settle for writing constellations into your coffee like foamy portents.

For the time being I think I'm going to step out of the advertising world and make my way through the subterranean venues of the art scene. I tried my hand at other projects I hadn't touched since grad school. I started afresh one morning. I put on *Abbey Road* and cleared my mind of anything and everything that spoke of branding. I looked out over the city and tried to see it the way I imagined Sedgwick saw it for the first time.

I need to wander on my own for a while, de-center myself, wandering around and in between the alleys, street corners, discount liquidation marts, pancake houses open past midnight, the hobo camps and the poor and battered places, lighting cigarettes and humming until I get a whiff of inspiration lingering around the corners and behind walls and under burnt out lights and blowing down the road with dead fall leaves and plastic grocery bags. In a way it'll be like searching for Sedgwick's weary ghost, or for a way to scrape it off my shadow.

Sedgwick appeared from time to time, like he was still a ghostly hobo impersonator floating from corner to corner. Songs, magazine features, belated retweets—he haunted the air. When some latecomer issued a sound remotely kin to his, some young sage would remind everyone that "Sedgwick totally started that sh—." Debates would pop up on the internet over the canonical title of *The August Session*. Showboat ticket sales went up, a profane indicator that his memory had become something for tourists. He had doomed himself to failure. He just had to attract enough attention first. He was no different than any fool with a guitar on his back holding his breath after stepping off the train and contemplating the skyline. It couldn't have even been said for certain that he was compelled only by his unrequited love for a young girl of quiet sophistication, but also by a corresponding desire to fill the shoes of an old hero whose body had outlived his soul.

He invested in Hoyt Murdock more than anything, in that unfailing song that resounded, unchanged, from his father's gramophone, until he saw it face to face. He would hop a ride to Music City and arrive a new creature. He was as much a contradiction as any of us.

I lived with, worked with, and went to venues with people just like him, young folks who just want to believe in an incoherent future rescued from the intolerable past. I felt sicker when his songs played. I felt like the only one willing to admit indifference to his music, because I knew it wasn't about the music at all, not for its own sake. I could have told his story to some magazine in a feature if I'd wanted, but I wasn't going to sell myself out and drag his skeletons out of the closet. I couldn't do it to his memory and I couldn't do it to Tab. For Sedgwick, it was about proving something—to the crowd, to Tabitha, to Hoyt Murdock. But Tab was married, Hoyt Murdock was dead, and countless critics couldn't make up their terrible minds.

I thought this would be the narrative of Garrett Sedgwick, but it turned out to be the narrative of us grown up kids from the South, from small towns, from religion, from sheltered and repressed upbringings, and from the nineties—for one reason or another we neglected to return to the stifling airs of whatever boorish or intolerant hole we grew up to roll our eyes at. Nashville is no less grotesque than any town, and I would be distorting the truth if I told you that the seeds of culture I saw sprouting were as satisfying as I imagined they would be. Moving to another city wouldn't make it any better for me. I had and still have inner resolutions to make. I've let my assumption of objectivity spoil the narrative. I can only react to my own portrait of events like a crowd does to a nude study in velvet. The portrait is untitled, and nobody can express what it means, only that it just might be of some value by merit of its raw…whatever.

This wasn't even the story of Nashville, because pockets of this crowd of mine are cropping up in the corners of every city. The subterranean world of all cities is distorted, but it knows it is distorted. All it cares for is knowing, and letting the rest of the world know, that it is not as distorted as the status quo. I dread that we are all so very sophomoric, this crowd—we roll our terrible eyes at heartfelt creations because we were not the first to appreciate them.

Our generation never requested to be pigeonholed, and we feel we can and should belong to any other previously revolutionary generation through the vicarious appreciation of their voices, voices that have faded from what place they held in the culture of their time due to their occupying ambiguous places of budding counterculture where conventional barriers were transgressed. This curse, this continuum of transition, urged the young and vibrant to move on, each time discovering themselves corralled and cramped into asylum with one another until they hit the road once again.

But for us there is no road. The information age removes the necessity of travel for the sake of discovery, our eco-conscious zeitgeist discourages us from burning fossil fuels across a never-ending pavement, and though we do not want to admit it, we feel the towns have all been visited and marked by the pioneers we've come to idolize, and it is our job to settle in and spread new roots. We make our discoveries in local Wi-Fi spots and in the midst of subterranean shows, anti-pioneers grown restless from migration both from and to the inevitably conventional.

There is no longer an "out there" for us to go to, but only an "out then and that" to wait for and take in. We find religion in the transformation of new sounds, in the frenetic sharing of new sounds. Like the beats who rejected settling home while yearning for a home, we have left fundamental belief in search of something we can fundamentally believe in. We are seekers, persistent seekers, and once we light our lanterns we do not come home, because we have made a spiritual pursuit out of seeking refuge after refuge in aesthetic ventures. In place of moving along the road, we move along from show to show, ever curious to go, never satisfied to stay, especially if the crowd follows soon after you arrive.

We all want to be a first generation something. We are too clever to follow a trend. Our modes are to create and critique, but we cannot do one without the other. We stretch our muscles to be pioneers of the shadowy corners our forebears have overlooked.

The previous generation's critics will search with great suspicion for some deficiency with which to label us. Suppose I just provide that for you. Suppose we are in a frenzy to seek refuge in meaning, but we have a habit of making refuge impossible for ourselves. Suppose we've cultivated the weariness of looking away from God's empty chair. Suppose we leave ourselves vulnerable to criticism because that's how karma works, and the truth is we can't dare create anything of our own. Our pale truths will always be absent. They look too familiar to be true.

We can be a nasty crowd. Wipe the smugness off our faces and we are all philosophers without the imposed structure of narrative. We yearn for a refuge of meaning but refuse to accept the ones bequeathed to us. We never felt rooted, and are afraid to settle.

We discard and criticize, but what are we all aching to do? We are aching to exhibit some will to power over the course of our future, sketching out the horizon and calling the sketches more real than the thing itself. We will either resign to settling or revolt against settling, but eventually we will all have to settle. I don't know yet what I'm going to do. I feel like the past five years haven't prepared me for anything substantial. There is no definitive positive proof of what lies ahead for me.

I'm being incredulous.

If you want to empathize with someone you have to simulate their life. Empathy and personality have to meet humanity at its most imperfect veracity. I hope I didn't disappoint you, readers. From the start my narrative was slouching toward anticlimax. I've arguably exploited myself, and maybe the lives of others too, because I can't afford psychotherapy, and I was hoping to possibly aggrandize my assets upon its publication.

I'm being sententious.

I have no moral meaning for you to extrapolate. I don't care for satire or epigram. I'm just trying to distill what I've drawn out of it all. At some point you'll find yourself in a struggle between expectations and possibilities. Hustle into something you love. Fight through the indefinite malaise. Adopt a socially progressive world-view. Don't be a phony. And if you must, submit to the inexplicable phenomenon of religion. Tell yourself that God is moving and other unprovable profundities.

You can always opt for the sweet cocoon of maturation, and in another few years maybe you can grow so optimistic that you just might get carried away in the current. Maybe the marvels you compose will flee like refugees from the ashes of the bonfire of the vanities kindled by the covetous and the arrogant, who have put you up on the stake to spite the sincerity of your song.

I'm being cynical.

Go back a bit to when nobody has yet heard of Garrett Sedgwick and anyone who knew Chance Merritt had forgotten him. Walk down the streets of downtown for a spell. You'll pass by the guy in the ten gallon hat singing outside Bluebird, then by the guy with the mic and drum who will rap freestyle everything he sees walking by. Keep walking. You have to almost disappear completely from sight. You'll see him eventually, wearing that handkerchief of his. He'll ask you to name a performer, anybody. He'll sing a few bars with rapt imitation. You'll laugh. He'll laugh. "The seventies," he'll say. Or "the eighties," or "the sixties," he'll say. "Crappy decade for music," he'll say, whatever it is, and in the moment you'll also dismiss the catalogue of an entire decade. Then he'll stop and sing one song he's chosen. Sometimes it's The Smiths, sometimes it's Zeppelin, sometimes The Doors. The whole decade trash — except for that band or that one song they do.

And just when you think he's finished, he lights it up. He's not even strumming now, just singing against the night. You're still laughing, but there is no punch line, so your laughter peters out, you and that girl with you huddling close. He's belting it out, he's possessed. He's almost to his knees, the vocals moving in him, drawing out some spirit of rapture. You've stopped laughing, you're so caught up in it. Maybe this is part of the act, but maybe not. Maybe this is Kaufman on Elvis.

Then you walk off. No change. He didn't have his case open. He was so lost in it he would have forgotten he was doing it for money, or for a woman, or for approval, or for anything. You just passed a conduit who took himself by surprise.

And there's only one song in your head when you go back downtown, one song you'll sing, and have everyone echo with you from street to street, taming yourself back into the scene, echoing back. And it goes like this:

Rococo. Rococo.

Rococo. Rococo.

A CALEB COY "NOVEL"

AN AUTHENTIC DERIVATIVE

An Authentic DERIVATIVE

AN Authentic DERIVATIVE

DERIVAT

AN AUTHENTIC DERIVATIVE

an authentic derivative

AN AUTHENTIC DERIVATIVE

AN AUTHENTIC DERIVATIVE

AN AUTHENTIC DERIVATIVE

AN authentic DERIVATIVE

Acknowledgements

I would like to give a special acknowledgement to the boys at The Podcast of Unnecessary Abstractions.

Special thanks goes out to all the contributors to my IndieGoGo campaign that made possible the independent publishing of this novel:

Charlene Guard, Luke Guard, Grat Tucker, John Michael Kennedy, Stefano Mugnaini, Justin Summers, Mary Gubala, Trae Bailey, Phillip McDoniel, Josh Whitlow, Will Norrid, Rebecca Sherman, Neil Brunett, Levi Galford, thecoffeespill, Blake Palmer, Kelee Barbour, Paul Heilker, Bob Martin, Roy Justus, Chris LaFever, Janine Kniola, Veronique Dobson, James Wolfe, Carl Jenkins, Happy Hiatt, Isaac Ganoe, Kimberly Brown, Sheryl Young, Seth Terrell, Michael Whitworth, Patrick Williams, Brian Chiglinsky, Sarah Plummer, Alisa Van Dyke, Morgan Ball, Michael Miller, Jordan Sowers, Katie Dredger, Kyle Gilpin, Laura Young, Joshua Mason, Clara Pope, Tyler Henley, Kara Clemons, Nathan Pelfrey, Kassie Bailey, and others who will remain anonymous.

Caleb Coy lives in Christiansburg, VA with his wife and son. He teaches college writing to high schoolers. *An Authentic Derivative* is his first novel. You can read his weekly blog on language, literature, and spirituality at calebcoy.wordpress.com.

www.ingramcontent.com/pod-product-compliance
Lightning Source LLC
Chambersburg PA
CBHW071452170626
46811CB00007B/2550